WITHDRAWN
FROM STOCK

A DANGEROUS GAME

A DANGEROUS GAME

Brian Reeve

Book Guild Publishing
Sussex, England

First published in Great Britain in 2005 by
The Book Guild Ltd
25 High Street
Lewes, East Sussex
BN7 2LU

Typesetting in Baskerville by
Keyboard Services, Luton, Bedfordshire

Printed in Great Britain by
Antony Rowe Ltd, Chippenham, Wiltshire

A catalogue record for this book is available from
The British Library

ISBN 1 85776 985 6

Sophie and Adam
I love you so much

Chapter 1

Near the Kruger Reserve, Jan Krige's farm, Republic of South Africa

Jan Krige came out of the rocking chair, biceps proud against his white vest, his features hard and leonine, formed from land on which he had been brought up. He went to a table, leaving the rhythmic motion of the chair to die in his wake.

'I spent fifteen years watching men kill one another.' His refined Afrikaans was low as he took a packet of cigarettes, ejecting one of the plain tips above the others. Fastening his lips on the paper he looked from the house to a *kopje*, the lone sentinel mound that erupted from the flat ground near the barns. With a flame to the leaf he inhaled, expelling blue rings at intervals into the evening air.

Perched expectantly behind him on a sofa, an older Afrikaner, Johan Muller, meaty and heavily boned, twitched his nostrils distastefully. He had never been able to understand how anyone could indulge himself in the toxic waste for a considerable part of each day. He eyed the farmer cautiously.

'I was born on this farm,' said Krige. 'My father's dream was to keep it in the family and for me to pass it on to my sons. He was disappointed when I joined the police.'

'But you came back, before he died,' said Muller.

'I did. And I want to stay here,' said Krige. 'You haven't

even told me exactly what this "job" as you call it entails, except that it is extremely important and that I might have to kill someone. That's quite charming.'

Muller didn't respond directly. 'Your credentials are impeccable,' he said. 'With your training and discipline you can do this job in your sleep, no need for lengthy preparation at some hideout in the bush. That's why we chose you. You will know the details as soon as we get your answer.'

Krige dragged on the cigarette and watched his wife Kirsty approach the house. He was of Boer descent and had inherited 3,000 acres of land near the Kruger National Park, the wild reserve bordered in the east by Mozambique and in the west by the old Transvaal. He had joined the police from school and risen rapidly through the ranks to become head of the elite Johannesburg murder and robbery squad. Then several years previously he had resigned and returned to the farm.

'Apartheid has gone,' he said. 'We have a new government. I'm not about to turn into one of your killing machines. Those days are long over.' He leant on the rail running round the verandah, and fixed his eyes firmly on Muller.

The fat man quelled his anger. He pushed himself up. 'Why did you leave the police, Major?' he asked bluntly.

'I came back to run the farm.' Krige frowned, wondering what Muller was getting at.

'That's not the complete truth, Major,' said Muller, confident. 'It was a cover-up. If you hadn't left you would've been put on trial for murder, the cold-blooded killing of a leading political activist in Johannesburg, another Steve Biko, but this one was not as well known. Even then you were lucky charges weren't pressed. The most lenient judge would have seen it as a criminal act.'

'It was self-defence,' said Krige unconvincingly.

'No, Major. The man was unarmed,' said Muller. 'There

was not a weapon anywhere near him. He had his hands up when you shot him in the chest.'

'There's no evidence,' said Krige quietly. 'What's this leading to?' He knew the answer, his gut wrenching as he felt the screw tighten.

'Evidence?' cackled Muller. 'This government with its investigative and prosecution powers will get it, dust it off and throw it at you with pleasure. A life term in a filthy prison is unpleasant to say the least. It would simply mean never being with your family again, never making love to your beautiful wife. To put it mildly, it would be shit on wheels. Not even Satan would enjoy it.' Muller released the hint of a smile. 'We also have other methods of persuading you.' Then he softened and added: 'Men of your ability and relative obscurity are not easy to find.'

'What do you mean? Spit it out,' said Krige, his face tense.

'This is not a game, Major, although it might appear to be...' Muller stopped as Krige's wife appeared at the door.

She was in a skirt and man's shirt, her burnished dark hair pulled from the exquisite structure of her face. For a moment Muller dwelt on her beauty, the thrusting breasts and finely curved, strong legs, the way she carried herself. He had bitterly conceded that in his physical condition he could only dream of going to bed with such a woman.

'Good evening, Mrs Krige,' he said in the most cultured voice he could muster, trying to conceal his desire. 'You are very beautiful.'

She laughed softly, slightly embarrassed, feeling some sympathy that he was so unattractive. She withdrew her hand from his flaccid grasp. 'Would you like dinner with us, Mr Muller?'

He glanced at an old watch on his wrist, one of the

early Japanese Seikos but still extremely accurate. 'I didn't think it was so late. The long evenings are deceptive.'

'There's no hurry,' she said, wondering what had brought him out to the house. 'But you have to drive to Pretoria.'

'No, I must go,' said Muller, a little reluctant to turn down the invitation. He would have relished being able to feast his eyes on her for longer. 'You're most kind. I won't be long.'

When they were alone again, Muller went on. He revealed more than he had intended to at this first meeting. 'I represent a political group of no name, which is aligned to similar groups or parties, but independent. There is, though, a recognized lead group, the one I'm in, which does not support black rule, like the other groups, and has as its members the men who governed this country before the blacks got into power.

'These men are the cream of our race and are part of this group because they have distanced themselves from the depraved and uncoordinated hysteria of the extreme right-wing parties, and certainly do not want to form any association with the African National Congress or the middle-road and weak opposition party, the Democratic Alliance.

'Personally, those small extremist parties that I have referred to, that have given themselves various political labels, have no chance, and some of their leaders are already in jail serving long sentences. But for us it's a case of waiting, and some of our members are already in positions of political, industrial and economic power.' Muller sat down, drawing air into his bloated body.

Then Muller at last revealed what he had come for. 'We want you to retrieve a file that names the leaders, members of the Nationalist Party of the time, appointed by the state during the apartheid period, who were in the police, security forces, the government, the state security council, and who held other positions of influence. The file is a detailed composition of activities executed and directed by those listed, and the evidence that would convict them if they were ever prosecuted and brought to trial.

'There are a lot of other documents or files that we have in our possession, but the sheer guts rests in this particular file. Reference to the other files is also made in this central file, and also where they can be found, exactly where I do not know. Such information was deliberately kept under the control of those assigned to compiling the file, to which I refer, people who had our total trust. As I have said, you will get further details when I hear from you, the name of the person who we believe now has the file and of course where he is.'

He paused and then added, as a possible incentive. 'For your interest, Major, you are not in the file but the evidence against you that I spoke of before still exists. You were never prominent enough to warrant inclusion.' A clap of thunder as if reinforcing Muller's mordant sentiments rattled the clouds overhead and large translucent drops began to beat the compacted earth in the yard, catapulting grains of sand away like trapeze artists. 'We're asking you to help us. For you, and as far as we're concerned, it's a one-off operation. After this you can go, we won't come to you again.'

He got up and went to the top of the steps. 'We want your answer tomorrow, Major. A night to sleep on it. This operation is, as I am sure you picked up from what I have just said, urgent and essential for the protection of the men who served us so well in the past. I'm sure we won't be disappointed when you reply.'

Krige turned from Muller and fed on the scented air coming in off the land, cleansed by the rain. 'I'll phone you then,' he said tersely. 'Now leave.'

'Thank you, Major,' said Muller. 'It's for a good cause and some of those you used to know will be grateful.'

Krige watched him go down the steps and dart to his Ford, with an alacrity that belied his bulk. He silently cursed the man. How had they found out about his past? It had been four years since he had left the police and killed the activist. Grimly he lit another cigarette, his mind racing ahead. They were playing the tune.

Muller was satisfied with his meeting with Krige and drove the Ford fast along the narrow track from the house, the thick tyres disgorging a golden plume of mud and spray that held itself in mock suspension behind the car. Twenty kilometres to the east lay Pretorius Kop, the southernmost camp of the Kruger Reserve and 3 kilometres inside the perimeter. Only 500 acres of Krige's land were used for tobacco, and as Muller sped south to the gate a vista of broad leaves gave way to wild terrain. Occasionally he saw small herds of impala browsing near the road, warthogs, the odd lone kudu bull, and he observed drily that there were a lot fewer sightings than in his youth as the animals had gradually acquired the good sense to stay in the park and protect themselves from increased hunting on the farms.

At the farming town of White River he took the turn for Nelspruit where he met the N4 freeway for Pretoria, one of the three governing capitals of South Africa.

Muller had been brought up in Pretoria and he prided himself on being pure Afrikaner, even though his father, who had come from the Cape, bore every indication of having coloured blood in his veins, with his flared nostrils, ursine features and short crinkly hair. But Muller's mother was of direct German descent and appeared to have eradicated any of the colouring and facial characteristics of her husband when she gave birth to her only son. His parents had died five years previously, within months of one another, and he had inherited the family house where he lived alone, never having married.

Muller's first political affiliation was to the Nationalist Party that governed through the apartheid years. He was a seminal member of the New Nationalist Party that appeared after the new ANC government was elected in 1994, but left it because it attracted the wrong men and was not going anywhere. Now in his early fifties, Muller was well rooted in a select tier just below the leadership of the political group which he helped to form, the group with no name. He was still right-wing, but had mellowed, having the vision and sense to adapt in part, and for the time being, to the will of the majority in the country. The group was central to his life, and its activities were substantially more important to him than his job as postmaster of a small urban post office, a little less than a kilometre from his house.

Pretoria

Three hours after leaving Krige's farm Muller reached the outskirts of Pretoria, but instead of driving to his home he went towards the quiet city centre, dimly lit by obsolete lamps, of beautiful architecture, a monument to the previous dominance of the Afrikaner. Just before he reached it he took the car north and a little later he came to a *Nederduitse Gereformeerde* (Dutch Reformed) church. He parked and after a moment of circumspection went down a flight of steps into the crypt. At an oak door he knocked twice and entered.

Three men were seated at a table and they looked up as Muller came in. No greeting was passed but one of the men, older than the others and with a head of steel-grey hair, nodded to an empty chair. His name was Gerrit Viljoen, a senior figure in the group.

Muller squeezed his corpulent frame into the space between the chair and table. Once seated, he gathered his breath and spoke, his words trenchant.

'Krige will call tomorrow,' said Muller. 'I'm sure he'll agree.'

'That doesn't surprise me.' Viljoen slid a thin pile of papers to his side and clasped his delicate hands. 'Does he know who we're after?'

Muller curled his lips. 'I told him what we want, that he might have to kill the man. He will be given further details when he is ready to go. He is used to this type of work and if anyone can succeed, it's him.'

Viljoen laughed briefly. 'Ring me at the farm,' he said. 'You may go.'

Jan Krige's farm

'It's about Muller, isn't it, Jan?' Kirsty Krige left her chair, gathering the dirty plates, and waiting for an answer. Their two teenage sons were at boarding school in Johannesburg and she and her husband had just finished dinner together in the long room at the side of the house. 'I had a feeling there was a reason for his visit.' She walked into the lounge, leaving the table to Maria the domestic servant who came in promptly from the kitchen.

The lounge was parallel to the verandah, that skirted the front and one side of the house, and was finished in carved panelling two-thirds up the white walls, nearly touching at each end the snarling heads of two leopards shot 15 years previously by Krige's father. Seating herself next to the front doors she drew her feet under her as her husband entered.

'Muller wants something,' she continued before he had taken a seat. 'It's written all over you. You know you can tell me about it.' She had removed the band holding her hair in place and it hung thickly, reaching below her neck.

'Muller's carrying out an investigation for his party,' he said. 'He's asked me to get information for him. I can't let him down.' He lit a cigarette and sank into the sofa opposite her, taking in the smoke and trying to be as casual as possible.

She lifted her knees, giving him an obvious view of amber-milk thighs up to black pants. 'Which party?'

'He describes it as a political group without a name, but comprising many of the leaders who ran this country under the old Nationalist Party,' he answered softly. 'This group is part of a network of similar groups, but apparently it is the controlling body.'

It was like sticking in a knife. 'They're killers,' she shot back with a look of blatant horror. 'You know what they stand for, and you're prepared to help them. They will never change from what they used to be. They have so much blood on their hands. And the leaders never appeared at the Truth and Reconciliation Committee hearings because they knew they had no chance of amnesty and any appearance would have put them under the lights.'

'They're not all the same. People like Muller accept those times have gone. I'll be gone for a few days at the most.'

'Not the same...?' She was astonished. 'You know as well as I do that it is still a party, even if it has no name, that has racists in its ranks, who vent their hate on helpless black mothers and their children. They're evil.

I'm sure that some of them are intelligent men and in positions of power, but they are still anti-black. I'm also certain that they will have thugs in their ranks. These people have failed to achieve any form of real political power in this new country of ours and yearn for the old days. Now they appear as clean, with no affiliation, but they silently go about achieving their own ends.' Her intense dislike for those who had shaped the past was apparent. 'I can imagine that this group is no different from the extreme right-wing parties who still resent black rule and believe their homeland has been taken from them.'

He walked across the rug, his posture military and powerful, the light from twin copper lamps shining on his sleek hair. He knelt on one knee in front of her, placing a hand on her knee. 'I'm sorry,' he said. 'I gave my word. It's not what you think.'

'I don't believe you.' Tears glistened in her eyes. She leaned over, gently pulling his head to her breasts. 'They've got a hold on you. Why won't you tell me?' She caressed him, taking in his male smell.

'You worry too much,' he said sliding his hand to the moist warmth between her legs. 'No one's got a hold on me, except you.'

She looked at him sadly, her honey-coloured eyes mellowing to her physical desire, knowing he was determined to do what had been asked of him. 'Be careful, my sweet,' she murmured, easing him aside and moving off the chair, her skirt riding up on her. 'You're precious to me.'

They made love on the rug, afterwards lying by the open door, savouring the cool breeze that came in from the yard. 'That was gorgeous,' she whispered. 'No other man can give me that.'

* * *

That night Krige slept fitfully, arching under the single sheet and jerking awake at intervals, like a child having a bad dream. Before dawn he dressed and left the room, thankful the night had passed, and stood at the window in his study waiting for the light to appear in the sky. He knew he had to comply with the request, that refusal would not be tolerated, that his wife and sons would be in danger.

His mind swept to his days in the police, the danger and blood that went with the work, the bitterness and low morale, the man he had gunned down in Johannesburg on that cold night. Strangely he had found it easy to pump the lead into his body and gloat as he died. And Muller was right, he had been unarmed.

He looked at the guns in their cabinet, fixed to the end wall above the desk. They were a fine collection, rifles of different size, from a .22 to a .458 magnum, shotguns and two pistols, some passed down to him and others acquired through the years. For a time he studied the weapons, perfectly bolted in tailor-made frames and moulds on the other side of the glass.

When he heard Maria lighting the fire in the kitchen he went out to his jeep and impatiently pulled himself behind the wheel. It was two hours before he could get Muller on the phone.

Berea, Durban

On the evening of the day Johan Muller had his meeting with Jan Krige, Andrew Cartwright was entertaining a friend at home, a Spanish-style house on Durban's Berea, a few kilometres from the centre of the city. Cartwright's wife was in Cape Town where their daughters were at university, and the two men dined alone. After a meal of fillet steaks cooked by the servant they retired to the lounge, a room with a panoramic view of bougainvillaea and verdant lawn, manicured to the perfection that wealth and taste can provide.

'Find a seat.' Cartwright selected a bottle from the cabinet and poured two measures of Scotch. Handing over a tumbler he sat near the French windows, vorticing the neat spirit in his glass before taking its fire to his mouth. '*Gesondheid*,' he said. 'Good health, to peace.'

Peter Kaplan sipped the whisky and watched the thin figure, strewn in the chair like a long bag of sand, fingers like a vulture's talons clutching the glass. He, like Cartwright, was a lawyer, a secretive man, and one of few who knew the central role Cartwright had played in formalizing African National Congress (ANC) strategic policy before and after their final coming to power. He recognized that Cartwright was seen as one of the finest criminal advocates in South Africa and knew that his involvement with the ANC went back much further when such an alliance would have, had it been known, led to imprisonment as a minimum.

'You must feel satisfied with the help you've given them. Here we are in 2005 and the ANC are in power again after securing another comprehensive majority last year. They wouldn't have come to power in 1994 and sustained it for ten years without the assistance of men like you.'

'The work never ends,' replied Cartwright in the clipped Cape accent he had acquired in his formative years. 'The ANC still has exiles, men who are afraid to return to this country which is the place of their birth. Clearly they want anything they were guilty of, relating to human rights, to be forgotten, even though they were fighting a just cause. They need some kind of reassurance to bring them back.'

'Some of them,' said Kaplan. 'Others should be put

on trial like the others who committed criminal acts in the apartheid period.'

Cartwright touched the crystal rim absently, sadness in his pale eyes. 'Unfortunately you'll never rid a political movement of its criminal element, men who use the cause as a catalyst to kill. Sometimes it's directed against their own people.' He went to the bottle and poured a heavy slug into his glass. His thoughts wandered to the past. 'Have you heard of a man named Thami Zulu? That's a *nom de guerre* for Muziwakhe Ngwenya.'

'The first name was short enough.' Kaplan shook his head. 'Who is he?'

'He was a celebrated son of the ANC and a gifted leader,' said Cartwright. 'He was tipped to replace Mandela.'

'Was?' said Kaplan.

'He died in strange circumstances, or rather he was murdered, but the killers got away with it,' said Cartwright. 'They were also members of Umkhonto we Sizwe, the military arm of the ANC, as you know.'

Kaplan swallowed his Scotch and helped himself liberally. 'Did you know him?'

'I knew him very well,' said Cartwright. 'He was an intelligent, sensitive man. After being turned down for Wits he went through the University of Botswana and then on to Moscow for training in guerilla warfare. They tried to keep him but he returned to the camps in southern Angola. Hani, the chief of staff, spotted him and made him regional commander of operations in Natal. His predecessor, Nyanda, was assassinated by South African agents.'

'The theatre of blood,' commented Kaplan cynically. 'They got what they deserved.'

'No they didn't,' contended Cartwright. 'They were at war. Thami wanted peace but in those days the whites were in no mood to listen.'

Kaplan grinned, sceptical. 'What happened to him?'

'His career came to an abrupt end. In 1988 nine ANC guerillas were massacred in separate ambushes as they entered the country from Swaziland. The killings had a paralyzing effect on the leadership which was reduced to paranoia about informers in its ranks.' Cartwright lit a cigarette. 'The ANC security section, independent of the military and with draconian investigatory powers, recalled Thami to Lusaka, Zambia. He was placed under house arrest and then formally detained.'

'I can imagine what their detention centres were like,' said Kaplan. 'Was he charged?'

'No, he was not. Hani and Joe Modise, commander of MK, or Umkhonto we Sizwe, made furious demands in the ANC national executive of the time to have access to him. They were refused. After seventeen months in detention, a large part in solitary confinement, Thami was released. Five days later he was dead, at the age of thirty-five.' He scraped ash from the cigarette. 'That started bitter controversy in the ANC and a commission of inquiry was set up. The findings were never made public but it's generally believed there was no evidence that Thami was a South African agent. Cause of death was given as tuberculosis, which he'd had for some time. The real cause was something else.'

Cartwright went to the French windows that led onto a wide verandah. 'The English *Guardian* newspaper obtained a copy of an analysis made of Thami's blood and stomach contents after his death. Diazon, an organo-phosphorous pesticide, was detected in both specimens. The pesticide is a particularly toxic poison. Only three men were known to have seen Thami in the twenty-four hours before he died. They served under him in Natal as part of the regional command structure.' Cartwright faced Kaplan. 'You talk about the theatre of blood; these three were the most wanton, ruthless killers ever to see service in the ANC military.'

'Why the hell didn't the ANC pull them in after Thami's death?' Kaplan got up and put his glass on the cabinet.

'I don't know. The senior of the three was a Xhosa named Elijah Ngubane. Last week I heard that he and the other two had secretly entered the country. Apparently their whereabouts are unknown. All I know is that at the moment and for a few years it is advisable that they keep low, as the key whites during the dark years have so successfully been doing with their uncanny ability to shred evidence. Blacks like Ngubane would still be convicted today if the evidence was given to the prosecuting authority.'

Kaplan felt this was leading to something. 'You are trying to tell me something,' he said. 'What is it?'

'You read me well,' replied Cartwright. 'Perhaps you're a better lawyer than I am.' He paused and then went on. 'You are my closest friend and I will tell about something I received this morning. It was delivered by special courier service from someone I knew a while back. He is a member of a powerful but secret political group and the message from him that came with the delivery said he and others had been working for that group on compiling a detailed dossier of all those appointed by the state in the police and security services who had had positions of power during apartheid and were clearly guilty of human rights violations. These guys had apparently been working on this dossier for a few years and it was designed to be protection or backup against any possible prosecution should these guilty be exposed.' Cartwright poured another liberal Scotch. 'The delivery I received this morning was the dossier, complete with all original documents and pieces of paper that would blow the perpetrators apart if revealed. It contains everything that should have been revealed at the Truth and Reconciliation Commission but never was. That's why the process effectively failed. I have never seen anything so damning and dangerous as this file in all my years in law.'

Kaplan leant forward, injected by the import of what he had just heard. 'Where is the file?' he said quietly, as if they were being overheard.

'Upstairs in my safe. And you are the only one who knows about it,' said Cartwright unambiguously.

'What are you going to do with it?' asked Kaplan. 'This guy's bosses are bound at some stage to find that it is gone and if he is accused and blabs they will soon be after you with everything they've got. You should make a copy and give it to someone you trust with instructions on what to do with it if the others come for you. Personally I would get it out of the house and hand it over to the DSO or Scorpions as they are appropriately called. If it's as good as you say they will feed on it with relish; it's exactly what they want and don't have.'

'Not yet,' said Cartwright. 'I think this guy has probably covered his tracks pretty well. He's not a fool. I also want a couple of days to digest it and then decide what to do with it. I might use the Scorpions and, for insurance, send it with a covering note to the leading newspapers in London and New York. The *Guardian, Times, Washington Post, New York Times* come to mind. They are a few of the really big newspapers.'

'Why did this guy send this dossier or file to you?' Kaplan was captured by the intrigue and potential devastation. 'Has he anything else?'

'In answer to the first, I would say guilt,' said Cartwright. 'It is hard to work intensively on something like that without feeling that those in it should be exposed. That is, of course, if you have any feelings or conscience.' Cartwright was enjoying his moment, the file of such importance that he held in his hands, and he poured another slug. 'In answer to the second, I suspect that they have an equally damaging file on others, black guerillas, militants, terrorists, call them what you like, who opposed the apartheid regime. I believe that when it suits them they will use it.'

Chapter 2

Central Durban

'He's a killer. I need your help.' Lieutenant Pat Mitchell of the Durban police service sat over the desk from his friend. He had first met Steiner a few years before at a nightclub in town.

'Where're the others in your unit? I'm not a member of the police.'

James Steiner, dressed in *a dogi*, the standard karate suit, his black belt hanging almost to his knees, wiped off the sweat with a towel. The two men were in his office, an extension to the hall where he ran a school in the *goju* style of Japanese karate. Half an hour earlier the second class of the evening had ended and the students had left.

'We're undermanned – they'd already been assigned when I heard the coloured was in town. There're a couple of others with him.'

'What's he done?'

'Everything from running township vice rings to multiple killings, black and white.'

'Why hasn't he been picked up?' said Steiner.

'He doesn't sit still,' said Mitchell growing impatient. 'Will you help?'

'Yes, as long as it's only to bring them in,' said Steiner. 'I want no more than that.'

'That's all I want,' said Mitchell. 'I can't do it alone, too dangerous.'

Steiner was born British, in London at the West London Hospital in the borough of Hammersmith and Fulham. He was educated through the state system, achieved superb grades in his A-level examinations and got a place at Cambridge University to read English and pure and applied mathematics, an unusual choice and combination. At the age of 21 he took his finals and graduated with a 2-1. He had hoped for a first in English at least, but recognized that his mind had been elsewhere, on something mentally and physically demanding that he had first read about in a fitness magazine. It was an article on the Japanese *budo* discipline, or martial art, of *karatedo*. The philosophy and demands described in the article that would face anyone wishing to follow the karate way enveloped him immediately and sucked him in like a moth to the proverbial flame. Shortly after graduating, his parents were killed in a car accident. Steiner was an only child and left with no family in England. Without hesitation he had left for Japan and immersed himself in what was to become his passion.

Steiner casually removed his jacket. He was 6 foot 1, of medium build, his physique conditioned from the 15 years he had spent in the art. Already he was seen as one of the few westerners who had gone beyond technique and achieved mastery of the deep psycho-physiological aspects of karate. He began in the art in his early twenties, later than most who achieved expert rank. When he started training in Japan it was unlike what he had expected but he immediately took to the Japanese *do* concept, or the spiritual way, one which prescribed mental and physical hardship within the technical bounds of the form for development of the spirit. In two years he was graded to *shodan*, first black belt level, in *gojuryu*, one of the five pre-eminent styles of karate.

After four years he went to South Africa, where his

father had been born. He had always had a desire to visit the country and enjoy its lifestyle and natural beauty. He also had dual citizenship, British and South African. He turned professional, opening his own club. He visited Japan several times in the ensuing years and at 33 was awarded the coveted seventh *dan*, an unprecedented rate of progress for a Japanese national or foreigner and an extremely high rank, a rank unknown in any of the main styles to be carried by one so young.

'Where's the coloured now?' He took his clothes off a peg and began changing, drying himself with the towel as he went along.

'They're in a building off Point Road – a couple of rooms that were used by the port authority. It's near the old Smugglers Inn.' Mitchell adjusted the holster at his waist. 'There's an alley that used to run through to the docks. The far end was blocked some years ago but this side is a way of getting in.'

'What's the other?' Steiner ushered Mitchell into the passage.

'Inside the docks – too much open space up to it.'

Steiner stopped, buttoning his shirt and long sleeves. 'How do you know they're there?'

Mitchell tapped his watch, rounding his mouth and showing gaps where he had lost teeth from poor dental hygiene and neglect. 'Thirty minutes ago they carried fish and chips and cans of beer down that alley. I reckon that gives us another hour before they'll feel like doing anything.'

Steiner went into the *dojo* to turn off the lights. It was a narrow room with a mirror down the length and equipment positioned at the ends. The floor was specially treated wood and a picture of a Japanese master hung opposite. He joined Mitchell and they left for the street.

Point Road was the longest in the city, running along

the eastern boundary of the docks from the nightclubs of the rich to a part where life was as cheap as the liquor, an area which used to have as its focus the Smugglers Inn, before this was closed and left as a derelict tribute to those who had died inside at the end of a knife or in other similarly brutal fights.

Mitchell drove slowly when they neared the inn and he parked the car at what he considered was a discreet distance away. 'This is far enough,' he said removing the key. He opened the door then said, as if as an afterthought. 'You can't mistake the coloured. He's tattooed from his neck down. I don't know the others, but they're niggers.'

'That's an old and derogatory term,' commented Steiner without a smile. 'These people rule this country, and it seems they are doing a good job.'

At ten o'clock it was too early for there to be many on the street, and then mostly the local beggars looking for food others didn't want. When they reached the alley, a long winding passage that soon disappeared into darkness, Mitchell went ahead, rubbing his hand along the wall to feel his way. They passed one door early on, an entrance to the inn, and then when they could go no further, a second door appeared.

'This is it. I knew we would find it.' Mitchell took a look through the keyhole. 'Tells me nothing,' he said. He tried the door knob, using his weight. He took out his gun. 'It needs your strength. I'm not good at breaking down doors unless I have a hammer. I'll go in first.'

'I can see why you asked me along,' said Steiner, wondering what they would find. He backed off and then went into a mercurial spin that seemed to appear from nowhere, gyroscopically whipping one leg round close to him and then thrusting the heel at waist height into the wood. The concentrated and exacting force released the door so it slammed into the wall, dislodging old plaster and paint. The room was empty except for litter. They saw the door to another room and as Mitchell ran to it, someone locked it.

Driven by a deep loathing for those he was after, Mitchell threw himself at the timber as if his continued existence depended on getting through. It parted like cardboard and he landed, ready for anything. Before him were the men he wanted, the coloured kneeling next to a bag, and the blacks close to the exit that led onto the docks.

'Halt! Police!' Mitchell's shout was that of the bewitched, and his knuckles whitened on the trigger. He screamed again. 'Face the wall.'

As he shouted, Steiner came in. The three men froze, transfixed by Mitchell's venom, their eyes going from one white to the other and knowing instantly they were in danger. Then with a scowl the coloured went to the wall and cruciformed himself on it, the others following. They were dressed in short-sleeved shirts and jeans and the remains of their meal and empty cans lay on the floor. The coloured was unmistakable, his arms and hands and neck, up to his chin, intricately patterned in red and blue ink, applied like graffiti in a poor town.

'I'll frisk them.' Steiner took a pace then halted as he saw Mitchell lift the gun and aim at the coloured. 'No!' he cried. Then he calmed and said: 'We'll take them in.'

But Mitchell was beyond hearing and he fired the weapon, hitting the coloured at the top of his neck, killing him with his palms still flat on the wall, grotesquely hanging on for his life. At first the blacks were too startled to move then they split up, one going for Mitchell and the other for the door.

Absorbed by the killing of the coloured, Mitchell was slow with the gun and the black grabbed it, trying to get his finger on the trigger and get Mitchell's off. He was a big man, his chest and arms heavily muscled from manual labour, and in a sudden effort pulled the gun down, releasing the white's hold. He took the muzzle to Mitchell's throat. Gleefully he slipped his thumb inside the guard and began to squeeze.

For a moment Steiner was immobile, then he wheeled his hips, bringing up his foot and connecting with the black's head with the force of a club. As the man's hands flew from the gun he hit him at the base of the skull, breaking his spine and sending him to the floor like a piece of meat thrown onto a slab.

At the door the second black freed the bolts, wrenching at the key to disengage the lock. In an instant Steiner was on him, hitting him in smooth combinations on the neck and head and driving him into the wall where he beat him again. With a massive expulsion of breath the man came off the wall in a ball, his resistance gone, and his life ebbing from him.

Angrily Steiner faced Mitchell who stood next to the body of the coloured, calmly replacing the spent shells in his gun. 'You shot him in cold blood,' he accused. 'His hands were up.'

'I assume the blacks are also dead. Thank you for helping me.' Mitchell holstered the gun and frisked the coloured, going past him when he had finished and doing the same to the blacks. Taking each man in turn he pulled them to the wall and lined them up neatly in a row. 'All unarmed,' he said. 'That'll create the sort of fuss we can do without. Things are not what they used to be. These people have now got rights.'

Steiner was bitter that he had come. He knew what Mitchell meant - attitudes had changed. And here were three dead men without weapons, one with two bullet holes in his head and the others killed by his bare hands.

After years of discipline he had lost control, in an art that was for the preservation of life, not its destruction.

'What do you suggest?' he asked in resignation. The deed had been done.

Mitchell thought, then said: 'No one knows. We either leave them here or get rid of them.'

'Where do we take them?' Steiner hated the thought of casting away the bodies of those he had killed.

'There's a small nature reserve on the skirts of Durban. I am sure you know it. It's the Palmiet gorge. An hour from now only the animals will know where they lie.'

On the second day after Steiner and Mitchell killed the three men, Dawie Gerber left his cottage at the top end of the Palmiet gorge and headed south on patrol. It was just after sunrise and his route that morning took him towards the ravine that curved in the shape of a bull's horn and passed under the bridge that carried traffic to Johannesburg and Pretoria, or the Reef as the area was commonly known after the fact that it held the most prodigious reefs of gold in the land.

Within minutes of embarking on his tour the warden entered the ravine, the undergrowth only in parts displaying his path. There was little he did not know about the reserve and the years had sharpened his senses, giving him an awareness second only to the small antelope that browsed on the green shoots. As he approached the bridge the old man stopped, unhitching the twelve-bore shotgun from across his chest. He had seen a breakage in the continuum of subtropical bush and he left the trail, treading cautiously between the tangled stems that covered the ground like wire mesh.

The horrible stillness of the coloured and the swarm of buzzing flies that clung to the congealed blood on his face told Gerber he was staring at death. Quelling incipient shock he waited without going closer, then he returned to the path. Hunching his shoulders purposefully he went back briskly the way he had come.

In an hour the police from Durban Central were at the body and shortly afterwards they found the two blacks, their bodies spread on a radius of 10 metres. Late that morning the bodies were in the Durban morgue under the security of the police pathologist. After an assessment he referred his findings to the head of the investigation department, Colonel Louis van Wyk.

Pat Mitchell was at his desk when he was summoned to van Wyk's office. Two senior officers from the special branch were present when he entered and he raised his eyebrows in surprise. He took up the vacant chair.

Van Wyk didn't mince his words. He spoke to Mitchell. 'On Monday you alone were given information concerning the whereabouts of three suspected criminals. Yesterday they were found dead at the bottom of the Palmiet gorge.'

Mitchell hung his head. He could feel Van Wyk's eyes boring into him.

Van Wyk lit a cigarette and continued. 'I ordered a search of the premises in Point Road where they were seen. We located the room with its smashed door. There was blood in the room and it matched the blood groups of the deceased. In addition we found two shells from a 9 mm parabellum, the same calibre that killed the coloured.'

Mitchell prepared himself for the final stroke. It came quickly.

'Lieutenant, I want to know who was there with you,' said van Wyk. 'The blacks were beaten to death before they were thrown into the gorge, probably from the bridge. You didn't do it alone.'

Acknowledging his guilt, and not prepared to carry the can alone, Mitchell quietly said: 'James Steiner. He runs a karate club in town. You can easily find him.'

After it was confirmed that the slugs in the coloured's head matched Mitchell's gun, he and James Steiner were arrested and charged with murder. A week later after their first appearance in the Durban Supreme Court they were released on bail.

The next day, as Steiner was preparing to leave his *dojo* for the flat he rented a couple of streets along, he had a visitor, Peter Smith, a man he hadn't seen for some years. Smith found the karate man in a black mood and he suspected he knew the reason.

'It's between me and my attorney,' said Steiner standing at the top of the stairs and wondering what Smith wanted. He hardly knew him. They had met when Smith had unsuccessfully tried his hand at the art.

'I can help you more than your lawyer can.' Smith grinned with cocky confidence, knowing he held all the cards. 'To be precise, you'll need the help and security that only I can give you. Unless you accept my offer you are definitely in for life.'

Steiner led him into the office where he showed him a chair. He was curious. 'Yes?'

'I won't ask you why you killed them,' said Smith. 'I'm more interested in how I can help you and in particular how at some future date you can help me and the organization I work for.' He fished out a flattened pack of Camels and held them up enquiringly.

'Go ahead.' Steiner pushed an ashtray along the desk. He didn't smoke, but recognized some had a requirement for the weed.

Exhaling with a satisfied hiss, Smith went on, irritatingly

unhurried. 'You never knew but I used to work for the National Intelligence Agency, NIA. I now work for the Directorate of Special Operations, or Scorpions as we are called. We need operatives, men who can act alone on special assignment, men who have, shall I say, particular skills.'

Steiner gave a hollow laugh. 'Why are you telling me?'

Smith crushed the cigarette. 'You have those skills in abundance,' he said. 'I'm offering you part-time service as a condition for your release. If you accept, the present charge will be quashed and you'll be able to carry on running this school or doing whatever else you want to do with your life.'

Steiner snorted. 'You're looking for a killer. Whatever the charge, I'm not an assassin.'

Smith lifted himself off the chair. 'Listen to me,' he said. 'You assume too much because of your fighting ability. I never said anything about killing anyone. But if necessary it's within the law, and besides, you've little choice. Have you thought what it's like to be deprived of your freedom for the rest of your life, to lose everything you have come to value? You are fortunate that this country no longer has a death penalty. If it did you would certainly end your days at the end of a rope.'

Steiner watched Smith like a hawk. 'What will happen to Mitchell? He won't go down without me.'

'He'll also be released, but he's of no use to me,' said Smith. 'His career is over.'

Steiner looked at the short unattractive man in front of him. 'So you can cut this shit adrift as if it had never happened?' he asked. He was still not sure.

'Yes is the simple answer.' Smith lit another cigarette, played with it for a moment between his forefinger and thumb, sucked on it, then prepared to leave. 'What's your answer? Are you in or out?'

'I have no choice,' said Steiner, wondering how he had been so stupid as to get himself into this mess in the first place. 'I'll be available.'

Smith smiled. 'It's the right choice. Some things are necessary in the interests of state security.' He sucked on the tube then added: 'I suggest you take a holiday abroad. Let me know when you get back. We're always looking for men who have intelligence and rare qualities. Such attributes are not easy to find.'

Chapter 3

Near the Kruger Reserve

A short distance into the town of White River, Krige pulled the jeep off the tar and stopped at the general store. He knew the old Afrikaner who ran it but instead of going in to greet him as he usually did he crossed the road to the public phonebox. From his pocket he took a scrap of paper and dialled the number scribbled on it. It was a direct line and after some seconds the call went through to Muller.

'Good morning Major,' said the fat man into the mouthpiece, pushing the door of his office shut. 'I was waiting for you.'

'I'll do it,' said Krige. 'I'm in White River.'

Muller's eyes shone. 'I'll be there in two hours. Where can we meet?'

'A kilometre to the north of town the road rises through a pass. You'll see me there.'

'Thank you for cooperating, Major,' said Muller, keeping the excitement to himself and pushing out his chest at what he had accomplished for the sake of the party.

Krige left the phonebox, his jaw set, the import of his commitment clutching his throat like bile. He bought a cold meat pie and wolfed it down in his jeep, surprised at his hunger and feeling more relaxed with food in his stomach. At a crawl he drove out of the town and headed for the pass to meet Muller.

* * *

Muller cleared his desk and after notifying the office girl of his departure left for his car. Under his arm he held a slim folder, the thumbed edges pressed into the folds of his shirt. On the way out of Pretoria he bought sandwiches and a Coke and ate and drank as he drove, his mind on the second stage of a plan he had begun to formulate three weeks before. The first stage, selecting the retriever and executioner, was complete and all that remained for him to do was brief his man and wait for the results.

At Nelspruit he turned off the freeway. It was a hot day, the sun already an ubiquitous laser, burning the arid earth and driving wildlife under the scattered scrub. In his regulation blue shirt and dark tie he dripped sweat, the heat squeezing it out of his white body to run in rivulets that were absorbed by his vest. He wished he had bought another drink and when he reached White River he was tempted to stop but he pushed on.

Krige's green jeep was easily visible against the rocks and Muller drew up behind, swearing at the five-second spurt of pinking that came in when he cut the ignition. He wished he had had the Ford serviced when he last thought about it. He watched as Krige walked towards him, admiring the ex-policeman's powerful bearing, his cat-like movement. He rolled out of the car, enjoying the cooling effect as he unstuck his damp vest from his shirt, and held out his free hand, the other clutching the folder.

Ignoring the gesture, Krige leant on the wing of the Ford, noting the folder under Muller's arm. Muller lowered his hand. When he spoke his local accent was marked. 'When we met I told you briefly what this is all about and I stressed its importance to the party and the urgency of this operation. We believe that it is essential that you retrieve the file in two days at the most. Any longer, and the risks of action being taken on it are multiplied and go up exponentially. The thought of such a thing happening is worse than hell. I hope that's clear. There is no room for mistakes.'

Krige pushed himself away from the vehicle and turned to face Muller. 'Get on with it.' He spat out the words. 'Who has the file and where is he? Who gave it to him?'

Muller felt he was in control. 'Let's take a step at a time, Major. I'll answer the last question first and give you some background. Then we will get on to the other.' He drew a deep breath, needing it to fuel his sense of importance. 'When the Truth and Reconciliation Commission was established we, in what was then the Nationalist Party, knew that those who were believed to have committed human rights violations during the reign of our government would be hunted down, prosecuted and probably convicted. In order to protect these people, who were after all operating on behalf of our heritage, we initiated the compilation of a detailed file. I told you what was in the file and how damaging its exposure would be to our political aspirations, plus our pride as a people who want their own separate identity and have a loyalty to their flesh and blood.'

Muller walked slowly in a circle, taking his time, with the self-given assurance that he was still in control. He continued. 'One of those who we chose to compile the file decided for whatever reason to break with us, and give away to someone who was never our friend the full contents of the dossier. This was the ultimate in betrayal.'

'When was this? How did you find out?' Krige probed, becoming interested in the story and letting his first question go unanswered for the time being.

'We found out two days ago,' said Muller. 'Someone became suspicious that there was something strange in the behaviour of the guy I'm talking about. He was openly questioning the work he had been doing and it became obvious that he had started to hate having to do it. I'm sure it was not the most pleasant job, dragging up the past, but he should have shut his mouth. The work was essentially complete and we were thinking of assigning him to another small group who were compiling the same file, except that it was about the opposition during those years.' Muller stared at Krige. He was absorbed by his own story.

'The file on the whites, shall I say, without being racist, was kept in a room in Pretoria to which only those few working on it had access. In the last forty-eight hours one of the group working on it found that the file and all its related documents, the vital original evidence, had gone. The guy had also disappeared.'

Krige grinned mirthlessly. 'I'm sure you found him,' he said. 'I'll bet it wasn't difficult getting him to confess to what he had done.'

'We found him,' said Muller. 'He confessed to taking the file. Under pressure he told us what he had done with it. To his credit, it was hard work getting that out of him. He said that he had sent it, within an hour of taking it, by courier to your man in Durban. That means early yesterday.'

'He's not "my man", as you so eloquently put it,' said Krige.

'He is your man, if the job you've agreed to do is going to be done,' said Muller. 'His name is Andrew Cartwright and he is one of the leading criminal advocates in this country. He is well known to us, and known to many in South Africa. He was educated at Natal University, then Oxford in England, and was a powerful player behind the scenes in securing Mandela's release and giving rise to the present government. He's a rabid ANC supporter.

He financed them heavily through the eighties and it hasn't stopped. He played a significant part evolving ANC policy, the very policy that forms the constitution of this country. Twenty years ago he would've been executed for treason, and as far as we're concerned his guilt remains. He is one person who did enormous damage to our people.' Muller looked away. 'And nothing has ever happened to him.'

'And what happened to the guy who took the file?' said Krige, knowing the answer.

'No one will ever hear from him again,' said Muller, satisfaction inscribed on his face. 'He paid the price for betrayal.'

'Where's Cartwright?' said Krige trenchantly, now wanting to get on with it.

'I'm coming to that.' Muller went to the edge of rock and surveyed the plain below, allowing his gaze to drift to the few buildings in the distance that comprised the town. He admired the beauty. It was the land that he dreamed of being his. 'He lives in Durban on the Berea, one of the most expensive and desirable parts of the city.' He finally handed over the folder. 'The address and particulars you will need are in there.'

His row of capped teeth shone yellow in the bright light. 'You may choose your method. The way you plan the operation is up to you.' He paused, taking in the dry air. 'There is however a requirement with which we expect you to comply. It is for our mutual benefit.'

Krige had known there would be more.

Muller went on, inexorably. 'You must take two men with you, men from the group. We don't want you to fail, and these men are purely there as back-up and support.'

'I don't want your thugs anywhere near me,' said Krige.

Muller rounded on him, his neck swelling in anger. 'Major, it is our wish.'

'Your party, or your group as you call it, is full of the type who can do this work,' sneered Krige. 'I wonder why you chose me.'

'These men will follow your orders, Major.' Muller came up close so Krige could smell his feculent breath. 'I've asked two men to prepare for this operation. They know it is of vital importance.'

'Who are they?' said Krige.

'You'll meet them,' said Muller. 'I suggest they join you at the farm before you move.'

Krige was silent. The farm was secluded and ideal for a meeting place. Muller was determined to have his way. He glanced at the folder. 'What if he's killed?'

Muller liked the question. Krige was cooperating. 'His death could point at anyone,' he said. 'He still has enemies, even eleven years after the end of separate development. If he dies, a report will appear in the press. No one will know the reason for his killing.' He went on ominously. 'If you are caught and prosecuted, there will be no link to me or the party.'

Krige watched Muller for a moment. 'What about Cartwright's movements?'

'He rarely leaves Durban,' said Muller confidently. 'He has an office in the city. You'll see it in the stuff I gave you.'

Krige lifted the folder and paged through the sheets, pausing at intervals. After several minutes he closed it and poked it under his arm. 'We'll travel in a large saloon. It must disappear afterwards. Your men can bring it out with them. I want Durban number plates.'

'What else?' said Muller.

'I want a Beretta R93 9mm parabellum pistol,' said Krige. 'It has special qualities that can be useful, and I don't think this job will be a church social. I am sure your people know where to get one. It must be silenced.

'I'm sure your men will wear plain clothes; no crude insignia of any affiliation they might have. These people still exist, of which I'm sure you are aware. Tell them to be at the farm tomorrow. I leave the next day. I'll have the job done in four days from now.' He looked at his watch, then went past Muller to the jeep. 'I'll phone you when we get back to Pretoria,' he said. 'By then you'll already know if he's dead. At least that should be satisfying.' He loitered on the running board, then got in.

Muller, his face an impassive red under the sun, watched him go. 'Good luck, Major,' he said under his breath. 'Don't come back without the file, and make sure you kill Cartwright. Your life depends on it.'

Chapter 4

Pretoria

The job was dangerous, that much John Bryant knew. If unearthed he would certainly be put to death by the men who believed they were fighting for the survival of their people. His death would be painful and slow, not unlike the Kaffirs who were killed, and those who hadn't learnt to keep to themselves. The vomit had risen in his chest when he had first seen a Venda hanged from a beam by his ankles, over a little fire that emitted enough radiation to pierce his head like a sword. The youth had arched himself upwards with the skinny muscles of his stomach but they had beaten him on the soles of his bare feet and when he could take it no longer he had hung limply as they wanted him to, his hair and scalp frizzling from the heat, bubbling like paint under a torch. After that he had died quickly and they had left him hanging.

Before closing time one Friday afternoon, Bryant received a phone call from Abe Richter, a young officer in the group.

'There's a dance at Gerrit Viljoen's farm,' said Richter in his deep guttural accent. 'You're invited. It'll be a chance for you to meet some of the women. They're better than you've ever seen. Men like you are thin on the ground.'

Bryant had met Viljoen once before. He knew he was one of the group's leaders, a close friend of others in that elite group who lived on the other side of Pretoria and the posh parts of Johannesburg.

'I'll meet you there,' he replied. 'Tell me how to find it.'

'I'll pick you up,' said Richter. 'There's something to do first. Koch and two others will be with us. Some niggers have got a lesson coming.'

Bryant had seen Richter in action before and it was a frightening sight, an unstoppable beast of great strength, no compassion, the emotions of hate and rage mixing to form the most evil transmutation. Koch was cast in a similar psychological mould and, like Richter, he was a big man, the muscles of his torso strapped to his bones like iron plates, developed from lifting weights and years playing rugby at provincial level. Both men were psychotic, persuasive personalities and in their presence it was not difficult to be controlled by their charm; an obvious reason, Bryant thought, for their ascendancy in party affairs.

'What time?' he asked.

'Six, at your place,' said Richter.

Bryant heard the line cut off, and replaced the receiver. Someone was going to die, he could feel it to his core, and he could do nothing about it except be there. It was the game he had to play. He left the office and drove through the city to his flat on the east side of the city.

Richter arrived promptly and they went to his five-year-old Buick. The others were already in the car, Koch in the front and two he had never met. They were introduced as Wessels and Malan.

'Do you remember a court case involving a farmer named Coetzee?' asked Richter once they had left Pretoria. He looked at Bryant in the mirror as he spoke.

'Yes,' said Bryant, surprised at the question. It was headline news. 'He killed his head boy and got off with a three-year sentence. It was ridiculed here and in the foreign press.'

'He should've been acquitted,' said Richter defiantly. 'The black ran over Coetzee's dog with a tractor and killed it. He was rightfully whipped and to my mind should have been killed.'

Bryant remembered the details well, the verdict of manslaughter despite the brutal flogging. To any civilized person it had been murder.

'At the trial,' said Richter, 'two men testified against Coetzee. They're still on the farm. Fortunately for us they're too superior to live in the compound with the other niggers,' said Richter. 'Some things haven't changed. They stay on their own and that's how we'll find them.'

After entering the farming district to the east, they covered another few kilometres before Richter left the road and halted at a gate. Once through, he held to the road until they came to a narrow track leading off into the long grass. He slid the car into it, the tyres rising and falling with the plentitude of potholes that pocked the unyielding earth.

'Who looks after the farm?' Bryant gazed ahead, guessing the answer before it came.

'Coetzee's manager. He's for us.' Richter pushed the car steadily on and after a while drew it up in the middle of the track. Except for Bryant, the men were wearing khaki-coloured clothing and they removed their jackets, baring black and red neo-swastika insignia stitched to their sleeves, which he knew was forbidden in the group and other civilized movements in South Africa.

Taking two coiled *sjambok* whips from under the seat, Richter led, setting off across the veld and then climbing a gradient to a flat ridge. When they reached it, he went to where the ground started to descend, raising a rigid finger and pointing to a clearing below. 'There,' he said.

'There, that's where they are.' A thatched rectangular hut sat in a circle of bare earth, the uneven mud walls baked hard by the sun, as strong as concrete.

Richter turned to Wessels and Malan. 'Come from behind,' he rasped. 'We'll get them out.'

The two left, backtracking for a while before disappearing over the hill. 'They've got to be there,' grunted Richter, moving down the slope. 'I'm not here to waste my time.'

Bryant kept up obediently. Above and beyond he saw Wessels and Malan emerge, moving round the hill like wraiths as they too closed in. He looked at the men in front, their powerful shoulders and narrow waists, the only ones armed, mute .357 magnum pistols sheathed in open holsters at their belts.

On level ground Richter speeded up, running to the door like a hungry dog with its mouth open, casually releasing the whips to drop onto the soil. He steadied, then took his boot into the panelling. The poorly constructed membrane collapsed like balsa under a hammer and he went through into the void.

Two male Xhosas were seated cross-legged on the earth, their chests bare, eating from a black pot, cans of Kaffir beer next to them. They stared at him in horror as he closed on the nearest, unhitching his pistol and taking it smoothly into his hand. For a moment the black was paralysed then he came up, defending with skinny arms and grimacing in expectation of what was to come.

In a flash the Afrikaner was on him, cutting the arms down like stalks of maize and bringing the weapon into use. He lifted off the ground as he heaved the barrel, striking the man on the head, penetrating to the bone and felling him like a tree under the axe.

In an instant he whirled and leapt for the other, raising the weapon as he bounded on. Already on his feet the black dodged wildly and at the last moment slipped out of reach, jumping over the pot and accelerating for the door. He was nearly there when Koch appeared, his embossed chest filling the space, like some bionic man. With a shriek the black stopped, trapped, desperate, and then they were on him, lashing him mercilessly with the cold steel of their guns, clubbing him down with undisguised delight.

Together Richter and Koch carried their victims outside into the low light, to the middle of the raked patch. Standing on the edge of the clearing Bryant watched, observer of a pagan ritual unfolding before him that carried with it imminent death. Coming from behind the building, Wessels and Malan also stayed back, content to leave the proceedings to the men who were masters at what they were about to do.

Already bleeding freely the Xhosas were still, emasculated, their eyes conveying defiance and dread. They had seen it before, when it was not their turn, the pattern forever engraved in their minds. They were proud men and steeled themselves in their determination to give the whites as little pleasure as they could, even when they were staring at death, the end of their lives.

Like actors on a stage the leaders uncoiled the whips, hanging the ends to their boots, and set about their work, driving the treated hide up and down, marking out the zones of flesh that delivered the greatest pain.

For long minutes the Xhosas endured the beating, for the most part suffering in near silence, writhing like snakes on a hot plate as their brown muscle was transformed into a landscape of crimson weals that would never heal – even if there was that chance.

Suddenly Richter lowered the wet hide, uttering a series of vile expletives and then: 'They had no guts. I want Kaffirs with fire.' He distanced himself from his victim, lazily unhooking the thong from his gun. For a while he stroked the blue steel, rotating the cylinder and delighting in the metallic clicking made by the ratchet. Koch had also moved off, the two mutilated forms heaving and sobbing in desperate gasps, spitting into the bone-dry sand.

Bryant looked on, aching to scream and somehow stop the killing, but without the courage, telling himself that he had a duty that extended beyond the deaths of those lying in the dirt. His stomach contracted as he saw Richter advance, and his muscles knotted into a ball that turned his breath into an old-man's wheeze. As the gun was levelled he closed his eyes, fighting to shut out the horror, waiting for the deafening din, but there was only quiet.

Then his ears were pounded by Richter's harsh laugh, a bark that split the stillness in the valley. He kept his eyes shut, bracing his body for the shot, but the laugh carried on. There was no sound from the gun. Opening his eyes, he saw Richter, his face creased in mirth, slipping the pistol into its sheath, and the others grinning like the insane, Koch his head rolled back as if he was about to burst into song.

Cautiously Bryant walked closer, but they ignored him, then all were laughing, the cacophony ringing across the veld.

When Richter took the car over the cattle grid onto Viljoen's farm several kilometres due east the two Xhosas were still, as they had been left, forgotten to all except Bryant, the memory a stain that would be with him until his death, continually asking the question how men could be so cruel.

In minutes they saw the buildings and a level field for parking the cars, where a servant immediately took refuge on the edge of the track for them to pass.

The guns were left under the seat, and they walked

past the house to one of the barns where music and excited voices intermingled and ruptured the calm of the night. The huge brick wall was bathed in an orange hue, reflecting the light cast by a trench of fire built in the ground. Above the turbulent flames two wildebeest rotated, attended by servants, skilfully turning the beasts and continually basting the skin in a rich marinade. At the end of the barn were massive doors, almost the height of the roof, and the little party entered, Wessels and Malan peeling off. Not knowing anyone else, Bryant kept up with Richter as he filed through the group to two women standing alone.

Richter embraced and kissed them, then turned to Bryant, smiling with the pride of a newly-wed. 'Bryant, this is my wife Marie and my sister Sarah.' He swept his arms gratuitously and Bryant shook the proffered hands, thinking it strange he had never seen them before. Both were attractive women, voluptuous and magnificently shaped, with flawless olive complexions and curling dark hair, thick and shiny and tied loosely in strips of ribbon.

At the far end of the barn a male quartet played classical *volk* music and people danced on a raised floor, with a choreography that Bryant had not seen before but that was in perfect accord with the music. Against one of the long walls, trestle tables were laid with traditional food, an abundance of *sosaties* (skwered lamb) and *boerewors* (the Boer sausage) ready for grilling, pawpaw and mango fruit salad, and tarts made to old Afrikaner recipes.

'Some of the men here, like me and Johan, were with smaller political parties before we joined the New Nationalist Party after the blacks came to power, and then this group.' Richter stood next to Bryant. 'They'd sooner die than share their land with blacks but they see that by forming a group like this, with powerful figures running it, they will eventually get their way.'

'They might have to,' answered Bryant. 'Die, that is. The population of South Africa is forty million, of which six million are whites, two million with your beliefs. You're chasing a non-existent dream. Give in and support the ANC. Some of your group already support the ANC, although they won't readily admit it.'

Richter appraised him coldly. 'That's enough.' He didn't like the truth, like others of his kind, and had no way of coping with it. 'We have the will and, as they say, the means.'

'I don't see how you can ever get what you want,' persisted Bryant. 'Ultimately you will have to adapt. A democratically elected government has been with us for over ten years. We have a ratified constitution, overwhelming support from white and black, and a system that makes your kind of thinking a non-starter. A reversion in change will never happen.'

'Never?' said Richter passionately. 'What do you think that was this afternoon?'

'Some kind of revenge,' replied Bryant, trying for more and hoping to get a lead to something a lot bigger. What, he didn't know but he was planted here for that reason.

'The desire for justice was peripheral,' said Richter. He watched Koch dancing with his wife.

'What's your group's military policy, their strategy, how are they going to achieve the dream they failed to see materialize before?' asked Bryant easily, looking past Richter at the band, casual, as if he didn't expect an answer. 'You must have formulated something or are you simply going to behave like a band of criminals and terrorists, like the Irish IRA cells?'

For a moment Richter studied him, then he replied. 'You already know.'

'Do I? said Bryant. 'You mean the commando units you keep hidden, whose existence you would deny? Even if they tried anything they'd be swatted out like flies.'

Richter laughed stridently, semi-maniacal, reminding Bryant of the two Xhosas in the sand, their horribly needless deaths.

'Don't be so sure,' said Richter. 'Of course we're a relatively small force but so were the commandos of the Boer War and look at the havoc they caused. The gradual expulsion of top white military commanders from the defence force has done us a favour. Many of them are now with us, training our men, arming them, converting them into a fighting unit that will yet make this land tremble. And look at what they're up against, niggers who're only used to carrying clubs, and whites who've lost the spirit of their ancestors.'

There was a spectral light in Richter's eyes as he carried on. 'But that's not all. There's also the silent game, the one the ANC tried to play during the seventies and eighties. I think we can be far more successful.' He spoke with the confidence of one who believes he's of a chosen few.

Bryant had the urge to question him further but felt he had asked enough for now.

Richter clearly felt the same. He said: 'This is an evening when we should be having some fun.' He went to his wife and guided her onto the floor, leaving his sister, who had been standing with her, alone.

'I've never seen you at group meetings,' said Bryant, going up to her and inhaling the strong musk of her scent. She was infinitely attractive and had a chemistry that immediately drew him in.

'That's not difficult to explain,' she replied, glancing at him mischievously. 'I've been away. And I've no interest in their politics.'

He raised his eyebrows. 'No interest?' he said. 'What does your brother say to that?'

She bridled indignantly. 'He's not my guardian,' she said. 'We happen to be individuals.'

As the band broke into a familiar piece he indicated the floor and she flared her dress sexily as she walked amongst the other couples and up on to the floor.

'I didn't think anyone would ask me,' she purred. 'The men here are not the most devastating.'

He smiled humourlessly, again thinking of the whippings. They spoke little as they danced and he was pleased she seemed interested in staying with him and in no hurry to find someone else. During the more intimate pieces she held herself to his chest, pressing into him with her breasts and flat stomach. She was around 5 foot 7, nearly his height, with a sophistication he hadn't thought he would find in such a place. He had never understood how women like her could be a part of men like her brother, connected by blood but nothing else.

When the band stopped for a break, people started going outside to watch the final turns of the beasts on the spit. The skewered lamb and *boerewors* lay on parallel grills, their spiced aroma commingling with the richly-soured smell coming from the game, a feast to adorn the finest table.

Wielding razor-sharp knives, the servants sliced slivers of meat from the animals, laying the pieces on heated trays placed on racks next to the fires. The guests helped themselves, liberally plucking the sausage and *sosaties* from the fires and forking venison onto their plates. The best South African wine was on tables nearby, reds and whites, Cabernet Sauvignon, Pinotage, Chenin Blanc and Sauvignon Blanc.

'Viljoen is a fine host,' said Bryant as he and Sarah found seats at one of the tables.

'He's very wealthy,' she said, looking at the house, a double-storeyed whitewashed building with layers of thatch covered by chicken mesh for protection, and the outhouses that were class accommodation and housed those needed to run the farm. 'He can afford to be. Few in these parts have his money.'

'Do you know him personally?' said Bryant. He dug his fork into a chunk of meat, took it to his mouth and silently applauded the subtle flavour.

'I've met him through Abe – once, twice, maybe more,' she said.

'He seems to be very popular,' said Bryant, savouring the flesh in his mouth.

'Yes,' she said cynically. 'Pity he's so vehemently racist, whatever his manner and charm might suggest otherwise. He was one of those who got away.' She dug into her food with the appetite of someone twice her size. 'Where do you stand in all this? Do you really want to be a member of this group? Do you share the views and aspirations of some of the others here, like my brother, Viljoen and that other monster, Koch. How I despise him. God only knows how Abe ever got so involved with him.' She sipped from her glass, the light of the stabbing flames magnifying her natural beauty and making it hard for him to keep his hands off her.

For a moment he was quiet. Then he said: 'One man, one vote is what we have and that is fair and the way it should be. I am certainly not racist and I will never understand why some people can hate others simply because of the colour of their skin. I came to Pretoria for work and met some who are in this party of no name. They seemed very intelligent and progressive. Through them I met Johan Muller and your brother. But in every basket you get bad apples. That is life.'

He ate some more. 'It is also true that some blacks will never renounce what they see is still their struggle, full access to white facilities, homes, schools. Cells of the old military wings of the ANC and the Pan Africanist Congress, Umkhonto we Sizwe and the Azanian Peoples'

Liberation Army, are still in contention and will not disband until their objectives are achieved, even though we hear little of them today. I think that the militant few, like some of this lot, have no chance of getting what they so mindlessly want.'

'But we have had a constituent assembly and a democratically elected government for ten years,' she said. Nearly seventy per cent of that is ANC. The blacks have total political power, with many whites now voting for the ANC.'

'Yes,' he said. 'But to the black radicals economic apartheid is as vibrant as ever. To them the present ANC leadership, with its old men, has betrayed them.'

'What do you mean?' she said. 'What more can we give them? They have the rights to direct their own destiny. Before that they were held captive by the whites.'

'Mandela always insisted on negotiating with de Klerk, sitting at the table with the old nationalists,' he said. 'He saw it as the only way forward, but he incurred the heavy criticism of dissenters in the townships and key industrial zones. They were gathering even before Chris Hani's assassination, a defiant ANC Youth League, resentment in Natal over any deal with Buthelezi, township ANC kangaroo courts, guerillas returning to neither a hero's welcome nor work, and going rogue. They claimed then and still claim that the Mandela who was released was a mere lookalike, that he was trained for years by the whites and then given to his people in 1992, programmed to secure white advantage. Bitterly they cite the lavish, millionaire lifestyles of the ANC leaders and demand to know who's paying for it. Representation in parliament is not enough. It's only a start to getting the privileges denied them, and they want a lot more.'

'That's the argument of some of those here,' she said. 'Are you racist?'

'Pragmatic,' he said. 'Do you want to see the Afrikaner culture abolished?' He changed tack slightly. He was becoming cautious, careful not to show a side that could brand him. However much she sounded like himself he had only just met her, and she was still Richter's sister.

'Of course I don't,' she said, angry at the assertion. 'I want people to share, learn to respect one another, work together and create a prosperous country. We have the resources, the talent and a first-world industrial base. We have to come together and use it.'

'You and Abe are different in how you see things,' he said.

'I believe it's something he has to work through,' she said, protectively. 'He's a gentle man. He loves the Afrikaner people. He's not like some of them. I think he'll change and realize the blacks aren't inherently a threat.'

They sat for a while, listening to the others as they finished their meal.

'Where do you live?' he asked, taking the last of his beer in a series of gulps that smarted tears and made him realize that he was drinking too much.

'I stay with my parents. They own a house near the university. I'm a student there, a postgraduate.'

'In what subject?' he asked.

She smiled, showing even teeth, her red lips beautifully full and convex, inviting. 'Astrophysics' she said with obvious pride. 'Not everyone's choice but it fascinates me and it is an incredible subject. Before this I got a degree in mechanical engineering at Stellenbosch University. That was hard work. What a school. That's the Oxford of South Africa.'

Most of the people had returned to the barn, the carcasses and remains of food cleared, leaving only the embers as a reminder of the feast that had so perfectly been put before them.

‘I feel like a walk,’ she said abruptly, moving her chair and straightening her dress. ‘Are you coming?’

‘Sure,’ he said casually. ‘Where are we going?’

He was a little behind her as she entered the garden and trees that came close to the barn, sheltering them.

She turned and he caught up, putting her arm round his waist. ‘I want sex,’ she said ingenuously. ‘Does that shock you?’

Before he could reply she kissed him, teasing him with her tongue and going for him in a manner that was the last thing he had expected. ‘You haven’t answered,’ she murmured, letting go.

‘You didn’t give me a chance,’ he said, concealing his surprise. ‘Of course I want you. We can go to my flat.’

‘That’s impossible.’ She was impatient. ‘Abe said he’d take me home. He’s also taking you. Even if you had a car here I couldn’t tell him I want to go screwing with you.’ She kissed him again, almost consuming him in her passion. ‘What’s wrong with doing it here? It’s isolated and perfect.’

‘And if someone finds us?’ he said, torn between his lust and the stricture that would inevitably follow if they were found.

‘You’re scared,’ she said. ‘I thought you had guts. Perhaps you don’t find me attractive.’ She tried to push him off but he held her, sliding his hand up her back and artlessly jerking down the zip that opened the door to what he so desired.

‘You know I do,’ he said, peeling the dress off her and lowering it to her waist. ‘I’m not scared of anyone.’

She smiled deviously. ‘I knew that would get you going,’ she said. ‘No man likes his pride dented. I like pride in a man. It’s appealing.’ She unclipped her bra. ‘Do you like them?’

He buried his face between the swollen glands, soaking

in their strange infectious warmth. He had never had anything like this before.

Casting a brief look at the undergrowth for any unlikely intruder, she scooped her dress to her waist and guided his hands to the wetness that had spread in a circle through her pants.

He went to his knees and for a moment savoured her. He led her to lie on the grass, taking his trousers to his calves. His penis was erect and she held it sliding the skin up and down until it was as large as a small pole.

He pulled her pants down a little so they were stretched erotically on her shaped thighs and then went in. She splayed her hands on his small buttocks, drawing and releasing, urging him on to the rapturous crescendo that was only seconds away.

But before they could climax a piercing cry came to them. 'Sarah ... we're leaving!'

As if confronting impending doom he extracted his unrewarded member and helped her up. 'His eyes are everywhere,' he said. 'This is what I feared.'

'Calm down,' she said, fixing her bra on her pouting, tumescent breasts. 'He can't possibly know what we were doing. How frustrating, that was going to be great. I'll get you another time if you want me.'

Walking apart they left the trees. He admired her composure, the way she strode confidently as if nothing had taken place.

Richter paced like a bear near the corner of the barn, silhouetted, his hands on his hips, his demeanour supercilious. Marie was with him, and as they got close he glared. Then he started off for the car and they followed in silence.

Chapter 5

Chelsea, London

'This is an unexpected pleasure. It's not every day students have the opportunity to see someone of your calibre.' David Lawson smiled, pouring water into cups of coffee. 'How long are you staying?'

'It will be a week, ten days at the most.' James Steiner perched himself on a stool, hitching his feet onto one of the cross-bars. 'I want a short spell in Japan, my spiritual home. It's been too long since my last visit. Then it's back to Durban.'

The two men were in Lawson's kitchen, part of a small mews house he had inherited from his uncle. The Englishman was of third-dan black belt rank in *goju-ryu karate*, four grades below Steiner, each grade at that level taking years of study. They had met on several occasions in Tokyo where both had pursued training in their art under a famous master named Chinen. Their friendship had formed through hours of hardship on the *dojo* floor, sparring and pounding the *makiwara* until their hands bled from the ordeal. That was years previously and they had not seen one another since.

'You can stay here.' Lawson passed a cup. 'There's enough space in this pad. I'm still single.'

'Thank you, I was hoping you'd offer,' said Steiner. 'Where's your training hall, the *dojo*. Let's have a workout this afternoon.'

'Unfortunately it's not as easy as that,' said Lawson. 'I hire a hall at Imperial College not far from here. It'll have to be when the class tonight finishes.'

For a week after his arrival in London, Steiner taught at Lawson's club in Knightbridge, staying on when the sessions ended to work alone with his friend. There were *kata* or set forms, an essential element in training, that the younger man had not learned and he welcomed the opportunity to penetrate the art more deeply, from the teachings of one who the Japanese considered was already a young master.

On the eighth day, as if on impulse, Steiner bought a ticket on Japanese Airlines for the next morning. He left the booking office in Hanover Square and took a tube to South Kensington station in Chelsea. Lawson was away, visiting his family in the country, and after disembarking at the station Steiner walked down the Old Brompton Road on his way to the house. It was October, the first signs of the coming winter evident in the morning chill and although he had spent hours meditating in icy Japanese streams he fastened his short jacket and pulled up the collar.

As he neared the intersection with Queen's Gate, a long wide road that ran up to Hyde Park, he saw a girl approach the lights from further down and stop, waiting for them to change. She was wearing a skirt that stopped a few inches above the knees and she had the legs and figure he had long ago decided were perfect. She was looking in the other direction and as his eyes rested on her dark-brown hair that hung well below her shoulders he was reminded of a girl he had last seen in Johannesburg three years before. He dismissed any chance that she was the same person, in the middle of London 6,000 miles away. But as she turned her head he halted. It was Sophie Carswell, the same girl.

Steiner clearly remembered the only time a woman had seduced him, in the lounge of her parents' house in a privileged Johannesburg suburb while they were asleep upstairs. She was then in her early twenties, a lot younger than he, unashamedly promiscuous, and they had made love continually until it was nearly dawn. Before the lights could change he went up to her. 'Do you remember me?' he said. 'James Steiner.'

She swung to him, searching the past. 'I do,' she said after a moment, her blue eyes sparkling alluringly. 'Johannesburg. That was a few years back. I apologize for leaving the next morning without saying goodbye, but that's how it was.'

They had met at a party over the road from where she lived, at the home of a friend of Steiner's father. Sophie's parents had offered to put him up for the night before he flew to Durban on the morning flight.

'What are you doing in London?' She could understand looking at him why she had found him so attractive that night, his dark, closely cropped hair, lean features and feline physique.

'I'm passing through,' he said. 'I've a friend here. Tomorrow I fly to Tokyo.'

'Tokyo?' She was curious.

'Yes.' He smiled. 'Our encounter was so brief I never got round to telling you my profession. That's how I got these. Didn't you notice?' He clenched his fists, displaying the faint but clear ball-like protuberances on the first two knuckles of each hand.

'I didn't,' she said. 'Perhaps I was too interested in something else, but I can guess. Callouses like that can only come from karate. My boyfriend is an aikido instructor and I know something about those arts. He also lived in Japan.'

Steiner smiled. 'Well done,' he said. 'It's the karate

style of *goju-ryu* to be exact. Where are you going now? I'll buy you coffee.'

She laughed infectiously. 'My flat's halfway up Queen's Gate.' She motioned towards Hyde Park. 'Come there, I've only got an hour before my class. I'm studying dance near Sloane Square.'

It was one of the large basement flats of Queen's Gate and after she had made coffee they sat in the living room, she on a sofa and he on a chair next to a dining table that had seen better days. He learned that she was living with her boyfriend, Paul Adams, and that she had been in London for a year. As she spoke, the hem of her skirt well up on her legs, his mind travelled back to the sexual experience they had had that night in Johannesburg. The intervening years had made her more beautiful, and he wondered if her boyfriend satisfied her. He knew he could.

When Steiner made his advance he expected a favourable response and he was mildly surprised when she said: 'I don't want sex with you. That was long ago. I told you, I have a steady boyfriend. And I love him.'

'You had a boyfriend when we last made love,' he answered. 'That's why I didn't see you the next morning. You'd gone to play tennis with him, so your mother said.'

'This one's different,' she said defensively. 'We're going to get married.'

'You'll enjoy it,' he said, getting off his chair. 'That is, sex with me. What's once more?'

'No, please leave.' She made to rise but he moved in a bound like a cat after prey and was there in an instant. 'Not without sex.' he said.

She looked at him and was for the first time aware of the smouldering determination. His close presence made her feel another strange energy. It reminded her of her boyfriend, but he had never frightened her. Steiner did now. She tried to slide past him but he pushed her back on to the sofa, her skirt rising high as if caught in a blast of wind.

'What kind of beast have you become?' she cried. 'To think we ever made love.'

'We did,' said Steiner. 'And you liked it. Get your pants off. If you don't I'll do it.'

She hesitated. If she didn't comply she was sure he would beat her, that she would ignite a terrible anger. She was sure he would have his way. Slowly, mechanically, as if in a dream, she removed her skirt and pants, thankful he had not asked her to take off her bra. She could feel his gaze feast on her naked parts and when the garments lay on the floor he peeled off his jeans. He was already erect, a huge circumsized organ that reached up almost vertically.

'Come to the edge,' he commanded, kneeling and parting her legs so they straddled his chest. He lowered his face to her pubic hair, stretching his tongue out and licking between the tumescent pink lips like a cat lapping from a bowl of milk. When she was wet on her skin he heaved her further over the edge and went into her, driving his loins in response to his lust. She shut her eyes, wanting the grotesque act to end, oblivious of the sporadic noise of cars outside and only hearing his deep, heavy breathing.

With a cry of gratification he finally ejaculated, quickly coming out as if eager to go, and fishing in his pocket for a tissue with which to wipe himself clean.

She waited while he dressed then left the sofa, taking her clothes. When she had finished putting them on she said: 'You're an animal. Now get out.' Her voice was composed, deliberate. She knew he had got what he wanted and no longer had any fear of him.

'I'm sorry you didn't enjoy it as much as I did,' he said unrepentantly. 'You've obviously changed.'

'That was rape, James. It was pure brutal rape. You'll be hearing from me.' She went to show him out. He left, and once on the pavement headed south towards the Fulham Road and Lawson's house.

That morning Sophie Carwell missed her class at the dance studio and for the rest of the day she was alone in the flat, infused by humiliation and anger, and a resolve to get revenge in whatever form. She was sufficiently informed that victims in rape cases seldom achieved satisfaction, and on the few occasions when the man was convicted the sentences were derisory, in no way compensating for the psychological trauma and debasing experience.

Her boyfriend Paul Adams arrived at the flat before ten o'clock that evening after a class he ran in Soho. He was surprised not to find her in the living room and more surprised to see her on their bed, propped against the headboard. She did not welcome him when he appeared and he went over, placing his hand on her hand.

'What's wrong?' he said gently. He was tall, handsome, his striking blond hair swept rakishly from his forehead.

She was still for a moment then reached for him, wrapping her arms around his neck and resting her head on his chest. In the relief of having him close she gave vent to a sob, and held him as if she dared not part, as if it was essential that she held him forever.

Then the tears were unrestrained and she blurted out: 'I've been raped, this morning here in our flat.' She broke down, weeping, her anguish expelling itself through the streams that ran onto his shirt.

At first he was too numbed to speak, then gradually he could only feel anger, coalescing into harnessed rage. 'Who was it?' he said, not expecting that she knew him.

She unfolded and sat up, wiping her hand and smudging her makeup, drained by the release of emotion. 'He was a South African and as English as you are. He was born and brought up here and has dual nationality. I met him years ago in Johannesburg.'

He moved from her, astonished. 'Did you have sex,' he demanded, 'when you first met him?'

She lowered her head, doefully, and then became defiant and cried: 'Yes, a one-off. I'm sure you've had plenty.'

He went to the end of the bed, tense, trying to absorb what had happened and what he'd heard. He forced himself to understand. He loved her.

She went on, his anger strangely calming. 'He came up to me in the street,' she said. 'I asked him here for a cup of coffee. I never thought he could behave like that. It was a terrible experience, someone take advantage of you without your consent. I was very frightened. And from someone I thought of as a friend.' She wept again, wanting and crying out for sympathy, something to lessen the pain.

Overcome by her piteous state Adams went to her, drawing her into him. Beyond feelings for her, his desire was for revenge. 'His name,' he said in a whisper. 'Where's he now?'

'I don't know,' she said. 'Oh Paul, he mustn't come between us. Please say he won't.

He nodded grimly. 'He won't,' he said. 'But he'll get what he deserves.'

'It's too late,' she said, remembering what Steiner had said in the street.

'Why?' he said, turning in surprise.

'Tomorrow he flies to Tokyo,' she said. 'He's in your business.'

'*Aikido*?' He frowned, disbelievingly, not accepting that anyone in such a revered discipline could commit rape.

'No,' she said. 'It's karate. He was specific.' She paused. 'The *goju* style, if that means anything to you?'

'It does,' he replied. 'In membership it's a small style but in technique it's very traditional and extremely powerful. Some of the truly great masters are products of *goju* schools.' An unfathomable expression came over his face. 'I may be too late to stop him leaving but I'll soon find him, even if I have to go to Japan. With his training I'm surprised he hasn't learnt how to behave.'

He thought for a moment then said: 'Phone your parents and tell them what has happened. It will help you. Don't hide it, or be ashamed of it. That man deserves what he is going to get.' He moved from her. 'After you have spoken to them I want to speak to your father. I assume you have told him of my existence?'

She nodded. 'Of course, they know all about you. Why do want to speak to him?'

'You've told me a lot about him, how you admire him, love him, how you respect his judgement,' said Adams. 'I want to see what he thinks before I go after this Steiner. Your father is also a commander in your country's National Intelligence Agency or NIA.'

Sophie was not slow in contacting her parents. She was naturally in tears when she told them that she had been raped. Her father was so angry she thought he would personally go after Steiner and exact retribution. He demanded to know where Steiner was, and calmed a little when she asked him to speak to her boyfriend.

'I'm sorry I wasn't here,' offered Adams to Sophie's father when he was given the phone. 'He didn't harm Sophie physically but it will take time for her to get over the mental trauma, the horror of such a violation. I will always be with her and we can get through it together.'

Adams let his concern for Sophie sink through to her father and give some reassurance. Then he said: 'I know

Japan and it won't take me long to find out where I can locate Steiner. The organization he is involved with, and the circles he is probably used to mixing in, are small. I will start here.'

Carswell was quiet for a while, thinking. 'What will you do when you find him? All countries have laws.'

'I'll work that out when we meet,' said Adams. 'I have close friends in Japan. I can be in and out in a few days, do the job and leave no trace. Sometimes it is justified in taking the law into your own hands, as the wise guys say.'

'I wish you luck,' said Carswell. 'Let me know what happens. I will see what I can find out about this Steiner, his past, if there is anything on him in this country. I might be able to help.'

Early the following morning, after several calls to London numbers, and when he was beginning to think he had struck a blank, Paul Adams reached Dave Lawson at home.

'James Steiner?' said Lawson. 'I know him, but he's gone.'

'Where's he gone to, and when?' Adams already knew enough from Sophie that would enable him to find Steiner once in Japan but it was always good to get some kind of confirmation.

'Tokyo,' said Lawson. 'He would go to the headquarters of our style. He left five hours ago.' Lawson added: 'Is he a friend?'

'No.' Adams was abrupt. 'He's got something to answer for. It's a personal matter.'

Lawson grunted in surprise. 'I won't ask. All I can say is that he's highly respected in our organization.'

'Where's your HQ?' said Adams, interjecting.

Lawson laughed, the sound he made empty. 'You're

not going over there?' he asked rhetorically. 'It must be serious.'

'I might,' said Adams.

'Do you know Tokyo?' said Lawson, curious about Adams' intent.

'I know enough,' answered Adams, eager to move on. 'I used to live there.'

Lawson hesitated. Then he said: 'James will probably stay in our *hombu dojo* in Yoyogi, a rail stop from Shinjuku. It's hard to miss. He will certainly contact them and they'll know where he is.'

'Thanks,' said Adams. 'I know the area. I spent a few years not far from there.'

'I hope it sorts itself out,' said Lawson, wondering if he had said too much. 'James is a great guy.'

Adams put down the receiver and thumbed the pages of the directory to Japan Airlines. In minutes he had made a reservation on the night flight to Tokyo.

Chaper 6

Pretoria

When Richter dropped him off at the flat and drove off along the road, Bryant had already decided not to see Sarah again. Much of the journey from the farm had been conducted without a word, and he was certain Richter suspected they had been copulating among the trees, and predictably he did not approve. Bitterly Bryant admonished himself for taking a chance when he was all too aware of local attitudes to such behaviour. That Richter had not actually seen them at it was some consolation, but he was convinced he had to break with her if the soured relationship between himself and her brother was to improve, a relationship that he was starting to believe more and more would be important to his investigative work.

A few days went by before Bryant attended another party meeting, in a community hall near the university. The turnout was as high as usual and he half-listened to the repetitious oratory, continually rising to a fanatical diatribe that brought a joyous outpouring from the people. He was astonished that this could still go on when these people were members of a group that appeared on the surface to support the governing ANC party. Surprisingly, Richter and Koch were not there but he could see Johan Muller sitting in the front row, a man he had met before, his jacket slung over the chair and his braces tenuously stretched to the top of his oversized pants.

At 10.30 Bryant drove to the flat, depressed at his slow progress, and with a feeling that he was going nowhere. His bosses were sure that there was something dangerous about elements in the group, with its powerful members, nowhere to be seen in any other predominantly white political group, and they wanted to find out more.

The dim lights of the block of flats revealed only patches along the corridor and only when Bryant inserted the key was he conscious of someone standing near him.

'John.' Sarah's dulcet tone was unmistakable and he turned to her.

'What do you want?' he grated, immediately regretting it as she stepped into the light, as pretty as he remembered her, delicately made up, her heavy breasts less obvious under a navy blue blazer.

'I want to speak to you,' she said, edging nearer. 'I'm sorry about the other night. I let myself go. It's not how I normally behave.'

'It's over,' he said. 'Anyway I wanted it as much as you did. Your brother wants to keep you a virgin.'

'I'm not,' she said. 'Do you think I could do that if I was? He's far too parochial. Things in the world have changed. It's known as liberation.' She lifted her arms in emphasis. 'Besides, there's something else, something more urgent than a quick screw.'

He smiled disbelievingly. 'I want to cool it, for a while at least,' he said. 'We were going too fast for Abe's taste. I don't want to fall out with him.'

'Why?' she asked innocently, never suspecting that he was anything more than what she saw. 'You don't really share their views.' She came up to him and played with the lapel of his coat. 'I can't understand you.'

'You don't have to.' He turned the key, pensive. 'What's so important?'

'So you're interested,' she said flatly. 'I'm not telling you out here. It was a conversation I had with Abe.'

He pushed the door of his basic, utilitarian flat. 'I'll listen,' he said. 'But not for long.'

'Thanks,' she said sarcastically.

He filed past her, going along the passage to the lounge, a room with little more than a sofa and a couple of seats. He indicated one. 'My ears are pricked,' he said.

She perched one knee on the other, adjusting her skirt and giving him a token view up it. 'No one knows I'm here,' she said. 'Relax and listen.'

He dragged one of the chairs into the middle of the room, lowering himself into it, stirred by the sight of diaphanous black tights to her apex. He searched her languid eyes. 'Well?'

'It could be nothing,' she said. 'Perhaps I'm too tense at the moment with my work at the university. I have to submit my thesis in four weeks.'

He moved on the seat to ease the swelling in his crotch, hoping it wasn't obvious.

'I saw my brother last night at a place in town,' she said. 'He was in a strange mood, elated, drinking excessively. I asked him if his party could ever accept the ratified constitution and live under this government. He said that no constitution could ever prevent the redistribution of land that the blacks want. He cited the Kruger Park farms that the blacks see as theirs, stolen from them by a minority regime over the decades, land that should be given to the people. He is convinced that the present government, and for that matter all blacks, only see the power they have as a stepping stone to that which will allow them to enforce their secret aims, economic wealth.'

'He didn't answer the question,' he said bluntly.

'I'm coming to that,' she said, straightening her skirt. 'I asked him again how they would react, beyond those ridiculous secret manoeuvres of their commandos on remote strips of veld.'

The corners of his mouth elevated. He knew what she meant. 'And what was his answer?'

'He laughed, saying it's not over yet,' she said, hanging her head. 'He was drunk, worse than I've seen him for a long time. There was no answer to the question but he said that in the next day he's going to Durban to help retrieve something that if it got into the wrong hands it would bring down those who have spent their lives defending the rights and heritage of the whites against the blacks.'

Bryant came to his feet, running his nails through greased hair. 'What does that mean?' he said.

'He clammed up,' she said, feeling that she had something even though it didn't come across as such.

He towered over her. 'That's nothing,' he said. 'Why did you come to me? I belong to the group. I like a lot of them.'

'You're sensible,' she said, looking at him appealingly. 'You're more rational. I'm afraid my brother's going to get into trouble. Please, can you talk to him?'

'About what?' he said. 'I can hardly ask him about something he is going to do in Natal.' He laughed soberly. 'Besides, he's not that approachable.'

'You scorn me,' she said. 'It might mean little to you but it does to me. I've never heard him speak like that. He was manic.'

'I think he was just getting you wound up, either that or he was fantasizing,' he said. 'That's not all you came for. I don't think you should be seen with me.'

'You're a bastard,' she said. 'Didn't you like what we were doing the other night? What kind of hold has Abe got on you? And that group?'

He was motionless. 'They have nothing over me,' he

said. 'And why should they? But if we meet it has to be on my terms. I don't want anyone else to know.' His lust had him, and she could see it.

She smiled, shedding her blazer and offering herself. 'If that is your wish, let's get on with something else, something that was so cruelly interrupted the other night.'

It was past midnight when Bryant let Sarah out and returned to the room where for nearly two hours they had copulated. He had never had anything like it before. It was like being in heaven, or so he imagined. He stood in the middle of the floor under the gaze of the frosted bulb then went to the phone. He dialled a number.

'Bryant,' he said, when he recognized the authoritative inflection on the other end of the line. 'There's something of interest to them in Durban that they are going to retrieve. It's certainly of more than a little interest.'

'Such as what?' asked Smith, one of the Durban commanders of the Scorpions.

'Don't know, and not likely to without some probing which is not easy,' said Bryant. 'If I ever found anything it would all be over, whatever it is.'

'That doesn't help,' said Smith, ever impatient with scraps he couldn't get his hands on.

'No,' said Bryant, expecting the response but still irritated by it. He wished Richter had said more to his sister, and he felt foolish.

'Find what you can,' said Smith. 'I can't send a squad running around the city looking for some guys who are fighting to save their people. Who's the source?'

'Someone who appears to be at the centre of it, whatever that is,' said Bryant. 'He bragged to his sister.'

The man on the other end laughed. 'And she told you,' said Smith. 'It sounds like pillow talk to me. Who is he?'

'Richter, Abe Richter. Verster Straat, Pretoria. I'm not sure of the number but I can easily find out. He's in the book.'

Silence, then: 'I'll have someone on him tomorrow. His name's Marais. The best we can do is to watch this Richter at source. If and when he moves we'll be on him.'

Bryant replaced the receiver. Something was going on, and it was important. He could smell it. That was what he had been sent to find out and for a moment, prematurely, he congratulated himself.

The day after seeing his sister at the bar Richter was in an angry mood, not only because he had a sore head from the neat spirit the night before, but also because he had let slip about the job in Durban. Normally he would have let it pass, but he suspected his sister was sleeping with John Bryant.

For a while he had felt uneasy about Bryant. Who would come to Pretoria, as beautiful as it was, from Durban, that was so distant, and take a low-paid job with the municipality and get involved so intimately with the political party, without the passionate conviction shared by some of the others? Bryant never missed meetings and was too interested in some party affairs that did not concern him.

Before lunch, in the privacy of his study, Richter phoned a friend in the city, someone who was a member of his group and worked for the local telephone exchange. He had contacted him earlier.

'Bryant made a long-distance call in the early hours,' said the man unemotionally. 'It was to a Durban number. We can determine the name of the receiver if you wish.'

Richter was standing next to his desk, resting the telephone on his bull-like neck. 'Get a courier to bring the contents of the call to me,' he said, disappointed. Only one call made in twenty-four hours. 'If it helps me after I've listened to the tape you can find out who the call was made to. Somehow I think I'll learn everything I want from the tape.'

A tape was delivered 20 minutes later and he went to his study, securing the door and switching on a portable cassette player. He waited impatiently while the tape rewound, drumming his fingers and thinking of the work in Durban. At last the speaker crackled and he went adroitly into a leather chair, rotating the volume knob a quarter turn and listening for the words. When they came he went rigid, and then closeted the tiny box as if it was made of gold.

'Got you,' he murmured. 'This is your passport to hell, my friend.'

In the dim light Richter replayed the tape several times, learning little more than he had on the first. He took it from the machine and went to the venetian blind. There were only a few parked cars. All were empty except one.

The rain was a shimmer of mist on the Sunday afternoon when Koch arrived at Richter's house. He was ushered in by his friend and they drank coffee in the kitchen before Marie and the children departed to visit an old aunt, leaving them alone.

'You must be wondering what I meant on the phone,' said Richter, draping his arms python-like as he sat on a high stool next to the breakfast bar. 'I'm afraid I've been careless. I told my sister that we were going to Durban for something that, if revealed, would wreak havoc amongst our people. She told Bryant.'

'Bryant?' said Koch, surprised.

'Yes, he's not what he appears to be,' said Richter. 'For

a while I've had my doubts. Yesterday I had his line tapped. This morning I was given a recording of a conversation he had with someone in Durban. You can guess what it was about. The guy he spoke to is certainly in the one the intelligence arms, the NIA, or even the Scorpions. Clearly Bryant is associated with them.'

Koch's expression narrowed. 'Why should Sarah tell him?' he asked.

'She's sleeping with him,' said Richter, convinced. 'She took a fancy to him at Viljoen's party.'

'What else? Where does it leave us?' asked Koch, starting to fidget nervously.

'Fortunately it's not serious.' Richter spoke confidently, getting up from the stool. 'They have nothing to go on, just a vague statement.' He went to the door. 'Except that a minor irritation has arisen. They've put someone on my tail.'

Koch followed Richter into the study, where he was led to the window. 'There,' said Richter. He showed Koch the parked car where the solitary figure sat behind the wheel. 'He's been there for hours.'

Koch left the window, as if he had already decided what to do. 'What about Bryant?' he said.

'He'll have the same fate as this one,' said Richter. 'We'll get Bryant when we return from the job in Durban. It will be a pleasure. I can't wait to see his face.' Richter passed his tongue over his lips. 'But, this one has to be dealt with first.'

At nine o'clock on the Sunday evening Richter finished the call in his study and went to the window. Whenever he looked out the man was still there, a leech, who seemed to need no respite from his task. Drawing the curtains and switching on a lamp, he unlocked a drawer in his desk. He extracted a snub-nosed .38 Ruger revolver, a silencer screwed to the end, and a small carton of ammunition. The pistol was lightly oiled, and after lowering the cylinder he wiped the weapon dry with cloth, deftly drawing a strip tied to a cord down the barrel. He filled the cylinder and put the gun in the pocket of his coat, agitating the fabric to balance the weight.

His wife looked up from the book on her lap as he entered the lounge, noting the jacket.

'You're going out. What's so urgent on a Sunday night?' She removed her glasses, the intriguing lights in her liquid eyes momentarily enticing him to stay. He still found her extremely attractive after years of marriage. He reckoned that he was one of the lucky ones.

'Something's got in the way,' he said distantly. 'I won't be long.'

She sighed, acquiescing, having learned through the years there was little to be gained by pressing the subject further. Besides, she loved him and she was sure it had something to do with party affairs. They were still embroiled in threatening times, or so she had been led to believe. 'God bless you. I'm always behind you. You know how much I love you.'

He returned to the study and peered through a slit in the curtain that draped the blinds. The car was still there with the man in it.

A few minutes passed, then another car appeared at a crawl. As it neared the first car the driver drew in to the curb. Leaving the engine running he went to the car ahead.

Richter left the study and let himself out of the house through the kitchen. At a run he went down the drive into the street and over to the cars.

Koch was standing next to the co-driver's door of the front one, his gun aimed at the sullen man behind the controls. 'It's hard to believe he's what you say he is,' he said as Richter came up. 'Except for the gun, it's enough to blow a hole in a tank.' He indicated a bulbous Colt semi-automatic on the floor of the car and made way for Richter to get in. 'His name's Marais.' He threw a wallet into the back. 'I'm behind in my car.'

Richter got into the car next to Marais, whose bony fingers were locked tensely around the wheel. 'Drive,' he said, taking out the revolver. 'You've got something to tell us.'

'You're insane,' said Marais defiantly. 'Get out and leave me alone.'

Richter cocked the revolver and held it to Marais's head. 'You heard me. Move this heap or I'll kill you.'

Reluctantly, beginning to fear for his life, Marais started the engine and went along the road.

'Take the freeway for Nelspruit,' said Richter. 'I'll tell you when to bear off.'

In minutes they were on the N4 heading north-east from the capital, Marais glancing in his mirror every now and then at the car on their tail. 'Where're you taking me?' he said when they had gone several kilometres. 'I don't know you, or your friend. The police will screw you for this. They'll get you and string you up.'

'Police,' said Richter. 'No one sits all day in a parked car with a Colt .45 in his vest for nothing. Who're you working for?'

'That's my business,' said Marais, still relatively composed.

'We'll see,' said Richter. 'I want the next turn.'

Marais left the road when the exit came up. He concealed his fear. They were strong, armed, and unlikely to let him go, especially if he admitted to what he was. He obeyed the terse commands and they were soon alone, the night black, the only illumination from the quarter-moon above and the halogen lamps. He looked out over the veld, sublimely peaceful, a silent observer of the wild antics of men.

'Go through the gate.' Richter briefly indicated white posts rearing up from nowhere. 'Keep to the right. You'll see a barn. Pull up next to it and switch off.'

The gate led onto someone's farm, the house fleetingly visible through a grove of willows. Marais stopped when he reached the barn, hesitating before complying.

In seconds Koch was at the car, roughly grabbing Marais by the sleeve. 'Out,' he said, turning on a torch. He hustled Marais to the building, Richter falling in, and shunted him inside. As Richter entered he brushed a bank of switches wired to a series of fluorescent tubes. Except for bales of hay packed to the ceiling at one end, the barn was empty.

'Start talking, no one will hear you,' said Richter cogently. 'That is, except us. Let's call it our secret.'

Marais was in his mid-forties, tall and thin, his pallid complexion and red vein-shot nose testimony to over-indulgence in alcohol and tobacco. 'I'll be killed whatever I say,' he said. 'How many others have you killed in this place?'

Richter took no notice. 'What about Bryant? He's one of you.'

Marais laughed through yellow teeth. 'I've never heard of him,' he said. He was sweating in dewdrop beads. He took a half-step. 'You're off line, mistaken.' He was starting to whine.

'What are you?' said Richter.

The answer was slow in coming. 'I'm a private investigator, missing persons, divorce, that sort of thing.'

Richter threw back his head, bleating like a beast on heat. 'Bullshit. Who's like that where I live? I know everyone in the district. You're lying.' He looked at Koch and cackled again, stroking the weapon.

He faced Marais. 'You're the missing person,' he said. 'Who you work for will go with you to your grave. Your disappearance will forever be a mystery. Not even the best cops will find you.'

Marais ran at him, reaching for the revolver, the desire for life welling inside him like a subterranean spring. But as he came close to the steel, Richter swept back, levering the revolver round. 'Get off,' he snarled. 'Your life's over.'

The barrel hit Marais on the head but it was a glancing blow, only briefly diverting him from his course. He pressed on, pivoting neatly and striking for the groin with his fist. Richter jackknifed but the fist caught him square on and Marais knew it had hurt. He threw himself after the weapon, his only hope. He found the barrel and took it with the pleasure of a child finding a present on Christmas day.

Richter fought to repel the attack but Marais held on, doing well although man-to-man combat was not his forte. For seconds Richter felt he was on a losing edge, then drawing on his cunning and superior strength he flowed with the force, disrupting Marais' balance and leading him in. Clasping the graying head he changed tack, butting the nose and transforming his victim's face into a sea of blood. Marais let the gun go, holding his nose, striving to see through the coloured flecks that blanked his sight.

'Got you,' shouted Richter victoriously, holding his bruised hand to his body and viewing his adversary scornfully.

He said to Koch. 'You're a calm bastard. He nearly got the gun.'

Koch patted his pistol. 'You're too strong.' He laughed evenly. 'Finish him off.'

Marais was defeated, still covering his face, tenderly stroking his nose and wiping away the blood. 'You'll get life for this, the rest of your days in a squalid pit with others of your breed.' He spat out the words through the blood that had reached his lips.

Richter's gun exploded and Marais staggered, miserably trying to keep upright as if that would stave off the dying moment. He gave his executioner one last wretched look and then he fell, his legs folding as their strength was at last severed.

'That was pretty good.' Koch nodded approvingly. 'Few can match your skill with one of those. I hope Krige gives you a chance to use it.' He went to the corpse and felt the pulse in the neck. 'He's finished, clearly yesterday's man.'

Richter put the revolver in his coat. 'I often wonder why Muller asked this guy Krige to take the lead in this job in Durban. He's an unknown quantity, not one of us. Any cock-up in retrieving the file will expose our group and rip it apart, and others.'

'We'll soon see how good he is,' said Koch. He gripped Marais's coat. 'Let's shift him.'

They took the body and laid it against the stack of hay, exposed, gaping up at the steel girders, a sudden metamorphism.

Koch scowled in disgust. 'Not the best sight first thing in the morning,' he said. 'What's du Preez going to do with it?'

'He's got a thousand acres,' said Richter. 'It'll never be found. By this hour tomorrow both this evil bastard and his car will have vanished. For us Marais doesn't exist and never has. He is of the past.'

Jan Krige's farm

On the Monday morning twelve hours after Marais met his death in the barn Krige started the four-cylinder engine of his jeep. He was on the edge of a field in the southern sector of his farm and he watched as a saloon car sped across the valley to the house, half a kilometre from him. He had been expecting them, Muller's men, the two he was being forced to take along with him.

They were talking to his wife when he pulled up in the yard next to their car. She was on the verandah, the Alsatians with her, and the men were at the bottom of the steps, relaxed and confident, dressed in the khaki those with paramilitary expectations preferred. He had expected the type who would be sent his way; not clear-thinking progressives but those forever tainted and chained to the past. He knew he had to forget his sentiments if the operation was to go smoothly. He just wanted to get it over and done with.

'Krige,' he said, going up to them, without offering his hand. 'I see you've met my wife.'

Richter put his heels together and saluted. 'Good morning, Major,' he said, grinning like the proverbial Cheshire cat. 'She's a beautiful woman.'

Krige nodded once, unsmiling, the compliment unwelcome. 'I've been expecting you,' he said. 'What are your names?' He looked at his wife. She had taken a dislike to them, and he could understand why.

'Richter, Major, Abe Richter,' said Richter. He indicated his friend without breaking his gaze. 'And this is Johannes Koch, a close friend of mine.'

'This is a fine farm,' said Koch, breaking his silence and alternating his attention between Kirsty and Krige. 'The best land in the district.' He looked at the dogs. 'Beasts like that are good for keeping the Kaffirs down.' The slant was intended, set to get a response, to find out where the Kriges stood.

Krige's wife lowered herself next to the dogs, stroking

their thick fur. 'We don't train them to attack blacks,' she blurted out, 'if that's who you mean. We're not racists.'

Koch gave a hooting cry. 'Anyone who wants to protect the Boer from the black horde is a racist,' he expounded. 'Or do you want them to take everything, more than what they've already got?' His benign expression had changed. She had seen it before, a caricature of hate and contempt for anyone who disagreed with white supremacy in its most violent form.

'I disagree,' she said, controlling herself and suppressing her distaste for the man. 'This country's for all of us.'

For a moment Koch bored into her eyes then deliberately took his gaze down to her gorgeously formed breasts. Calmly he turned to Krige. 'Disappointing,' he said, understating the anger that settled in his gut. 'Clearly your wife's not of Boer stock, Major.'

'You're here for a job,' said Krige softly, so Kirsty couldn't hear. 'Not to argue politics with my wife.'

Koch's mouth stretched elastically. 'I can wait,' he said, inaudibly.

Kirsty left the verandah and went into the house, her walk angry, condemning, the hate she was not used to feeling building in a surge.

'They're at their most attractive when they're like that,' said Richter watching her until she disappeared. 'What's the plan, Major?'

'Did you bring the gun I asked Muller for?' said Krige, mentally making a note of what had happened.

Richter nodded. 'It's in a box in the back of the car,' he said. 'I've never seen one like it before.'

'Leave it there for the moment,' said Krige.

'Where are we staying?' said Richter. 'Muller said we move tomorrow.' He lit one of his rare cigarettes, dropping the match onto the soil as if the land was his.

'You'll find it over there near the barns,' said Krige.

'It's comfortable.' He climbed the steps. 'Relax,' he said, insincerely. 'I'll join you here for lunch.'

Krige left them in the yard and went looking for his wife. She was in the kitchen, sitting at the table, picking nervously at the uneven surface, uncertain and afraid.

'You didn't tell me those men were coming to the farm,' she said accusingly. 'And they're staying the night. Anyone can see they're thugs. Oh, what are you caught up in?'

He came to the table and embraced her tentatively. 'They're helping me with the work for Muller,' he said, knowing what she was feeling. 'We leave in the morning. You'll never see them again.'

She was dissatisfied. 'Oh God, what kind of work is this? These men are obviously killers. Their appearance and the first words they spoke tell me that. They're everything we don't want to see in this country anymore.'

He went to the end of the table, on edge, glancing out onto the yard. 'I'll return before the weekend,' he said. 'You're getting worried over nothing.'

She sighed achingly, resigning herself to the fact that he was going through with it, whatever it was. Stretching out sensuously she drew him over and kissed him, her wide mouth full and moist.

'That's enough,' he said gently. 'We'll end up in bed. I'll keep them out of your way.'

'When are you going?' she asked, releasing herself from his hold.

'It'll be mid-morning tomorrow,' he said. 'Now I want to see Claasen. He'll check the barns for me.'

He went along the straight passage into the lounge. The two men had gone. She was right, their extreme beliefs and truculent manner exposed them for what they were, killers of their party, the type who would willingly lead their people into a savage covert war. He thought of Cartwright in Durban, the brilliant lawyer, the one who apparently now had the weapon to bring the top cats during the apartheid period to justice – not men like Richter and Koch but men who were in a completely different league. He knew he might have to kill Cartwright. That was his decision when the time came. Perhaps he was no different from the likes of Richter and Koch, whatever the reason for accepting this job.

At noon when Krige returned to the house, the men were on the porch, Koch seated and Richter pacing like a caged lion, dispensing ash from his cigarette onto the spotless stone.

'I'll get something to eat,' said Krige, thudding up the steps one by one and throwing his jacket over the rail. Pre-empting his call, Maria appeared and laid cold meat and bread and a pot of tea on the table. 'Anything else, Master?' she enquired, holding the empty tray flat against her freshly laundered skirt.

Krige shook his head and she left them, scurrying away like a mouse as she crossed the porch. Grating the chairs over to the table, Krige said: 'I hope you like your room.'

'It's perfect, Major.' Richter lowered his bulk. 'You're a lucky man. This is the kind of land we're fighting for.'

Krige leant on a wooden post, lighting a cigarette. 'These people don't want war,' he said. 'The Venda tribe lived and hunted here before the Boer but they didn't put up fences.'

Koch said: 'We have a name for people who think like that, *Kaffirboetie*, brother of the Kaffir.' He sat still, his contempt evident.

With an iron will Krige canned his anger, his arms braced as if ready for a bar-room brawl. 'This time I'll let that go,' he said. 'Next time you come up with that crap you're off the job.'

Koch smirked but shut up, instead stuffing various meats between thick chunks of liberally buttered bread. He was prepared to wait.

They ate in silence, washing down the food with sweet tea. Krige's wife stayed in the house, her absence from the table conspicuous, but Richter and Koch seemed not to notice as they wolfed their meal from the enamel plates. When the food was gone Krige took his jacket and put it on. 'Bring your car and follow me. I'll tell you how much I know.'

For several minutes they drove behind him due east towards the Kruger Reserve, first between the fields and then through wild virgin land, keeping to tracks that at times were invisible in the feral richness of the veld.

A couple of kilometres from the reserve Krige stopped, leaving his vehicle and going to the car as it came up. 'Let me have the gun,' he said as Koch got out. 'I've never used one like it before, only read about it in a magazine.'

The Beretta pistol was in mint condition, as Krige expected it would be, liberally oiled and greased. Removing the wrappings Krige cleaned it, stripping and drying the working parts, and drawing the barrel through until it shone like a mirror made from the finest glass. With the other two watching he paced out 25 metres and hung a cardboard target from the branch of a tree. He returned to the vehicles, picked up the pistol and inserted the ten-shot magazine. Using the bonnet of the jeep as a rest he squeezed the trigger, savouring the burst of fire that came every time he pulled the trigger. The R93 model was a standard Beretta 9 mm parabellum pistol except that it had the facility to deliver three rounds each time the trigger was pulled. The mode could be changed back to a simple single shot for each pull, like the usual semi-automatics.

For ten minutes he fired at the target, making adjustments every few rounds to the sight, not that he expected to need such precision for the close-range work he might have to deal with. Finally he cleaned the pistol and sheathed it in its shoulder holster.

'Satisfied, Major?' said Richter, sauntering over from where he had lolled against a tree. 'We're impressed.'

'What are you two carrying? Mind you, it's unlikely you'll be using them,' said Krige.

'What do you mean, Major?' said Richter. He was motionless, on a half-step. 'Then why the hell are we here?'

'In case I miss my chances of getting what I'm going for,' said Krige curtly. 'Your guns are under wraps until I say so. I don't even expect to use mine.'

'That's not how we heard it,' said Richter, holding his ground, belligerent.

'What did Muller tell you?' said Krige.

'He said we'd be involved, active support. That means that we'll share what has to be done,' said Richter.

'Not while I'm in command,' said Krige. It'll be as I say, else you can return to your homes.'

Koch came up to his friend. 'What's the problem, Krige?' he demanded icily. 'Do you want all the glory for yourself?'

'Killing people is not my kind of glory.' Krige put the pistol into the cubby hole in the front of the jeep. 'If you don't like what I say, speak to Muller.' The more Krige heard from them the more he knew they were going to give him trouble. His worst fears were beginning to materialize, the start of a bad dream.

They were quiet. Then Richter said: 'It's all yours, Major. But if I've got someone between me and Hell, he'll go first.'

Krige closed the tailgate of his jeep, resigning himself to the fact that he couldn't afford to lose his cool. He had at least to try and work with them, however distasteful that might be.

'Where are your guns?' he said. 'I want to know what's behind me.'

'They're in the car,' said Richter, going to the saloon. 'They're .357 magnums, revolvers, and silenced.' He took his pistol from the car, plucking it proudly from its custom holster and holding it up, admiring the excellent workmanship.

Krige's face creased in a fleering spasm. 'That shit's useless for this kind of work. Silencers are no good at velocities above the speed of sound. Those bullets move at twice that. Neither do silencers work on revolvers, whatever you might see on film, a James Bond movie. There's too much noise at the breech. That's one of the reasons I chose the Beretta. But have a go and let's see how good you are with that kind of power.'

Richter fed six cartridges into the revolver and brought the weapon level. For seconds the weapon popped repeatedly, spitting out the soft snub-nosed lead, splintering the bark of a tree 10 metres away and ejecting the wooden chips as if chiselled loose by the beak of a bird. He released the cylinder and emptied it of the spent shells. 'It's the perfect weapon for close-range work. The 9 mm doesn't have the stopping power.'

'Plenty for any man,' countered Krige. He silently acknowledged Richter's ability with a handgun. The man was as good, if not better, than he was. He expected Koch to be in the same class.

He took a manila file from a side pocket on the inside of the jeep's door and placed it on the bonnet. 'Now let's get on,' he said. 'I am sure that Muller has given you some details of what this operation is about. Even though I don't particularly want to get involved, I and anyone can see how crucial it is to get back the file.'

Krige was pleased that the others had his attention. 'First, I must emphasize that the file sent to Andrew Cartwright in Durban, the guy we're going after, is not simply a copy, as damaging as that would be, but the original, which makes it a lot worse. That means that all the supporting evidence that would undoubtedly convict those referred to in the file is shown in its original form, memoranda, minutes of meetings, signed orders, reports of work carried out and executed. The file also contains, of course, a comprehensive statement compiled by leading lawyers of how any competent prosecution would nail those accused. Quite frankly, there would be no escape and it would be a case of a string of life sentences being handed out, as easily as giving sweets to a child.'

Krige paused and then added: 'The prosecutions of a couple of the apartheid leaders that followed the Truth and Reconciliation Commission's hearings, and I reiterate the word couple, were blown apart by the defence. Sure, there were allegations that could have filled a room, but the damning evidence, even the most meagre, that would have convicted them and tied them to the alleged crimes was not there. Without such evidence you are barking up the wrong tree.'

Krige rested his hands behind him on the jeep, taking a breather. 'The prosecutor who is trying to get the Serb leader on war crimes at the court in The Hague admitted that nothing connecting him was written down, or anything that could be found. She also said, most poignantly, that Hitler didn't write anything down.' Krige turned to the others and said: 'But in this case it is written down and bloody well documented as I believe.'

'Why was the file prepared in the first place?' asked

Koch. 'Why didn't they just shred the evidence that they felt would have been so incriminating?'

'They shredded a lot,' said Krige. 'I know that for a fact. But you can't get rid of everything. Not even the cleverest criminal can manage to do that without leaving a trace that would finally convict him.'

Richter and Koch didn't like the reference to 'criminal', but they kept quiet.

'In answer to your first question, I see it like this,' said Krige. 'This is also what Muller told me. When the TRC was formed the nationalists, primarily the government of the apartheid period and the seminal leaders of the group of no name to which you belong, decided to search for any remaining incriminating evidence that could be linked to the so-called perpetrators of human rights violations, namely themselves and other guys in the file. The aim was to get everything that conceivably still existed, put it together in one dossier for safe-keeping and, if the heat was put on these guys by the powers now in this country, to use it if necessary in forming an escape route. The existing evidence would then have been destroyed or placed in a bank vault in a foreign country, France or Germany.'

'What do you mean?' said Richter. 'Some of those men are present leaders in this country, industrialists, academics, surgeons and lawyers.'

'The escape would have been through new identities, names, passports, birth certificates, everything that would effectively create another person,' said Krige. 'These documents have already been prepared and are apparently in safe-keeping to be used when and if required. If the heat on these guys gets too great they would simply vanish, if they have the time. It has been done elsewhere. How do you think the Nazis and others got away?'

Krige let this sink in, without any real purpose that

he felt he had needed to convey, and added: 'But if this file gets into the hands of people like the Scorpions, incredibly adept at what they do, these men in the file won't have the time to vanish. They could be charged and held within days from now if the file is released.

'For your interest, this file is not the only one that has been so meticulously compiled. A similar team in the party has worked on a file, and might still be at it, that comprises the same information except that it covers the opposition. At the TRC there were people from the black resistance movements, the armed wing of the ANC, or Umkhonto we Sizwe, and that of the Pan Africanist Congress, who should have been but were never brought to trial. Again, it was lack of evidence, but many of their deeds were equally criminal to what was done by the whites in power. The culprits if caught would claim political retaliation, but would fail and go down on criminal charges. The senior and powerful members of these militant groups never applied for amnesty because like the whites they were not sure if judgement would swing against them and that they would end up doing life behind bars.'

'Where is the file, this one on the blacks or others who shared their beliefs?' asked Koch.

'It is safe, apparently under greater security than the other, the one we are supposed to retrieve,' said Krige.

'What's the second file for?' asked Richter, stating the obvious question.

'I can only assume that if any of those in the first file, as we can call it, are brought to trial the second file will be thrown into the open and result in trials that the present ANC government would certainly not like. But I don't believe that this second file has the evidence that is contained in the first. It is not easy, close to being impossible, to compile evidence on the opposition without being a part of its ranks. That's the problem the present prosecuting forces face, and the vital importance of the file we are after. In short, evidence is everything and, figuratively, it's about being seen with your hand on the gun when you pulled the trigger and killed someone, or in some of these cases a lot more than one. It is worth noting that the people listed in these files are not the foot soldiers, some of whom are already in prison. They are the commanders, the top dogs.'

'Tell us more about this white we are going after,' said Koch impassively, unsure about killing a white if it ever came to that.

Krige sorted the sheets. 'As I told you, his name's Andrew Cartwright,' he said. 'If we go by your party's sources he funded the ANC extensively during the eighties. He's a lawyer, and apparently much of the success the ANC had in their negotiations with the Nationalists is owed to him. Muller loathes him and wants him dead for what he calls direct complicity in white deaths. I get the feeling that that is as important to him as retrieval of the file. That's called hate, and can easily obscure clear thinking.'

Krige drank water from the bottle he always took with him when out on the veld. 'It seems Cartwright's still giving money and continues to motivate powerful sources amongst the Asians and whites to do the same. It's not difficult to see that his death will assist in cutting a supply of finance the ANC still wants in order to establish a stronger political base, if that's possible when their present success and vast popularity is taken into account. But our objective is clear. It is not the death of Cartwright, unless we have to kill him, but to retrieve the file.'

'And who'll get the blame if Cartwright is killed?' said Richter trenchantly, wondering about Bryant and his contacts. 'Who else wants Cartwright dead? If we kill him the police will be onto us.'

'Not necessarily,' said Krige, patiently. 'After Cartwright's death, if that occurs, a report released in the press will reveal his allegiances over the last decade. Few whites will mourn his departure, including the influential leaders in your group and aligned groups. If you look at the complex political history of this nation it could be anyone, extreme right-wing groups or mavericks in the Inkatha Freedom Party under Buthelezi, which I am sure you are aware refused to take part in the TRC process. Absence of the IFP at the hearings and their refusal to recognize it and cooperate was another failure in what the Commission set out to achieve. And, like the whites in the file, there was nothing concrete to get them on.'

For a while Richter and Koch were quiet, thinking of their chances on a mission that required a measure of luck and a degree of skill. They didn't want to let down those who were obviously relying on them to be successful.

'Nevertheless we'll have to be very careful,' said Koch at last. 'And how good are you at pulling the trigger, Krige?'

'I have said that I hope it doesn't come to that, and I can do this job on my own,' said Krige acidly. 'Muller insisted you came along. If you're not happy, have it out with him.'

'Relax, Major, just checking,' said Richter running his eyes down the brief text next to Cartwright's name. 'You haven't told us how we're going to get to Cartwright. And what do we do then? What kind of security has he got? I sense that you think it'll be easy, that you know more than you're saying.'

'Whites are surrounded by elaborate security,' said Koch, joining in, uncertain what awaited them. 'Their homes are wired like Fort Knox.'

'Durban's not a Johannesburg suburb,' said Krige impatiently. 'Perhaps the whites down there aren't so scared.'

'And if Cartwright's not there?' said Koch.

'I'll wait a couple of days, no more,' said Krige. 'After that Muller can do it himself.'

Richter gave another raucous laugh. 'He'd love to hear that, Major.'

'You tell him.' Krige took the folder off the bonnet. 'We leave at ten in the morning. I expect to be in Durban by early afternoon. I'll take the jeep as far as Pretoria and leave it there. After that, we're together.'

'What about on the way back?' said Koch. 'I wanted another chance to speak to your wife.'

Krige looked at him viciously. 'She wants nothing to do with you,' he spat. 'If she knew what I was doing she'd kill herself.'

Richter raised his shoulders in a semblance of an apology. 'He means no offence, Major,' he said. 'What do we do when we get there?'

Krige sliced his nail into a fresh pack of cigarettes, peeling off the cellophane and crushing it into his pocket. 'Simple,' he said. 'We'll stay in a hotel somewhere on the Berea. It's a residential area that's effectively part of Durban, prestigious and wealthy. Cartwright lives there. We'll stake out his place, ascertain his movements and then go in.'

Muller's two men didn't see Kirsty Krige again until the next morning, after the maid had served them a decent breakfast of sausages and eggs on the porch. It was a few minutes before nine o'clock and Krige had gone to see Claasen on the neighbouring farm. The morning was crisp and clear, tiny flecks of white cloud traversing the sky and a faint wind blowing over the *kopje* into the yard. Tapping an unfiltered cigarette on the sole of his boot, Koch saw Kirsty passing the verandah on her way to the back of the house.

'Beautiful and stubborn,' he said. 'She's wasted on the farmer.' He took his feet off the table and went to the rail at the end of the porch.

'A fine morning, Mrs Krige,' he said suavely, doffing a non-existent cap and bowing as if to an appreciative audience.

She was several feet from him and stopped, glaring up with disgust. 'I believe you're leaving,' she said. 'Men like you are a disgrace to the Afrikaner. You're motivated by pure hate. You're killing your own people.'

He chuckled admonishingly and leapt over the rail, landing near her. 'I'm a realist,' he said, 'and you're white. Join us or die. These people will spit in your face as if they didn't know you. Do you want to be an icon for some Kaffir cause?' His boots dug into the sand and he clenched his fists.

'You're revolting,' she said, pushing out her ample chest.

He went up to her, the humour gone, his face set as if chiselled from stone. 'If you were mine I'd screw you rigid.' His thin colourless lips bared his teeth and he gripped her arm, callously tightening to the bone.

She pulled against his strength, helpless. 'Let me go, leave us alone.' She started to weep. 'Why have you come here? What do you want of my husband?'

'It's for the party, the group with no name as we call it. There are many influential and respected people in its ranks.' he said. 'Or didn't your husband tell you? He's doing as he's told.'

'Leave her.' Richter was leaning on the rail looking past them to the barns.

Koch turned his head and saw Krige's jeep coming along the stretch of track. He released her reluctantly. 'You're saved by the bell, Mrs Krige. One day I'll get you between the sheets.'

She glanced at the approaching vehicle, her hand going

to where he had held her. 'You'll never have me, in that way or any other,' she said, and ran up into the house, holding her arms across her breasts.

Krige drove into the yard. He stamped on the brake and pulled up the jeep. It slid in a blanket of dust before coming to a halt. He took exit through the co-driver's door and went straight to Koch. 'Where's my wife gone?' he demanded. He had seen the way she ran off when he approached.

'She went into the house,' said Koch, still on a high from feeling her warm body, an enormously tantalizing taste.

'Get the car,' said Krige flatly. 'We're leaving.'

'That was close,' said Richter as Krige went into the house. 'If he'd seen you playing with his wife it would've blown the job. She might still tell him.'

'I get a hard-on every time I see her,' said Koch. 'She drives me mad with desire.'

'What were you going to do, screw her in the sand?' said Richter. 'Krige would've chopped your balls into small pieces and fed them to the dogs.'

'She won't breathe a word,' said Koch. 'He came back earlier than I thought.'

'Let's get the car,' said Richter. 'Krige might still want some answers.'

They fetched the car, pulling up on the tail of the jeep and staying inside. In a while Krige came out carrying his jacket and a small bag. He went to the car and spoke to Koch, who was driving. 'Let me get ahead and keep on my tail to Pretoria.'

Koch started up. He watched the farmer as he got into the jeep. 'Nothing about his wife,' he said, a little relieved. 'He couldn't have seen it. She obviously didn't tell him. Maybe she likes a bit of passion.'

'It's over,' said Richter. 'Forget her. There's this job to

be done.' He signalled ahead moodily. 'Give him a couple of minutes and then we'll follow.'

From a window in the house Krige's wife watched them go. 'Goodbye, you dogs,' she said to herself, tears wetting her tanned, silken cheeks. 'I hope you rot in hell.'

Chapter 7

Tokyo, Japan

At Narita Airport Steiner travelled by limousine coach to the Shinjuku area of Tokyo and then on the Chuo Line one stop to Yoyogi station. It was a short walk to the training headquarters where he had spent so much time, seemingly endless hours on the equipment peculiar to the traditions of the art, and the *kata*, or set forms, and freestyle sparring. It was after lunch when he met his master in the *dojo* office.

Chinen *sensei* bowed, the correct height for the relationship he had with Steiner, as master to student, then in Western style offered his hand. 'Ah, Steiner *san*, you are most welcome.'

James Steiner returned the bow, lower than the master, and took the proffered hand, briefly, feeling the softness, like a child's, free from tension and conveying the internal power that had come from a life dedicated to karate. 'I am here for several days, *Sensei*.'

They were in the *hombu dojo* of the particular sect of *goju-ryu karatedo* of which Chinen was chief instructor on the main island, Honshu. He was also successor to the headship of the worldwide body, at present under a man in his eighties who lived on Okinawa. The old Okinawan had been the foremost disciple of Miyagi Sensei, the founder of *goju-ryu* karate.

'You must have your old room,' said Chinen, a little

disappointed at the brevity of Steiner's visit but too polite to enquire further. The South African instructor held the highest rank he had ever awarded to a foreigner, and amongst the Japanese teachers under him was rated in the top five in his understanding of the *do*, the way of the martial arts, and was more powerful than anyone he had ever met or trained.

'Thank you, *Sensei*.' Steiner bowed again. Conversation between them was mostly reserved for the *dojo* floor, and then on aspects of the art itself. Chinen had given his life to karate and little else interested him. Steiner respected that. It was how their close bond had been formed, none of the jabbering that some of those from abroad seemed to think necessary, like the Americans, people who at times never seemed able to shut up.

'Tonight we go to *unagi* restaurant,' said Chinen. 'You like *unagi*.' He beamed hugely and for a moment, with his round eyes, looked more Western than Oriental. He was a little over five feet and rotund in build.

Steiner smiled. Grilled eel on a bed of steamed rice with soy sauce was his favourite dish and this was its particular season. He waited while Chinen left the office, then took his two bags and went upstairs to his room. It was sparsely furnished, straw matting with the great semi-intoxicating smell that only it could produce, and cupboards which housed the futons. There were no washing facilities except a sink in a second room that was also a small kitchen. Bathing was done in the local community bath houses.

London, England

For the remainder of the morning after the call from Adams, Dave Lawson's mind was on the conversation and he regretted revealing as much as he had. He knew of no blemish on Steiner's character, and Adams's obvious grievance was a mystery. Nevertheless it was real, and before he left his house to see a friend in the city he sent a telegram to the *hombu dojo* in Tokyo, addressed to Steiner. He was sure Adams was on his way to Japan, and he was convinced that Steiner should know about it.

Tokyo

The day after his arrival Steiner went to the morning class run by one of Chinen's instructors. Afterwards he stayed on the floor and was performing a sequence of moves in front of the wall mirror when the office girl appeared, waving a scrap of paper. 'James *san*,' she called, standing at the edge. 'I have got a telegram for you from London.'

Steiner wrinkled his brow and went over, bowing his thank you and taking the folded sheet. She returned to the office as he read it, once, twice, the look of surprise converting to an impassive screen. He remembered the name of Paul Adams from Sophie Carswell, and he knew what it was about. If the man was flying to Tokyo he was bitter, as Lawson said. Untying his belt, he went to the changing room, mechanically stripping off his *dogi* and spreading it to dry. He had no idea what Adams would do when they met. If he came to the *dojo* and remonstrated in front of Chinen, he would leave dissatisfied. The master would never believe him. But Steiner knew Adams would never give up and that he wanted what he was coming for, revenge.

The other students from the class had left and for a while he sat naked on the bench, allowing his body to cool after the heavy exercise, his thoughts all the time on Adams. Finally he changed and went to his room where he packed his bag with items for a couple of days. As he left the *dojo* he poked his head in at the office and said: 'Tanaka *san*, I'm not here for a day, maybe two.'

'So soon, James *san*,' she replied in a voice that had never ceased to captivate him. 'You have only just come.' She had always fancied him, his tall, lithe physique and arrogant predatory looks. Her brown eyes opened wide, sensually calling him to her.

He knew what she was thinking, but Adams was more important. He would have her later. 'An Englishman, Paul Adams, will come here to the school asking for me,' he said. 'Tell him I'll be staying at the *ryokan* at the top of the Nikko reserve. There's only one. He can reach me there from tomorrow.'

Nikko was a wild reserve north of Tokyo. It was two hours by train from Ueno in the capital to Nikko town, which was on the south-eastern extremity of the reserve and near the Toshogu shrine, dedicated to Ieyasu Tokugawa, founder of the Tokugawa Shogunate that heralded the Edo period in Japan's history. The region was mountainous and comprised several lakes, spread out and rising with the terrain, from near the town and station to Yumoto spa, the highest point, with magnificent views of much of the reserve. The slopes of the mountains were shrouded in forest, and two rivers joined the middle lakes, each with its own waterfall, the Ryuzu cascade and the Kegon falls.

Steiner had visited Nikko frequently with Chinen and other instructors, and he knew the area, especially the upper reaches beyond the Ryuzu cascade and near the Senjogahara plateau, a large marsh that had a surreal quality to it, endlessly appealing in its own right. Despite its renowned beauty and the resulting popularity, Nikko easily accommodated the summer tourist traffic and from October through to spring the wooded trails around Yumoto spa and the nearby marsh, 30 minutes by coach up the main road from the town, were essentially deserted.

Later that morning Steiner arrived at the station in Nikko town and after lunching on *miso* soup, rice and fish at an eating house caught the bus for the *ryokan* where he had booked a room.

Tokyo

Minutes after Steiner reserved a room in the Spa *ryokan*, Paul Adams booked in at a business hotel in Shinjuku, its hundred box-like rooms designed for city businessmen who after a night in the bars were too drunk to catch the last train home. The accommodation was functional to the limit, offering hard metal-framed Western beds, grey partition walls and communal facilities. But it was inexpensive and met his need.

Adams did not wait in the hotel. The headquarters *dojo* of the style of aikido he followed was in Ushigome, a sub-district of Shinjuku, and five minutes by bus from the station. He chose to walk, and took a route through the alleys of game parlours and one-owner restaurants, with synthetic displays of the available foodstuffs in their windows. In 25 minutes he neared the *dojo*.

Like Steiner, Adams had attained high black-belt rank, sixth dan, one below Steiner, and of his 15 years delving into the esoteric mysteries of the art he had spent long periods in Tokyo. His master was a man named Shirai, but at this time of day he was very seldom around the *dojo* and Adams hoped he wasn't there when he arrived, for he did not want him involved in what was a personal matter. Instead he wanted to speak to Oshima, a senior instructor, of his age and a close friend.

The *dojo* was a rented space of 40 canvas-covered *tatami* mats, small but adequate, on the first floor of a high-rise block of flats and reached externally by a flight of stairs. There was no class in progress and he made for the office beneath on the ground floor. When he saw Oshima alone, poring over the paperwork, the reason for his visit was briefly forgotten in the pleasure of seeing his friend. Oshima, still clad in white *dogi* and black *hakama* – the recognized aikido dress for black belts – was as pleased to see Adams as the Englishman was to see him. In European fashion they embraced, greeting one another in English and Japanese. Each had an understanding of the other's language but after several years in the West, Oshima's command of English was a lot better, and that was what he used once they were seated. 'Adams *san*, you did not tell us you were coming.'

Adams's eyes hardened. 'There was no time,' he answered laconically. 'I'm not here to practise. I expect my visit to be short, a few days at the most.'

Oshima's lean face twitched slightly. The Japanese seldom showed emotion, except in bed. He sensed Adams was troubled. 'Why have you come to Tokyo, Adams *san*?' he asked. In his travels he had picked up Western directness, and he was talking to a friend.

Adams replied with equal candour. 'A man who is now in Tokyo raped my girlfriend.'

'Is he Japanese?' Oshima stiffened, beginning to conclude that a fellow countryman had committed the crime.

'No, he's an Englishman who is also a South African national,' said Adams. 'He's a high-graded *karate-ka* who spent years training here in the *goju* style of karate. My girlfriend is South African and knew him from before.

Yesterday they met by chance in a London street. He raped her in my flat when she refused to have sex with him.'

Oshima rested his fleshy hand on Adams' arm. He was a little overweight, but in superb condition. His muscular strength was prodigious but he had learned not to use it. The training demanded development of the superior coordinated power, *ki*, without which the art was reduced to an exercise in physical force and mechanical leverage.

'Where is his school?' said Oshima.

'It's in Yoyogi, not far from the station,' said Adams.

Oshima did not ask Adams how he knew. Instead he said: 'What are you going to do, Adams *san*?'

Adams said: 'I'm not sure. I only know I want to face him and have it out. At the very least his master will hear about it.'

'Informing his master will serve you little,' said Oshima. 'Unless you have proof he won't believe you. These people protect their own whatever the crime. They're like the *yakuza*, the Japanese mafia, in that respect. You said she had met him previously.' He lifted his wide shoulders, not pressing the point further. 'There's not much you can do except meet him.'

He paused. 'But I don't see how that will give you satisfaction. He deserves punishment but I don't know how.' He breathed deeply then continued. 'You can't destroy him.'

'Can't I?' Adams spoke quietly. 'The English legal system is of no use because I can't get him back there, and then there's no hard evidence.'

Oshima watched him. The techniques of aikido were strictly for self-defence. 'Adams *san*, you'd lower yourself to his level if you killed him,' he said. 'I assume that's what you consider an option.'

Adams got off his chair. 'It may be the only alternative,'

he said. 'But before then I must find him. I'm going to Yoyogi.'

'Adams *san*,' said Oshima, coming over to him. 'I'm going with you.' He walked to the changing room, loosening the straps of his *hakama* and the black belt underneath. He folded the *hakama* meticulously in the established way, then dressed in jeans, shirt and jacket.

Paul Adams and Oshima soon found the *goju-ryu dojo* near Yoyogi station, a small station but in the centre of the broad cosmopolitan area. The *dojo* was plain and of traditional design, with glass-panelled *shoji* doors set well back from the road, innocuous, and belying the often intense physical and mental training that went on inside. The doors opened onto a practice area surrounded by a neat assembly of black and white photographs, scrolls and primitive Okinawan weapons on the walls, a small shrine at one end. Leaving their shoes in the footwell at the entrance, the two men went round to the office in the corner. Like other *budo* schools there were seldom classes in mid-afternoon and the place was quiet. The girl, Michiko Tanaka, was working in the only filing cabinet in the room when they entered. Japanese regarded blond foreigners with a curious mixture of reverence and awe, and she held her eyes on him before bowing faintly, and greeting them in her tongue.

They returned the greeting, then Adams addressed her in English. 'An Englishman, James Steiner, is a member of this school,' he said. 'I believe that he is in Tokyo.'

She closed the drawer of the cabinet. The foreigner or *gaijin* was obviously Paul Adams. 'He's not here,' she said evenly, unused to the direct tone, like most of her people. She was immediately taken by his exquisite good looks. She passed on the message given to her by Steiner.

'He went to Nikko, the *ryokan* at Yumoto spa at the top of the reserve. He'll be there in the morning. He goes there to practise.'

Adams thought of Lawson. It seemed obvious. 'I'm Paul Adams. Is he expecting me?'

'No,' she lied, disengaging her eyes from his. 'He loves Nikko. It is very spiritual and he is a very spiritual person. He wouldn't have achieved his level without being so.'

Adams looked at Oshima and then at her. 'Thank you,' he said. 'I know Nikko, it's one of the most beautiful and attractive parts of Japan and, as you say, very spiritual.'

She bowed as they left, wondering what it was about. They clearly weren't friends. But, Steiner could look after himself. Her protective instinct told her not to mention it to anyone. She returned to the cabinet and carried on with her duties.

Outside in the street, Adams and Oshima stopped a short way from the *dojo*. 'He knows you're coming,' said Oshima, 'and he is setting you up. She was lying. You know the Japanese as well as I do.'

Adams gazed along the street, nodding slowly. 'It suits me. Nikko is quiet at this time of the year.' He started to go towards the station. 'I'll meet him on his ground. In the morning I'll be on the early train and then I'll meet him. I'm not turning back now. He's got this coming to him and I'm going to give it to him.'

Oshima caught up with him. 'You're very strong, Adams *san*, but this man is dangerous and I'm sure that he knows exactly what he's doing,' he said. 'He's drawing you into position. We'll go together. He won't stand a chance against two of us.'

As he spoke Oshima felt a cloud envelope him. They were deliberately going into the camp of their enemy, knowing it could mean death. Their actions were contrary to the precepts of the *do*, the belief of non-resistance, that you should never go against a perceived antagonist, and instead let them come to you if that was their wish.

That afternoon, shortly before she began tidying the office to leave for her home, Michiko Tanaka received a call from Steiner. 'He was here,' she said as soon as she recognized his voice. 'There was a Japanese man with him.'

'Did you give him the message?' He was lying on the futon in his room, and dressed in a *yukata*, the full-length informal Japanese garment used for privacy and pleasure. He was ready for a soak in the bathhouse where the natural waters of the spa emitted a sulphurous vapour that hung like mist and enshrined those in the bath, men and women.

'Yes,' she said. 'He knows Nikko.'

'Good,' said Steiner. 'What does he look like?'

'You haven't seen him before, James *san*?' She was astonished and mystified. What was all this about.

'Tell me,' said Steiner abruptly, wanting facts.

She controlled herself. 'I'm sorry,' she said. 'He has blond hair.' Adams's colouring was still with her and she felt that was enough for anyone to notice him.

Steiner rolled off the futon. 'Did anyone else see him?' he asked.

'No,' she said.

'Thank you,' he replied. 'And Tanaka *san*, this is private, you haven't seen these men, to you they don't exist.'

The express from Ueno was on schedule and at 8.10 Adams and Oshima left the station in Nikko town and caught the bus for Yumoto spa. It was the end of the two-week spell when the unsurpassed autumn colours of red and gold were past their best, but the landscape was still inherently superb. Through each season Nikko was irreplaccable, like other parts of the world renowned for their natural beauty.

There were few on the lumbering vehicle, local people who worked in the reserve and came up to their chosen places of work each day. By the time they reached the spa *ryokan* only one other person remained on the bus. He was an old Japanese man and he sped off round the building to get on with his work as they went in.

There was a young man behind the reception desk in the small hall and he reacted dutifully as they walked up, quickly putting desk papers away under the surface so that everything was as tidy and neatly arranged as possible, the foundation of his upbringing. Adams expected the negative answer he got to his question of whether Steiner was there, but the attendant carried on, bobbing his head obsequiously. Steiner had given him a message. He had been curious but too polite to ask any questions.

'Steiner *san* is on the other side of the marsh,' he said. He pointed through the window across the lake, Lake Yunoko, from where the beginning of the Senjogohara marsh was visible. 'He said to meet him there.'

Adams led Oshima into the hotel lounge and over to the window. 'Beyond that ridge,' he said, 'a raised footway crosses the marsh. I'll take it.' He indicated a low ridge clad in maples that went along the far border of the lake. 'If you walk down the road past the marsh you'll see a path. It'll bring you to where I come off the footway. That's where I think Steiner will be waiting. We'll get there at about the same time, but hold back. The complication of someone else might chase him off.'

'A man who goes to this trouble won't give in without a result,' said Oshima. 'I'll leave after you. I hope you get what you want.'

Nikko, Japan

A little before Adams and Oshima boarded the bus in Nikko town, Steiner left the *ryokan* and headed for the lake and the opposite shore. When he reached it he went into the trees, climbing to the top of the ridge. Finally he stopped and looked down on the marsh. He saw the start of the footway. It was built of planks and transverse beams and was supported above the water on thick posts. It provided a carriageway a metre wide, constructed for the convenience of visitors drawn by the indescribable magnetism that the marsh had for people. At first it was like a long straight jetty, then it curved as it followed the U-shaped waters out of sight.

From his position Steiner had a clear view of the hotel, the mountain of rock behind, and the flat open area where the bus stopped. He could also see the final stretch of road. After a while he squatted where the ground formed a hollow, casually digging at the moist cohesion with a twig, ever alert and aware as his training had taught him to be.

He did not have to wait for long before he heard the chugging diesel engine of the first bus as it passed the Ryuzu cascade. When it appeared he made out the three figures sitting apart but it wasn't until they disembarked that he had confirmation Paul Adams had come. The striking blond head of the man was all he needed. Michiko Tanaka was spot on in her description. He watched as the first occupant went past the entrance, then focused on the Englishman as he bounded out of the bus. Adams was nearly at the entrance when he slowed for the third man to join him, and they went inside. Steiner remembered Michiko's words and he thrust the twig into the earth. Adams had brought the other man with him. He looked at the hotel, working through what they might do. Much depended on whether they would stay together or look for him separately. It had to be a combination of both, a planned and coordinated approach.

Minutes later he knew the answer as he saw Adams emerge and come towards the lake. Shortly afterwards Oshima appeared, taking the road. To Steiner their plan was obvious and he left his position, going over the ridge to the footway. He ran onto the planking and followed it until he was at the far end. When he touched earth he carried on, soon picking up the path parallel to the edge of the marsh that he guessed Oshima would use. The vegetation became thicker as he went on, the trees closer and the ground hidden by perennially green bush. He wanted as much distance as he could get from the footway where he hoped Adams would wait. From the speed of Oshima's walk he judged how far he could go before seeing him, or betraying his own presence, and he was not far from the road when he stopped and went into the undergrowth.

For moments Steiner was engulfed in silence, except for the irregular chirping of birds and the gentle pulsing of wind through the trees. Then he heard the rustle of leaves along the path. After what seemed an unending delay Oshima came into view. The distance between them was no more than 10 metres, and when it was half that Steiner came through the bush onto the path, folding his arms and blocking Oshima's way like the warrior of a people he had been chosen to serve.

Oshima had never seen Steiner before but the beautifully proud, upright figure in front of him could be no one else. He stopped, relaxed, his arms loose, the elbows slightly bent, then he advanced until they were a couple of strides apart. Their eyes locked together, searching, each gauging the opposing strength, the internal power of *ki*.

'You're with Adams,' said Steiner after a moment. 'This is not your business.' From years of facing trained exponents of the *dojo* floor he could tell Oshima was strong.

'You wronged him,' said Oshima softly. 'He wants to speak to you. Go and meet him.'

'Not until you leave.' Steiner went closer. They were on the edge of *maai*, the distance recognized by those trained in the martial arts as that within which either one could launch a telling strike without taking another step. He guessed Oshima's schooling was in aikido, that his defence would be second to none. He also knew Oshima would stay. He probed deeper, trying to sense how rapidly the Japanese could evade or counter. Then he moved.

The attack was without warning, disguised, a low kick for the groin, a feint, followed by a lunging punch for the heart that carried Steiner to Oshima with the speed of a duellist's sword. He had performed the combination frequently, invariably with success, though then he had exercised control and only delivered a little of his power. Now, as with the men in Durban, the blow was for real.

As if he had been caught short, the big Japanese swivelled his impressive chest, slicing onto the arm with the speed of a falcon diving for its prey. In a blending movement he took the wrist that grazed him, leading the bunched hand in a quarter-circle then sweeping it in the reversal of the *kotegaeshi* technique of aikido, a mainstay of their practice sessions. Steadying himself he slowed, drawing his opponent nearer into the centre of his imaginary sphere. When Steiner was fully outstretched he folded his free hand over the other and concentrated his power in a short stroke. Steiner lifted, tumbling over the pivot of his trapped fist, his feet thrown above his head by the centrifugal force. As his legs began to descend, Oshima released the wrist, casting it off as if throwing crumbs to a gathering of birds.

Untrained in the art of breakfalling, perfected by *aikidoka*, Steiner hit the ground heavily, his shoulder slamming against the solid earth, and he felt the strength sucked from him. When his legs came down, the momentum generated by his mass and speed slid him along and he ended up partly under a bush. He was slightly dazed from the shattering impact, enough to concuss most men, and he shook himself, immediately sensing Oshima's calculated advance. Getting up, he stood as if nothing had happened, giving a mocking smile, forcing himself not to reveal the uselessness of his arm and the mounting pain.

But Oshima knew the fall had had effect and he kept coming, confident, shuffling and staying calm and centred. Though the techniques he had learned were primarily for defence, the aikido ethics, he had a powerful repertoire of lethal strikes at his command, and now he was not going to wait. With Steiner motionless he went just outside *maai*, relying on his acute senses to propel him into action at the slightest opening. He tried to create it with his power and he was surprised when Steiner did not give. At that moment his concentration lapsed, which for someone as highly trained as he was, it should not have done.

For Steiner it was enough and the energy welled in his legs as he again turned into a machine, smashing an instep onto the inside of Oshima's thigh and without retrieving the leg throwing his body back and sweeping for the head with the other. The blow caught Oshima on the neck, the hands of the Japanese still low, with a force that would have felled a bull. His eyes glazed over, recognition of his assailant gone. He swayed then fell.

Steiner landed on his feet and keeping a distance looked at the figure. He had delivered everything he could in the kick. A bruised lump the size of a pigeon egg was starting to form on the man's neck, like that from an executioner's rope, and he knew Oshima was dead. He went to the body, bending to look closer, and then hoisting it in a fireman's lift onto his back. He winced from his hurt shoulder, momentarily concentrating his mind to forget the pain, and then went into the bush. A short way from the path he threw the corpse onto the ground and turned it over so it was covered by a screen of leaves. He thought of Adams. His patience would run out and he would come looking for his friend. His injury was an impediment and Adams would be skilled. He had no choice other than to withdraw, reluctantly. He had to have a while to think.

Instead of going to the path he made for the Ryuzu cascade in the direction of Nikko town. For a spell he used the main road until he had bypassed the waterfall, and then he went into woodland and circled Lake Chuzenji. It was nearly two hours before he arrived at the station and a little later he boarded a train for Ueno in Tokyo.

Chapter 8

Durban

In the dark of the evening Krige, Richter and Koch reached the outer suburbs of Durban. The convolution of freeways that entered the city from the interior were empty, and their car sped towards the city, Koch behind the wheel, Richter next to him and Krige in the back.

'Where are we going, Major?' asked Richter, absorbed by the expanse of three-lane tar rushing under the wheels. 'We need food and sleep.'

Krige stretched himself out. 'That'll come later,' he said. 'The plan's changed. We're going for Cartwright now. At first I thought we could go for him tomorrow, but we can't wait.'

Koch reduced his speed to the national limit. 'You said we'd lie up, check his whereabouts. We don't even know he's there. What kind of game are you playing, Major?'

'It's a dirty one,' said Krige, grinning as if enjoying a personal joke. 'By Muller's account Cartwright is as regular as clockwork, a workaholic who sticks to a routine of office during the day and home at night. He seldom travels, preferring to send his minions about serving his interests, and reading their reports in the privacy of his home, except of course when he's in court.'

'How do you know?' said Koch. He adjusted the mirror infinitesimally so he could see Krige's face.

'He only feeds us bits and pieces,' said Richter caustically, still suspicious, failing to understand that Krige had given everything to them that he'd been told by Muller.

Krige sat quietly. After a while he said: 'I'll tell you what you need to know and what I've been told. That's how this job is run. I'm keeping it like that.'

Richter was dissatisfied. 'You've never liked us coming along, have you, Major?' he said.

'I've had to put up with Muller's choice, and you're it,' said Krige, refusing to be drawn by men he regarded as animals.

Richter laughed. 'Let's get to the white, Major. If you can kill him I'll forgive you.' The mirth glistened in his eyes.

Krige stuck his feet on the back seat. 'In a short while, one, two miles, you'll see a turn-off to the Berea,' he said. 'Take it. That's where we'll find "the white" as you keep calling him.' He added, condescendingly: 'Have you people ever been out of Pretoria?'

'You've been here before,' said Koch steering through a long sweep in the road.

'Ten years ago, during my time in the police, then only for a month, but enough to give me an idea of the layout of the general area,' said Krige. 'Cartwright has apparently lived for twenty years on the Berea, an extremely expensive suburb that rises from the city which it virtually surrounds, like the sides and rim of a bowl. The house is Spanish, double-storeyed, six bedrooms, palatial. It's on a couple of acres, quite unusual for such a location in an area that can be termed an estate agent's dream.'

'What about access?' asked Richter, 'to the grounds and the house?'

Ahead of them there was a sign to the Berea and Koch filtered into the left lane, his bull-like arms pulling on the wheel, without any finesse.

'The grounds are easy, iron gates and a low wall at

the front,' said Krige. 'The house is more difficult. No apparent sound systems but standard burglar guards on the windows. My plan was to get him when he returned from work and not have to break in, but now we'll need a bit of luck.' Krige coughed then said: 'There are also the dogs, two Alsatians.'

'Dogs, that's all we need,' spat Richter. 'Are they in the house or out?'

'They're in kennels in a courtyard next to the building,' said Krige. 'We'll probably have to get rid of them first.'

'Why?' Koch pulled up at a junction. 'Which way are we going now?'

'Go to the left,' said Krige. 'You'll meet the old main road between Durban and Pietermaritzburg. It'll take us into the heart of the Berea.' He continued: 'The dogs roam where they like and I don't want them biting my arse while I'm getting in.'

The other two laughed coarsely and then went quiet. When they reached the end of the dual carriageway Krige said: 'Take the next right and then the bridge. We'll be in Ridge Road. The second road along is King James Avenue. Turn into it and stop. We'll be near the house.'

'Who goes with you?' asked Richter as if it had just occurred to him.

'You do,' replied Krige. 'I'm getting used to you. If those dogs are not asleep I might need help.' He smiled thinly. 'A fully grown Alsatian is quite an adversary. They move like lightning and the momentum they generate is enough to make anyone lose their nerve, especially when they're coming at you. I've seen them at work in the police.'

Richter could understand what Krige was saying. He had also seen Alsatians at work when they were directed by him against blacks. He thought for a second and said: 'It makes sense for the two of us to be with you.' They were close to Ridge Road. 'Koch's pretty lethal when he gets going. You might have missed that quality in him.'

'Koch stays with the car,' said Krige. 'We can't leave it alone. Police cars regularly patrol this sort of area at night. That's the privilege of being born in the right class and getting the education that goes with it.'

Shortly after entering King James Avenue, Koch steered the car up to the curb. The steep road was lined with trees, interlinking down the pavement and spanning the tar like a huge elongated umbrella. Further down, two roads fed off, the nearest dropping on a steep gradient.

'The house is down the first road,' said Krige. He looked at his map where he had marked the road in pencil. He spoke to Koch. 'Go for a drive and meet us at the bottom of this road in an hour. Take this map.'

Koch took the map and located their position. 'If you're not there I'll come back every five minutes,' he said. 'I hope the dogs don't get you.' He grinned at Richter. 'How long do I wait before I come searching for you?'

'Keep waiting and be patient,' said Krige crisply. 'If by morning we don't show up, clear out and return to the Reef. But we'll be there. I'm not about to end my days in this part of the land. I still know where my roots lie.'

'You almost sound like a Boer,' said Richter.

Krige levered the catch on the door. 'I am Boer, but first an Afrikaner, one who can see what's best for this country.' He said to Koch: 'If we don't see you go straight to Muller and tell him what I've just told you. Even if you don't see us and clear out, this operation might not be over. The retrieval of that file is absolutely vital to the success of this job, and I told Muller I would get it.'

As Richter and Krige left the car, Koch released the handbrake and let the vehicle roll from the curb. Krige stood on the pavement, watching the red tail-lights recede, and then he walked on with Richter. Together they reached the nearest side road and turned into it, walking slowly, purposefully, as if they were local residents. The road was narrow, without pavements, the irregular edges of the tar touching 20-metre grass borders that lay like synthetic fibre, meticulously mown and nurtured. The light was low, with only inadequate street lamps and a quarter-moon that submerged itself for long periods behind the cloud.

'Which one is it?' asked Richter.

'It's the fourth driveway on the left, where the road levels out,' said Krige. He scanned the houses through the trees. They were in darkness. Either the owners weren't there or they were unafraid of the dark, probably so well protected from any conceivable intrusion.

The iron gates to Cartwright's house were closed, a chain linked through the bars. They went further along the verge and when they were almost past the place Krige stopped next to the wall. 'Over here,' he said, placing his hands on it. He sprang onto the top, keeping flat on the surface, and rolled into the garden. Richter followed, mounting the stone with ease, his athletic training showing itself.

They landed in a bed of poinsettias, fully grown and packed along the length of the wall, the bright red petals forming a continuum perfectly in tune with the large green leaves that were part of the plant.

'You certainly take off, Major,' said Richter, 'It could have been a bed of roses.'

'Scared of a few thorns?' Krige parted the leaves and went onto the lawn. The house was more or less secluded, in a sanctuary of trees and rockeries that had been landscaped harmoniously after an obvious infusion of money. The gravel driveway curved on the lawn, terminating in a roundabout at the front with a short piece up to a double garage.

'Fast asleep,' murmured Richter, joining him. 'Where are the dogs?'

'Somewhere over there,' said Krige. He looked to where the garage blocked the space between the house and the front garden beds and lawn. 'The courtyard's on the other side. While they're alive they're a threat.'

'So you told me,' said Richter. 'Where are we going now? You're supposed to be running this show, Major.'

'We go to the left and to the back,' said Krige. 'If we're lucky we'll find the dogs asleep and kill them where they lie. That, or they may find us first and it'll be target practice on the move, with my pistol, not that cannon of yours.'

Skirting the central lawn, the two men went through the trees that ran in a man-made corridor. When they had gone far enough Krige halted.

'We need slabs of poisoned steak,' said Richter. 'That would soon get rid of them.'

'It wouldn't,' said Krige. 'Not if they're well trained, and I suspect they are. It's a case of getting in range and pumping lead into their brains.' He thought of his own dogs on the farm, devoted to him. Did Cartwright have a similar relationship with the two dogs that they now wanted to kill? He probably did. 'Let's go,' he said, going low as he went clear of the trees.

They had a rockery between them and the house for most of the way. In a minute they were working down the back of the house, past a long verandah of black stone, laid before double doors that served the main reception room. At the end they came to a series of steps that led to an elevated lawn, recently mown and as flat and smooth as a bowling green. Not far from them a goldfish pond spewed a jet of water in a lazy arc, and nearer the house white garden chairs were fastidiously arranged in a ring around a matching table. The moon was enclosed in cloud and without the street lamps visibility was poor. For a time the two men studied the landscape of the grounds.

Krige looked at the mass of cloud. 'If we wait for the moon we'll be here all night,' he whispered, starting to feel the excitement of raw drive. 'There's an archway over there that leads to the courtyard. Follow me. They're quiet, but any noise will set them off.'

Richter came nearer, the adrenalin priming him. 'Keep going,' he said under his breath. 'I'm not scared of dogs.'

They went past the garden furniture and into the recesses of shadow. As they adjusted to the change in light they saw the courtyard wall, above head height and between the building and the fence. The wall was white and crowned with the curved, rectangular tiles of Spanish design. Close to the house a narrow arch with an open wrought-iron gate led into the yard.

'We only have to close the gate,' urged Richter in Krige's ear.

'Maybe,' said Krige. 'But if they hear us and find their way blocked they'll create a hell of a fuss. Have you ever heard an Alsatian go crazy with frustrated energy just bursting to be released? The noise is enough to raise the dead in the city morgue.'

Cautiously they went to the arch. When they reached it Krige looked in. Near him was the kitchen and opposite him other doors to the garage and what he guessed were the servant's quarters. Furthest from him he saw the gabled outline that was obviously the dog kennels. From what he could see the yard was bare and he took the range to be 15 metres. At first he couldn't make out the animals and assumed they were inside. Then in the shadow he saw a mass expanding lazily on the ground. 'I can see one,' he said over his shoulder. 'The other must be in one of the kennels.'

'I can't see anything,' said Richter. 'What about the gate?'

Krige couldn't see the hinges clearly in the dark, whether they were oiled and in good condition. Even if they were, they might make a noise and he didn't like taking that chance.

'Shut the gate,' repeated Richter. 'If they hear us, kill them through the bars.'

'Risky to do that in this light,' said Krige. 'We'd have to go close and take our time to be sure. They'd go insane.'

'Shoot them from here,' said Richter, acquiescing. 'It's hard to miss with several bursts from that gun of yours. But if you haven't the confidence I'll do it.' Richter couldn't resist the jibe.

Krige replied, bullishly: 'You're not getting anything with that. Why do I have to repeat such basic facts?'

Richter said: 'Thanks, Major. But I plan to stay alive.'

Krige held from comment. He engaged the rapid mode on the Beretta and raised it, hooking his thumb through the enlarged guard and resting the foregrip in his palm. He aimed where he had seen the movement and let off three rounds, keeping the gun steady against the strong recoil. The mass didn't move and he aimed at the kennels, giving them four bursts, springing twelve brass cases like tracers. There was no sound.

'They must be dead,' said Richter. 'Otherwise we'd hear something.'

'Give it a minute and then we'll go in,' said Krige. He put in a new magazine.

As two minutes came up Richter lifted himself, losing patience. 'Come on, let's do it,' he said. As he moved his eyes caught a speeding ball coming over the lawn. 'The other dog,' he cried, groping for the revolver at his belt. 'It was out there all the time.' He plummeted to a squat, the gun at eye level, his body and balance melding instantly with the gun. With that in his hands he was an artist.

'Hold it,' rasped Krige, turning and immediately lifting the Beretta to the target. 'The noise will be too great. I'll get it with this.'

But he was too late. The magnum leapt in Richter's hands as he fired at the charging dog, the sound deafening in the yard. Undeterred he fired again, the weapon blending with him perfectly as it jetted another of the flat-nosed projectiles at a velocity of 1,700 feet per second against the animal.

The bullets hit the black and tan Alsatian below the jaw, mushrooming as they entered, as they were designed to do, boring into the body with brute force. Their combined effect lifted the head of the dog high above the earth and for a moment the stricken beast seemed to dance on air, pirouetting as if on a stage. Then like a gymnast it somersaulted onto its hindquarters, the hair on its chest vermilion from the visceral blood that ejaculated in waves.

'That's why I carry this gun.' Richter casually opened the cylinder and ejected the spent shells. 'It's just great.'

'Not in this game.' Krige faced him. 'If we lose Cartwright you're in shit. You lost your nerve.' He took a look at the dead dog a few metres away, lying in an ignominious heap, and walked into the courtyard. He crossed quickly. The other dog was lying in blood, its head screwed unnaturally by the bullets, the lips agonizingly resting on the fangs. He returned to the arch where Richter lounged sullenly, his revolver obediently in its sheath.

'That's blown it for a quiet entry,' said Krige angrily. 'We'll try the porch.'

He went at a sprint along the house to the verandah. Richter followed a few metres behind, complimenting himself on the accuracy of his shooting and bristling at Krige's outburst. Few men, he told himself, could handle the power of the pistol with such skill, against a moving target in poor light. One day he would prove it to the farmer. He settled into a run.

When they reached the verandah Krige went up the steps to the doors. They were of wood and inset with square panes of glass, delicately aligned in horizontal rows. There was a lock, and two simple catches at the top and bottom. He broke the panes next to the catches with the pistol and reaching in, slid the catches. Impatiently he pulled the doors to him, the mortise parting uneasily, and like an ineffective guard revealing the expanse within.

The sound of the falling glass had been minimized by the carpet that butted to the door and the men skipped over the shards into the room, resplendent in panelled oak, fine paintings and leather chairs. Running round the furniture they went through a set of swing doors into a cavernous entrance hall. Sweeping down in a half-spiral, a wide stairway came into the hall. Outside the moon emerged from cloud and the improved light shone through an overhead window, magnifying the stairs in a surreal glow that was strangely tempting.

'It's odd,' said Krige. 'The noise from that cannon of yours was enough to make a deaf man hear. Yet there's no sign that anyone's here. No sound, no lights, nothing.' He glanced at Richter. 'I don't think our man's at home.'

'He's probably smart and sitting up there in the dark,' said Richter, itching to find out if he was right.

Krige closed on the stairs and sprang up them, taking three at a time, Richter behind. At the top they came into a long high-ceilinged passage with several rooms leading off at intervals. It was truly palatial and perfectly Spanish.

'I don't know which one,' said Krige. 'My guess is the

master suite is usually at the end.' He ran on again, his feet gliding over the floor, well used to this kind of activity.

When they reached the room, Krige went in, oblivious to any risk, simultaneously banging the switch. But no one was there. It was like stepping into a harmlessly inviting space.

Concealing his disappointment he went to the double bed, neatly made, its ornate headboard guarded by banks of built-in cupboards, adorned with moulded brass that had clearly seen the skill of a highly competent craftsman, with a finely painted canvas hanging above and a little to the side of the bed. Opposite the bed a mahogany dressing table was positioned between the windows, and a superbly woven Chinese carpet covered most of the floor.

'Not here.' Krige stated the obvious, the disappointment beginning to show. Failure crossed his mind, but he dispelled it. He could never accept such a thing as failure.

'We should've checked him out first,' said Richter, fidgeting in spoiled expectation.

'As leader I took the chance,' said Krige irritably. 'There's little hope, but I want to see the other rooms. Then we can join Koch.'

They went methodically through the remaining rooms. All were empty except for pieces of furniture, and in three, single beds were laid for use, as if prepared for a family homecoming.

Krige turned off the lights and they left the house the way they had come in.

They went over the wall, leaving the dead dogs where they lay, and set course for the meeting with Koch. He was at the assigned place, the car tucked against the curb near an intersection. As soon as they were in he pulled off, with the self-assurance of one who had for the past hour become familiarized with the roads in the area.

'Where to now, Major?' asked Koch as they came to the nearest lights. 'You tell me you didn't get Cartwright. What went wrong?'

Krige wished he was alone, anywhere away from the others. Their presence, and that he hadn't found Cartwright and the file, grated like white ants relentlessly eating away at wood.

'He wasn't there,' answered Richter quietly. 'It was a waste of effort.'

'What about the dogs? Did you kill them?' asked Koch, persevering in his desire to find out what had gone wrong up at the house.

'They're dead,' said Krige caustically, still wondering where Cartwright was. 'Take a right at the bottom of this street and leave the city. You'll find a road leading south along the coast. We'll spend tonight in a seaside town, Amanzimtoti, ten kilometres from here. This area makes me uncomfortable.'

'And then? What happened to your plans, Krige? How are you going to kill Cartwright?' Koch steered the car slowly down the street.

'We'll be back,' said Krige. 'Now you can get your sleep.'

When the three men reached Amanzimtoti they split up and spent the rest of the night in guest houses in the town. A couple of hours after dawn they met at a rundown cafe near the beach and filled themselves with sausages and eggs. Richter and Koch had changed out of the khaki clothing they normally wore, and had on casual clothing more in keeping with preferred dress on the coast.

Finally satisfied, Krige distanced himself from his plate. 'The first thing is to locate Cartwright. The police might also be sniffing around and one of us will have to take a look at the house.'

'Why are the police suddenly involved?' asked Koch, frowning. 'What's this got to do with them?'

'Richter clearly hasn't told you yet,' said Krige. 'He let rip at one of Cartwright's dogs with that piece of artillery he cradles like a lovesick boyfriend. It was enough to scare the neighbours shitless.'

'It was us or the dog,' said Richter defensively.

'A noise like that on the Berea brings the police out like rats leaving a clean sewer. Guns, dogs and everything else they can bring into play. Cartwright might have come back after we left, but we had to run.' Krige enjoyed making the point.

Richter sat quietly, brooding, resenting the assertion.

Krige carried on, tapping the table. 'I'll get out in Durban and ring his secretary. If the police were called to the house I think that they'll treat it as burglary. Nothing was taken, but they'll think we were disturbed. It's too much of a mental leap for them to think we were there to kill him or, more specifically, know the reason we were there in the first place.'

Richter drained his cup, reaching for the teapot, not so sure. 'And if the police conclude his life's in danger?'

'We'll never get near him,' said Krige curtly. 'Then it'll be up to you or others in your group to find him when he's available.' Krige lit a Texan cigarette. 'I'm not coming back, as Muller knows.'

Koch grated his chair. 'You will be,' he said. 'We're not picking up your mistakes.'

Krige smiled mockingly, content to ignore the comment. He needed the edge, and a reply would serve no purpose. Outside the surf crashed onto the beach in a turbulence of white foam, drenching and grading the sand.

He spoke to Richter. 'The road past the house goes up a steep rise. It may offer you a spot that's not obvious and from where you can see the premises. At nine o'clock join Koch where we met last night. Collect me at the corner of Smith and Broad Streets. They're on the city map. Our plan after that will depend on what we find out.'

Durban

Before seven o'clock Koch dropped Richter and Krige off at different points in the city and drove to the beach where he planned to pass the hours until he met them later.

Richter didn't take long to reach King James Avenue and after climbing up the long incline they had come down the night before he reached Cartwright's road. The street was as quiet as when they had left it, and he went towards the house. Maintaining his pace he went past and up the rise Krige had referred to. His breathing was heavy and against his high standards it told him that he was out of shape, not in the condition he wanted of himself. He had heard of the hilly terrain of Natal but he never imagined he'd experience it as a member of a squad trying to retrieve a file of such importance.

In the daylight and at the slow speed Richter was able to pay more attention to the area he was in. It was peaceful and quiet, extremely well-off, and clearly for those who had acquired wealth. He wondered how Cartwright with his beliefs could live there. Compared to where he had been brought up it was another planet.

When Richter felt he was high enough he went among some trees lining a garden fence. He looked through the branches down the slope. Apart from a section hidden by the house and most of the courtyard, he had a good view of the grounds. As he regulated his breathing his gaze went to the lawn where he had killed the dog. He expected to see it there, but it had gone. Except for the fountain and furniture the mown grass was a symbol of unused green baize, serene in the morning light.

He studied the rest of the garden, concentrating on where the shadows made an accurate sighting difficult. He switched his attention to the courtyard but it was largely obscured and much to his annoyance he couldn't tell if the dog shot by Krige had also been removed. He watched for another hour, the stillness beginning to get to him, and at ten to nine he went up the hill to the top where it came into Ridge Road. He went along to the avenue and then down to the junction where he was to meet Koch.

A while later, and growing frustrated, he saw his friend pull up at the opposite curb and he ran over. 'One of the dogs has gone,' he said as he thudded onto the seat. 'The one I shot on the lawn. I couldn't see if the other dog has also been removed.' He was pleased with his observation and his report. He concluded: 'Something weird is going on up there. I don't like it at all.'

Koch took the heavy car through the traffic lights into Smith Street, quietly digesting what Richter had spewed out. A couple of blocks further on, they saw Krige standing in the entrance to a store and he came over and got in when they stopped. He sensed something was wrong. 'What?' he asked as Koch went into the flow of traffic. 'Who's up at the house?'

'There was no one in sight and not so much as a whisper,' said Richter and opened the window. 'The dog I shot has vanished. I couldn't see the other but it would have been the first to stare them in the face. They would have looked around and found both.'

'Where were you?' said Krige, not liking what he'd heard.

'I was up on the rise, where you told me to go for a

decent view. I could see everything except the entire courtyard and the rear.'

Krige thought for a while and said: 'My news is better. Cartwright's in Cape Town. He returns on the seven-ten flight this evening.'

'Cape Town,' said Koch. 'I thought he never went away.'

'His children are at the University of Cape Town,' said Krige. 'I told you at the farm. His wife stays there during term time.'

'We knew about his kids, not his wife,' said Richter. 'I wonder how you were going to deal with her if we found her at the house.'

'We're three weeks into the fourth term,' said Krige, irritation creeping into his voice. 'I was sure she wouldn't be there.'

'If she had been?' pressed Richter. 'I bet you would've spared her because she's a white woman. You discriminate, Major, like the rest of us, but I'm sure you won't admit that either.'

Krige quietly listened, admitting to himself that there was a segment of truth in what Richter had said, and that maybe the strong white male superiority in the past had made and taught them all to discriminate – sex, race, religion, tribes. He spoke to Koch. 'Go to the esplanade at the end. When Richter regains his cool I'll tell the two of you what comes next.'

Richter said: 'Like always, Major.' He still resented Krige's appointed leadership of the job.

They parked obliquely, overlooking the south beach where a gusting wind blew the upper layers of sand in stinging clouds above the surface. A waitress from a nearby cafeteria attended them and they ordered coffee that was duly delivered and placed on a tray hooked to the window. Krige said: 'Our last chance is to get Cartwright when he returns to the house tonight. It's best that I go in on my own. If the police are with him I might have to get out and there's less chance of a screw-up if there's only one of us.'

Richter slurped from his cup. 'You're not sure, Major. I can see Cartwright living through this and us going back with empty hands.'

'Then you can tell Muller you screwed up with the noise from that gun,' said Krige. 'But before then you're going up that rise to see if anything happens the rest of the day. At seven o'clock this evening I'll meet you where you met Koch. If everything's okay I'll carry on.'

'How?' asked Koch, curious. 'You can't keep jumping over the front wall, can you?'

'You're smart,' said Krige sarcastically. 'There are other ways to get into the property.'

'You sound like a professional,' sneered Richter. 'Pull this off and Muller will never let you go.'

Koch giggled. 'You'll be a hero, Major.'

'You bastards are stuffed,' said Krige evenly, unable to stop himself from being needled. 'I'd love to see the two of you on the next job Muller has lined up. You'd never be able to coordinate stealing toilet paper from a bog in a one-horse town.'

Richter turned to ice. Krige watched him closely. After a while Richter said: 'We'll talk in Pretoria, Major.' For a moment he spoke as if he was in charge.

Krige lit a cigarette, exhaling the smoke in twin streams through his nose. If he had ever been meant to pay for a past crime it was on an operation like this with these two. He lowered the window a bit and rested his arm on the toughened glass. 'Let's move on,' he said. 'Make sure Richter finds something to eat. He's in for a long day.'

'Where are you going?' Koch reversed the car, belligerently turning the wheel.

'Drop me in the centre,' said Krige. 'I want to give Cartwright's secretary another ring.' He added, dryness etching his words: 'He may have changed his mind.' He adjusted the Beretta in his shoulder holster and slipped on his jacket.

Later Krige got out at a junction in the city and waited as the car sped off to the Berea. In a nearby arcade he found an open cafeteria and after buying a cup of coffee at the self-service counter sat with the *Natal Mercury* newspaper, flattening it on the table. He swept over the front page, skimming a report on the ambushing of an ANC minibus in eastern Natal, allegedly by members of Inkatha. The tribal faction rivalry and internecine fighting still went on. Most of those in the van were killed, before the attackers were disturbed by a police patrol and fled into the bush. The deceased were another mass of nameless people, dead and forgotten, only their families weeping.

A little before midday Krige left the cafeteria and sauntered back into Smith Street. The town was becoming busy, a massive mix of black and white people, incongruously ordered and calm compared to other parts of the country. From his position in the street he could see Cartwright's office. It was on the ninth floor of the Sanlam Building, 50 metres closer to the beach and over the street. Near him was the phonebox he had used earlier. He went to it and took out the piece of paper that contained the lawyer's number.

The phone was answered on the first ring and he heard the woman he had spoken to two hours before. Her voice was refined and she spoke in English. 'May I help you?'

'Collingwood,' he replied, trying his best to speak without the heavy northern accent. 'I'm in Durban for a few days. I'd like to arrange a meeting with Mr Cartwright.'

She went silent and he thought she had hung up. But

he could make out her breathing, faint and hollow in the room.

'Are you there?' He spoke close to the mouthpiece.

'Mr Cartwright's not here,' she said in a whisper. 'He's flying in this evening from Cape Town. You can contact him here in the morning. May I ask what it's about?'

'It's confidential. A mutual friend suggested I call him. Is it possible to ring him at home this evening? I don't want to miss him.' Krige couldn't suppress a grin at his choice of phrase.

'He won't want to be disturbed,' she said. 'He's usually here at seven in the morning. The line's straight through at that time.'

'I'll phone then.' Krige hooked the receiver into its cradle and left the box, walking slowly up the street in the direction of the Berea. His thoughts were on the beginning of the conversation, her hesitation when he'd asked for Cartwright. She was cautious, perhaps suspicious, her response in stark contrast to the call he had made earlier. There was nothing irregular about the request; dozens must contact Cartwright in the course of a week. He thought about the information she had given. It was the same as before, and she had no reason to suspect him. He assumed it was correct. There was nothing else to go on, simply to get on with it.

Berea, Durban

After leaving Krige, Koch let Richter out in the road that ran parallel to King James Avenue. Taking a circuitous route, Richter finally entered Cartwright's road at the upper end and he went to the spot he had taken up previously. The blue sky of the early morning had turned to cloud and he felt the first tentative drops of rain. He could think of few things worse than spending the rest of the day in damp clothes.

Because of the inchoate rain and the need for effective concealment over a long period he went deeper into the foliage where the leaves formed a canopy. The view of the property was not as good, but he had sight of the drive and the lawn that lay at the entrance and gave access to the back. He settled in for the wait, resting himself on the weathered trunk of a tree; hard, but it offered upright support. The house was still quiet and the minutes summed into an hour, during which he saw nothing except three cars, one a palatial Cadillac coming from a mansion up the road and cruising as if it had not a care in the world. The rain had established itself as a drizzle and he pulled his knees up to his chest, exposing as little of himself as possible, a natural response.

Another three hours went by, much the same, and he began to see his vigil as a total waste of time. If the police were involved and they had stationed someone on the far flank, the part he couldn't see, the person had stayed there for four hours, not even walking the grounds periodically as watchmen usually did. He thought everything was too still for there to be anyone there.

It was nearly three o'clock when Richter made the effort to check the grounds again. He wanted to stretch his legs and relieve the drowsiness that had come since eating his cheese and tomato sandwiches half-an-hour ago and drinking a can of lager, but he did not want to attract attention by wandering about.

As he watched the patch that had come to bore him he was astonished by the emergence of a black male, clothed in the blue-grey raincoat and cap of the South African police service, from the rear of the house. The man walked stiffly, as if aggravated by rheumatic joints, and took a path to the driveway and the closed gate.

Briefly the black went behind the row of trees in the middle sector of the drive before appearing again, only metres from where the raked gravel came to an end. When he reached the gate the policeman leant somnolently against the bars of iron, and looked at the house, a bleak monolith in the rain.

For Richter it was like seeing a man levitate from the grave, and he stared at the policeman finding it difficult to believe that he hadn't even momentarily revealed his presence over a period of five hours, unless he had come to the property when his vigilance was not as sharp as it should have been. But Richter's surprise at seeing the black gave way to the hard realization that the police were right in the centre of things. No longer could Krige base his strategy on chance. Police involvement was now a certainty, and it was closer and more invasive than the lone policeman he now saw.

During the ensuing ten minutes the constable glanced frequently at his watch, clearly waiting for someone, and in his sporadic movements seemingly becoming impatient. Almost predictably, a little later, a small Ford Anglia van turned into the road and drew up at the drive. Acknowledging the arrival, the black unlocked the gates and allowed the van to crawl to the house. As the van reversed and parked, Richter was able to read the blue and red inscription on the van's side panelling. It read: Security Fittings Pty Ltd. Durban 857367.

With the same air of disinterest the black shut the gate and went to the house. He said something to the Asian driver who had alighted from the vehicle and with a nod walked towards the back of house, expecting the newcomer to follow. The driver grabbed a metal box and went after him, as if he was scared of getting lost.

In moments the tranquil setting had returned, and except for the van it was identical to the one Richter had watched diligently for the past hours. It wasn't difficult for him to conclude that the new arrival was there to mend the door, with a lock that didn't yield so easily to the aspirations of the would-be thief. The rain had intensified and the vegetation and soil were soaked. Although he was well screened from the bulk of the water, drops deflected by the leaves had sprayed him and his clothes were wet. The light was fading fast and he longed to get out of the place, to a warm bath and hot meal. He was beginning to get cramp from lack of any movement, and as he waited for the van driver to reappear he started to feel that Cartwright wasn't worth the effort, and that they should return to the Reef. If Krige got caught, breaking in again and possibly killing Cartwright, it would only be a while before they arrested him and Koch, in Durban or in Pretoria if they got that far. Cartwright might escape with his life and the file, with all the damage such a dossier could cause if thrown into the state arena and the international market.

Daylight went, and the man from Security Fittings had been at the house for nearly two hours when Richter saw a flashing torch coming to the van. It was the Asian. He threw his box into the vehicle, clambered in and took off along the drive to the gate and the road.

Shortly afterwards powerful external lights went on at various points, dispersing a yellow moat that illuminated the courtyard and every vestige of vacant space around the house.

At 6.30 when Richter was about to leave the policeman appeared, walking onto the gravel where the van had been parked and then in his easy manner to the gates. Without locking them he went up the road and into the avenue that led to the city centre.

Richter stayed under the tree for a little longer, not knowing what to deduce from the departure of the policeman. Withdrawing from the trees he traced the route he had taken in the morning and was soon near the spot where he was to meet Krige. He saw him coming from a corner tobacconist and he hurried to him. They walked a short way up an adjacent road, Krige lighting one of the high-tar Texan cigarettes that were favoured by many above any other brand, primarily for their strength.

'What did you find?' said Krige.

'The police are in on it,' said Richter, gratefully releasing his burden and irritated by Krige's composure. 'There was a black cop stationed at the house.'

'Was?' Krige pulled on the cigarette, leaving the resulting stem of ash intact. 'Where's he gone?'

'He left twenty minutes ago,' said Richter. 'I didn't see him for hours and then he showed himself and let in some guy who'd come to fix the mess you made.'

'How do you know that was the reason?' asked Krige.

'It was splashed all over his van. Some outfit called Security Fittings. You've got no chance. I guarantee that place is now like a fortress.'

'Bullshit,' said Krige. 'I'm not giving up now because of a black cop and a mended door. Even if the police were called because of dead dogs and a break-in there is nothing to arouse their suspicion that Cartwright needs protection.'

To return without the file was negative and he had the professional pride to accomplish what he'd been asked to do, whatever it was. He also remembered the look on Muller's face, the obsessive and fanatical desire for the white, and the hold that Muller and his bosses had over him.

'Why did the cop leave? Where's the other guy?' He pulled at his wristwatch, aware that time was passing quickly, and that if any more of it was lost the objectives of the operation could be cancelled out as unachievable.

'How the hell do I know why the cop left?' said Richter. 'The security guy finished up an hour ago and pulled out. There're so many lights on up there it's like noon. What have you found out?'

'The same thing I found out before, except that the girl seemed more reluctant to reveal anything,' said Krige. 'But as far as I know Cartwright's due in at seven-ten.'

'If you are right and you pull this job off, Muller will give you a medal,' said Koch.

'You can have it,' said Krige. 'It'll sit well on your chest. Now I'm going. Make sure you're at the bridge at the top of the Berea. After this I want out fast and back to my farm.'

Richter shook his head, still sceptical, an attitude that was not in Krige's repertoire. 'You're always one for risk, Major. The deck's stacked against you. If you get caught we'll catch it as well, Muller and above.'

'You're scared for your skin,' said Krige scathingly. 'I'm still doing the job. Besides, I don't trust the two of you. If I pull away now from this you'll play a different tune when you see Muller, and spin some weird concoction that I lost my nerve.'

Richter stared at Krige, showing no feeling, realizing that the farmer was set on going ahead. 'Carry on, Major,' he said softly. 'As long as you understand the consequences I'm not really in a position to complain. But for the record, I still believe Cartwright will be surrounded by police.'

'All you have to do is meet me at the bridge,' said Krige, going to the corner. 'I told you that you couldn't handle this kind of work.'

Berea

Krige moved quickly up to the road below Cartwright's. It was surprisingly straight and flat, only dipping slightly after several hundred metres. He chose the second house along and went into the garden and along the fence. When he was as far as he could go he worked out where he was in relation to the house he wanted. Nothing of it was visible, but he knew the general direction and that was all he needed.

It was 7.15 when he vaulted the last wall to Cartwright's grounds, at a place from which he could see the verandah where he had forced entry. Richter was right, the lawn and drive were well lit.

Krige went up the length until he could see the gates. There were at least 30 minutes to go before he expected the lawyer, if what the secretary had first said was anything to go by. The rain had ceased and the wind was dispersing the cloud. He longed for a cigarette but he refrained from lighting up, remembering his spell in the military when it had been demonstrated how easy it was to spot the glow of a fag at night. He fondled the Beretta, thumbing the safety on and off and willing his target to appear so he could get the wretched file and get out.

At a few minutes to eight, with clandestine quietness, a large American saloon appeared in the road and came to the gates. A thin man swung them in and drove up to the garage. Before he had quenched the engine a second car came in and ponderously snaked after the first. When it halted a thick-set man got out. He was joined by the driver of the other car, and as the thin man came under the porch lamp Krige recognized him as the one he wanted. He had no idea who the other person was and it didn't particularly concern him, except that if he got in the way he might also have to die, if that was to be Cartwright's fate.

Chapter 9

Tokyo

As Steiner caught the train in Nikko town, Paul Adams found the body of Oshima, already stiffening in death, his arms soullessly spread out at right angles to his chest.

Adams had hung about in cover at the end of the footway until he was certain Steiner would not show. He had sensed Oshima was in trouble. Taking the path to the road, he had come across the damaged foliage where the two men had fought, and he had begun a meticulous search, describing a pattern above and below the path and going progressively deeper into the bush. As he examined the body and touched the lump on the neck, he was filled with a brooding sadness that was changed to a feeling of guilt and then desire for deepest revenge. The man had done it again and committed another crime.

From the road Adams called the *hombu dojo* and asked for Shirai. The master knew Adams was in Japan and greeted him warmly, though he was surprised at the phone call rather than a visit in person. He soon had the reason, and he listened as Adams related the events culminating in Oshima's death.

When Adams waited for a reply Shirai said: 'Shioda will come for you Adams *san*. Bring the body with you and then we will talk. You have met Shioda *san*.'

Adams knew the man. He had been one of the younger

instructors, an *uchideshi*, the inside disciples of the art, when he had last visited Japan. 'Yes,' he said.

Shirai went on: 'He'll meet you on the road at the top of Nikko in a few hours. You'll recognize the same large black Mazda saloon we always use.'

The train journey to Tokyo gave Steiner enough time to lay his plans, and on arrival in the city he took the circle line to Shinjuku station and phoned Michiko Tanaka at the *dojo* in Yoyogi. It was Wednesday and she was eating her lunch of *tonkatsu* and rice from a small tray she had purchased on her way to work. The skewered chicken was a popular dish in Japan, easily affordable and in some ways similar in popularity for lunch to the sandwiches of the Westerners.

'James *san*, where are you?' she said, immediately recognizing his voice. 'Chinen *sensei* was asking for you. Will you be coming here?'

'No,' he said curtly, without intent. 'Michiko, I'm leaving Japan. The first direct flight is on Saturday. Until then I'll be in Takamiyama in the Fuji area. I have friends there at the school.'

She knew the village to which he referred. It was in the shadow of Mount Fuji, the dormant volcano with its peak at 3,500 metres, 45 minutes by coach from Shinjuku. The village was renowned for its picturesque setting and the organization had a *dojo* there which, she remembered, Steiner had visited on numerous occasions.

'But when will you see Chinen *sensei*?' she asked, taken aback by his abrupt departure. 'He will be most disappointed if you don't speak to him before you go.'

'I will write to him and explain,' he said. 'The men you saw are dangerous and I have to deal with them on my own. I do not want the master involved. You must not tell him I have spoken to you. This is a personal matter and those men wanted to kill me.'

'Did they find you, James *san*?' She knew from her formal Japanese upbringing that she had no right to ask the question, but Westerners were not of her culture and she was spurred on by curiosity.

'I saw them,' he replied vaguely, not giving any more away. 'But I returned to Tokyo. They might speak to you again. You are to tell them you haven't heard from me, and that you believe I have left Japan. They are not to be trusted, Michiko.' He added bluntly: 'They're killers.'

'Your secret is safe with me,' she stammered loyally. 'I'm so sorry this has happened to you James *san*.'

He fed his last 100-yen coin into the box. 'There's one last request,' he said. 'This is your half-day?'

'Yes,' she answered, puzzled.

'I have a bag in the room,' said Steiner, 'and some clothes in the cupboard. Please bring them to me at the coach depot in Shinjuku.'

'When do you want them, James *san*?' She was eager to comply. 'I finish at two o'clock.'

'As soon after that as you can,' said Steiner. 'I'll be at the east entrance. You won't miss me.'

Adams's master, Shirai, lived in a flat on the seventh floor of the block that rose above the *dojo*. Shioda, the instructor sent to pick him up, parked the car in the triangular forecourt and went with Adams as far as the lift. He did not return Adams's brief bow as the doors slid together, and Adams's parting glimpse was of the hard inscrutable face that had remained unchanged since their meeting in Nikko Reserve nearly six hours ago. The body had been collected in silence, and on the drive to Tokyo Shioda had said nothing except when absolutely necessary, and then only in monosyllabic grunts. To Adams it could only be that the Japanese held him responsible for Oshima's death.

Shirai's wife, a woman of a little over five feet, let him into the flat. After he had replaced his shoes with a pair of purple slippers from a rack next to the footwell she ushered him into the *tatami* room where Shirai squatted next to a black lacquered table. The woman withdrew behind another set of screens and the men were alone.

'Please sit down, Adams *san*,' said Shirai, bowing his head slightly. 'Your journey has been long and hard. You must take refreshment before we begin to talk and you let me know what you are really involved in.'

As if on call his wife came in with Japanese tea. She poured the yellow liquid into the little cups and when she had gone Shirai sipped appreciatively before speaking.

'I did not think I would see you again so soon, Adams *san*,' he said. He was in his sixties, a few inches taller than his wife, and he carried the aura of calm that distinguished the select group of true *budo* masters. And on the mat he demonstrated the enormous power that came from acutely developed mind and body coordination, the essential aim of the art. 'I am sorry the circumstances are not better. Tell me what brought you to Japan, and your business with the man who killed Oshima.'

Adams told the Japanese what he knew about Steiner, and the events that had taken place after he had raped Sophie Carswell. Shirai did not interrupt, and when Adams had completed his account he drank his tea thoughtfully.

'From what you have said I believe there is little evidence to convict this man for murder in the courts of Japan. Therefore we will not go to the authorities and waste our energy.'

Adams was patient, wondering what Shirai was coming to.

'Also,' said Shirai, 'the man's deed, the killing of one my most loyal students and your trusted friend, is too serious for us to get satisfaction by simply speaking to the master of his school. If he believed the story he might expel Steiner from his organization, but that would not be sufficient punishment. This man should die for his crime.'

Adams was silent. Even men who lived by the highest ideals favoured the ultimate penalty if it meant gaining revenge. He let Shirai go on, curious.

'Because of our principles of non-resistance the techniques we teach have been developed primarily for defence against an attacking force, physically and psychologically. We are not skilled in the methods of surveillance, detection and assassination, nor do we want to be. But others are, men who live by the ancient *ninja* code and who do not need moral justification before they go about their work. Steiner's death must not be a blemish on the members of this school.'

'Who are these people?' said Adams. 'I know *Ninjutsu* is still practised in Japan and some has filtered to the West. But these are modern forms, boy's games played by men, and their methods of combat are technically flawed. I have seen their demonstrations and read their books. Steiner is in a different class and will not be easily killed.'

'Not all are like those you describe,' said Shirai. 'The genuine *ninja* schools trace their roots to the pre-Edo period and according to ancient custom still jealously protect their secrets. It is not possible for foreigners to learn their art, and even for the Japanese they have very strict entry requirements.'

'Do you know them?' asked Adams, still thinking Shirai was conveying legend, and that the sects he spoke of had ceased to exist.

'In my home village of Kinagawa, when I was young, I met a man who was connected to the *ninja*. He was studying judo and karate as a part of his preparation for initiation into a sect. He wanted me to follow his path and I always remember him saying their training was designed to eradicate all forms of human attachment, that there is no place for compassion or conscience in the *ninja* arts. I found it sad that he should have such beliefs, but now I am glad such people exist. Sometimes in our society, like others in the world, they are necessary.' Shirai held his head as if ashamed of his sentiments. He resumed: 'His name was Kanazawa and he is now head-master of the sect. This afternoon before you arrived I spoke to him. His men will kill this man Steiner. He awaits my call.'

Adams looked at the old man at the table, clinically impassive about the death of a student he had taught since boyhood and just as unemotional in the way he planned to order the execution of someone he'd never met. The callous reality of his master's words, so simply delivered, made him want to get out and think alone.

As if knowing his thoughts Shirai said: 'It has to be like this Adams, *san*. When you go I will speak to Kanazawa and I want to know the name of the school and where it is. You have been there and spoken to the girl. It is our only lead to the present whereabouts of this Steiner. He might even have left the country and if that is the case we have lost him. We would never go on a job like this in a foreign land.'

'The *dojo* is in Yoyogi, near the station,' said Adams. 'The master is Chinen.'

'Ah, Chinen, a respected teacher,' said Shirai. 'I've heard much about him. He's a man of great prowess and an exceptional teacher of the arts. I wonder what Steiner is doing in his organization.'

'What will you do with Oshima's body?' said Adams, wanting to press on.

'He has no family except his father,' said Shirai. 'I will see him personally and explain that his son died honourably. Honour is more important to the old Japanese than death. Oshima will be cremated quietly.' Shirai uncoiled himself. 'You should return to England. This business is over.'

'Not before Kanazawa's men have done their work,' said Adams, after a pause. 'I'll stay until then, *sensei*.'

'No.' Shirai was emphatic. 'Your continued stay here will not serve a purpose. I will contact you when the job has been done, satisfactorily concluded as your people would say.'

Takamiyama, near Mt Fuji

Steiner woke early the next morning and lay for a while, taking in the smell of the straw, woven exactingly on the six *tatami* mats that covered the floor. He was in a *ryokan* a kilometre from the centre of Takamiyama and on the road that led into the mountains from Mount Fuji and the vast plain surrounding it. The establishment was of ten rooms and isolated, the nearest buildings located in the village itself. The accommodation was modest, but contained a traditional feudal charm that for him set it apart from the modern equivalents of Tokyo.

It was raining as he left the inn and started for the village. The road was rough, forgotten, flanked by a stretch of bamboos that swayed in the wind like giant ostrich feathers and melted into the indigenous oaks and maples that clad the hill.

The *dojo* was near the village centre and sole access to the sliding door was down a narrow footpath that ran 50 metres from the road and wound slightly between the houses. He had forgotten the class schedule and learned from the leaflet pinned on a board that morning sessions were only on Wednesdays and Fridays. The next class was that evening. The list of instructors was short, and he saw no name he recognized. The men he had known and trained with in his formative years seemed to have moved on. He went back along the path. He would take the classes as they came, and up to when his flight was due leave for the Republic of South Africa.

In some ways he regretted coming to Takamiyama. He was starting to feel alone and wanted to be back in his second country. He didn't believe Smith of the DSO would have anything of significance to give him, perhaps a few errand-boy jobs, and it was reassuring to know that he would be returning with a clean slate and able to get on with his chosen profession as a karate teacher. Guys like Smith had undoubted influence in the highest places.

Tokyo

Michiko Tanaka seldom worked late, but on the Thursday evening she stayed until after the class, filing accounts and invoices that in the modern age were essential to the business. Gone were the days when tuition in the art was freely given and purely dependent on a student's willingness to train.

She let herself out through a side exit and walked briskly along the street for Yoyogi station. She lived in Kichijogi, the first stop west on thc fast train from Shinjuku. As she passed a deserted plot of land two men came from the shadow and fell in next to her. She kept going, the lights of the small station a twinkle in the distance, but in less than ten paces one of them took her by the arm and roughly halted her.

'Tanaka *san*,' he said, 'tell us what we want and you can catch your train.' The man's name was Morio Oita, a senior disciple of the powerful *ninja* sect referred to by Adams's *sensei*, Shirai.

'Let me go,' she cried, trying to resist his bullish grip but quickly realizing the futility of her physical attempt. She tried something else. 'If you don't let me go I'll scream.'

'And how will that help you,' he said. 'There's no one else on the street. You're alone, Tanaka *san*.'

He spoke the truth, and with a tearless sob she gave into his strength, relaxing her arm to appease the blood-stopping hold. 'Why are you doing this?' she pleaded. 'Who are you?' The second Japanese, Koichi Sato, joined his colleague, and she added: 'I don't know him either.'

Oita pulled her closer and she averted her face at the smell of his breath. 'James Steiner,' he said. 'He's a member of the *goju* organization, the headquarters of which you have just left. I am sure you know him. We want to find out where to contact him.'

'He's not here,' she said, naively hoping that would satisfy him. 'He left Japan.'

'So soon,' mocked Sato. 'He only arrived a day ago.' He was younger than Oita, both men in their mid-thirties, and, like others in Kanazawa's organization, schooled in the *ninja* arts since their late teens. Each had enormous strength and the physical structure that, had they desired, adequately suited them for the noble profession of sumo wrestling. They were highly skilled in the traditional martial arts and proud of being efficient killers.

'I'm not his keeper,' she said. 'I've told you what he said to me. Now can I go and catch my train?'

'That's not enough,' said Oita, increasing the pressure on her arm until she shrieked. 'You're a liar, and my patience is wearing thin.'

She shook her head despairingly, as if trying to rid herself of a bad dream. They could tell that she was lying. She hoped Steiner would understand, but she also knew in her heart that he could look after himself, whatever his surprise if and when confronted by these men. 'He's in Takamiyama,' she said with a heave and a sob. 'It's a village near Mount Fuji. On Saturday he flies from Narita.'

'Why Takamiyama?' said Sato, taking her with deceptive softness at the nape of her neck. He knew the area and the village. It was famous for its pottery and works of art.

'We have a *dojo* there,' she whispered. 'It's in the centre of the village. He has friends there and has trained there a lot in the past. He wanted to see them before leaving the country.'

'When's that?' asked Sato.

'He's leaving on Saturday for South Africa,' she said, weakening further under the increasing pressure.

'Thank you,' said Oita, freeing her arm. 'You have been wise, but if what you tell us is a lie your gods will not save you from death. We always have time. Now go, you will miss your train.'

Takamiyama, near Mt Fuji

When Steiner entered the hall on the Thursday evening it was 6.45, 15 minutes before the class. He changed and took up position in front of a *makiwara* – thc favoured post for developing coordination and power – that was set along the mirrored wall, and he was soon punching and striking the straw binding with a power that quickly had him soaked in sweat. A few of the students gathered around him, noting enviously the speed with which he changed posture and delivered combinations that stressed the foundations of the post to its limits.

When the beginning of the class was called, Steiner's reading of the list pinned outside was confirmed – the three instructors were strangers to him, several years younger and men who carried low black-belt rank. They were the new wave in the expansion of the organization. He had seen it before – as teachers acquired higher grades on their testing ground they were moved on to start new schools and through that earn higher grades and increase their standing in the organization.

Thirty or more students filled the floor, and the teachers conducted the first hour of the two-hour session in the usual pattern, from basics on the spot to moving sequences, and then semi-free sparring against an opponent. Although all those present were well below his technical proficiency, Steiner gave each partner attention. To him even a novice was dangerous. When the instructors joined in at the end of the line they found his defence impenetrable, while he frequently got through their guard, and they commented among themselves with obvious respect for his undeniable ability.

There were four people watching the group train, and as the students spread out for *kata* practice, the set forms, Steiner was near one of them, a male who sat alone on a long bench. His wide-eyed innocence appeared as that of a man who was interested in the art, possibly with the intention of becoming a new convert. But Steiner's glance told him more. The loose tracksuit enveloped a powerful athletic physique and the ridges and knuckles of his hands showed scar tissue like his own. They weren't the hands of a beginner.

For the rest of the class Steiner worked on his *kata*, striving for perfection, forgetting the man. At the end, after they had all bowed to the front, he showered and returned to the hall, going to the exit. The man was looking at old black and white photographs further up and he was still doing so when Steiner went out into the night and set off along the path.

When he came to the road Steiner went towards the *ryokan* and then crossed to a bar, small and nearly empty. He bought a beer and sat at a table with a video game under the glass top. He fed a coin into the slot and as the screen lit up some of the students appeared from the alley. Almost on their heels, so did the man Steiner had seen watching the class in the *dojo*.

Morio Oita was not interested in the pictures on the wall, but it required some of his patience to pretend that he was. Neither did he find it difficult to know what was going on in the hall and when Steiner left he too went to let himself out, slowing behind others who were at the door first. Ahead he saw the tall silhouette of Steiner approach the end of the alley and then go from view. He held his pace and when he came to the road turned the other way. In the shadow of a shop awning, he saw his friend Sato lounging, and continuing up the pavement he held his arm across his stomach in a pre-arranged signal. He had had only the vaguest description of Steiner, one that would have fitted several *gaijin*, but very few *gaijin* had the technical skill and power he had just seen on the *dojo* floor. He was easily recognizable from that, and his killing would be a challenge. Oita had difficulty concealing his desire for Steiner's death, and was grateful to his master for giving him the job.

Steiner swallowed the last of his beer and after placing the bottle and glass on the counter went outside. Except for a couple of lovers further up, the street was deserted and most of the small houses were already shuttered. High above, the half-moon and shimmering stars were visible and he was glad of the light they offered as he left the village behind.

When he came to the inn Steiner nodded to the clerk at the desk and went to the flight of stairs. Some people were drinking in the lounge, and as it was still early for him to sleep he decided to join them after dropping off his bag. He had a first-floor room, and after laying out the futon and hanging his *dogi* to air he retraced his steps to the lounge. At the top of the stairs he glanced through a window that overlooked the road leading to the village and began his descent. But after a couple of steps he brought himself up short and went back to the window. The passage light was out, and he stood in front of the glass. A man was watching the inn from over the road, at less than 100 metres. He thought of the man in the *dojo*, but he had seen him come from the alley when he was in the bar. He had gone in the other direction, and surely couldn't have known he was there, even if he was after him, which was doubtful.

The man departed as if he had seen enough, walking for a while along the verge before going off it, travelling closer to the trees. When he was no longer visible, Steiner carried on to the lounge. He ordered a measure of Japanese whisky and parked himself on a stool. Casually he swilled the liquid in the glass, sipping it, enjoying the quality that was well known for its excellence. Was he becoming paranoid? His only enemy was Adams, and Adams would want to meet him face to face. He wouldn't send others, particularly if he'd found his friend's body. And only Michiko knew his plans. He drank more of the whisky, then swallowed the remainder and ordered another.

He stayed in the lounge until after the bar had closed,

and no one else was left. He extinguished the light and went to his room where he changed into the darkest clothing he had. He went to the foyer and into the kitchen then through to the garden. He waited a while, then ran round the inn to the road, going over and into the trees. His honed intuition was taking control and he had come to rely on it completely.

At a *ryokan* in the village Oita got up when he heard a knock on the screen. He slid it in its groove and Sato came into the room.

'He's in an inn on the mountain road.' said Sato, seating himself on the floor and helping himself from a flask of heated sake. 'It's perfect for us.'

'How far is it from here?' asked Oita.

'Two kilometres at the most, and there's nothing out there except the night,' said Sato, pouring the cup of sake down his throat and reaching for another.

'Good,' said Oita. He was in the black garments of their trade, ideally concealing for what he had in mind. 'Change your clothes. We'll give it a while more and then go and find him.'

In the small hours of the morning they slipped from the inn into the darkness, and wove between the houses away from the lamps of the village, moving parallel to the road, their cat-like silhouettes virtually indistinguishable from the dark that embraced them, the dark that was their friend.

As the minutes accumulated into an hour since leaving the inn Steiner came from his cover, rubbing himself to restore circulation. He was angry he had allowed his imagination to override simple logic, to suspect a man who he had never seen before was there to kill him in a remote village. He scuffed bits of vegetation from his trousers and began to go to the inn.

Then from nowhere two figures emerged, going along the ditch next to the road, only the upper parts of their bodies outlined on the sand. Their heads were hooded, the cloth framing relative whiteness of their faces. He knew who they were, their mission in life, and everything fitted into place. They hadn't seen him, and he held his position as they went to the inn and passed inside.

Oita spent only seconds finding what he wanted in the register on the reception desk. 'Room seven,' he said, straightening his jacket. 'It'll be on the first floor.'

They went up the stairs and at number seven Oita slipped the lock with the blade of a knife he pulled deftly from his waist. As the screen parted he shot through like a striking snake, but just as quickly drew up when he saw the empty futon, lit only by the moon and bitterly mocking.

'The *gaijin* knows we're hunting him,' he said as Sato went to the windows. 'He's clever. Something must have alerted him.' He thought for a moment then grinned, his yellow teeth a perfect portrait of evil intent. 'He'll be where he can watch us come and go about our business, the woods by the road. He must have seen us when we came in.'

'Maybe he's got a woman,' said Sato, less certain. 'He could be making love to her now.'

'No,' said Oita. 'There'd be no one in this place to interest him. The young girls are all in the city.' He joined Sato at the window and opened it, judging the drop to the ground. 'We go out here,' he said. 'I'll go first. Meet in the woods.' He went up to the opening and then he was gone. Sato let him get clear, before also mounting the ledge and dropping into the emptiness.

Steiner knew Oita and Sato would search for him when they discovered the empty futon, and that they wouldn't bother with the rest of the inn. When the men vanished he had thought of evading them, but they were not the type to give up, and their presence instilled in him contempt for what they stood for, certainly not the type of training with its beliefs that he'd learnt under his master, Shirai. Now as he watched the inn he thought he heard something, but it was only a murmur, unrepeated. Minutes passed and he became uneasy. Their black costumes would assist them. He walked along a bit, placing his feet carefully and wondering where they were. Then he knew.

Oita came out of the dark, light from the half-moon starred in tiny shimmers on his knife. His stance was wide and he scuttled through the dead leaves like a crab, his Mongoloid visage like that of a villain in a horror film. He moved quickly and, when he was a few metres from Steiner, Sato materialized at right angles, nearer than his friend and with his arms cocked like a boxer.

In his eagerness Oita increased his speed and then lunged with a martial cry. His body described a parabolic arc, and when his boot touched the earth and he felt sure of his target, he stabbed.

A moment from taking the blade in his chest Steiner advanced, gliding past the steel so close it sliced his shirt. With his forefinger and thumb forming a 'V' he hit Oita across the throat, halting the *ninja*'s charge as if he had reached the end of a rope.

With the weight of a swinging pendulum, Oita's lower body came up level with his head. Breaking loose, Steiner chopped down onto the chest as if trying to disintegrate a block of ice. Oita was slammed to the earth, the jolt of energy to his heart killing him instantly. When he landed, Steiner faced Sato, who was already arrowing in, his fist recoiled at his hip like a bolt in a crossbow.

As Sato came within *maai* and his fist shot out, Steiner altered his balance and with his instep swept the *ninja*'s foot in a perfect execution of *ashi barai*, the deadly foot-sweep. He blocked the blow, cutting onto Sato's neck with the knife edge of his hand, again invoking all the strength at his command. The strike was devastating and like his comrade Sato died before he hit the ground, his glazed, lifeless eyes staring at the branches overhead, never having a chance to know what went wrong.

Steiner left the bodies where he had killed them and made for the *ryokan*. He was not interested in sleep, only the need to get out before anyone else came for him. He was sure Smith's work with the Scorpions in Durban, if the man had any, could not be like this.

Chapter 10

Cape Town

When Krige made his second phone call to Cartwright's office the lawyer was reclining with the morning newspaper in his Cape Town flat. His wife had gone shopping in a nearby arcade and as was his custom he went straight to the financial pages. Halfway into the share index he was startled when the hall phone started ringing. Aside from the family circle, only his secretary had the number and she was under instructions to ring only on matters of extreme urgency. Resting the paper on the arm of the chair he went into the hall, his surprise at the intrusion adding deep lines to his permanently creased brow. He reached the phone and grabbed the receiver.

'Cartwright. Who is it?' he demanded with creeping apprehension, for what reason he didn't know.

'Mr Cartwright, Fraser, Captain Fraser of Durban Central Police. Your house was broken into during the night. We got your number from your secretary.'

Cartwright's expression was vacant, his thoughts on the Alsatians. They were trained, capable of ripping anyone to shreds. 'How did they evade the dogs?' he asked. Then he feared the worst. 'Where are they?'

'The dogs were shot to pieces by heavy-calibre hand guns, a .357 magnum and a 9 mm parabellum to be precise. Whoever did it knows how to use them.' The Captain's voice was a monotone. 'Going by the different bullets there was certainly more than one of them, unless one guy carried both weapons which is highly improbable.'

He stopped, giving Cartwright a while to soak in the information. Then he added: 'The verandah door gave them entry. Nothing appears to have been stolen. We don't think theft was the motive.'

'What do you think was? Tell me what you know, Captain,' urged Cartwright.

'We think it's possible they were after you. Men of prominence like you who have adopted a definite political alliance always have enemies.'

'Sure,' said Cartwright, thinking of his support for the ANC. 'But we're ten years into a democratic country and there are others who are far more influential than I am. My guess is they were common burglars. Obviously someone disturbed them. My servant was in his quarters out in the yard.'

'Burglars with the fire power I described?' pressed Fraser. 'Unlikely. Your servant was in his room. He heard the guns but was too scared to appear, until half an hour later when he contacted the police. Have you ever heard the discharge from a magnum and a parabellum? It is enough to rupture your eardrums. The dogs were a mess. Whoever did it wanted to make sure they wouldn't bark, or more importantly pose any physical threat to their presence at your house. I wouldn't like to face an Alsatian in a close fight.'

Cartwright felt sick. He'd reared the Alsatians from puppies, both of the finest pedigree. 'What are you saying, Captain?'

'You need protection,' answered Fraser unambiguously. 'At least until we can sort this out. It's not safe for you to return to the house.'

'I'm going there tonight.' Cartwright was emphatic. 'If you want men around the place, keep them so they can't be seen. I'm not some Mafia boss. I land at seven-ten. I've invited someone for the evening. He's a man named Kaplan, an old business friend and a lawyer. I'll collect him on the way.'

'My men will be there,' said Fraser. 'You won't see them, and I'll pull them off when these maniacs are behind bars.'

'Thank you, Captain. The sooner that is done the better.' Cartwright was getting the point of the police officer's words and realized that his life might well be in danger. 'What was the damage to the house? How did they get in?'

'As I said, they broke in through the door leading onto the verandah,' replied Fraser. 'A few of the panes are history and there is possible damage to the lock. It's not secure enough, and should be replaced.'

'It'll be attended to today.' Cartwright hung up and returned to the room, thoughtfully gazing through the sheet of glass that overlooked Adderley Street, the main street of the city. He couldn't believe he was the target of an assassination squad, after all these years and when he had merely aided a cause rather than led it. And he was white.

The murdered Chris Hani and others of his prominent stature were the prime targets for the maverick Boer resistance parties and right-wingers, who, since the election of the new ANC government had lost any conceivable credibility and whose days of achieving anything had surely gone. Despite their ceaseless invective, a pathetic patter, they had not to his knowledge assassinated anyone in recent years who was overtly, or less obviously, involved as he was with the ANC. And no one else would want to kill him.

Cartwright went back to the phone. He dialled his secretary and gave her instructions to get someone to the house to repair the damaged verandah doors, and replace the locks with bolts that he knew would render the opening impregnable when closed, like the front doors.

Durban

'Cartwright's at the centre of the operation in Durban that Bryant told me about. I confess I didn't think of him, but it fits with what happened last evening. I still don't know the precise reason why he's in it, but we'll find out.' Peter Smith of the Directorate of Special Operations, the Scorpions, swung in his chair and faced the young man seated across the desk.

'How do you know it is him? Someone killed his two dogs. That's next to nothing.' David Johnson scratched his chin, quizzically watching his superior. 'If I were this country's right wing, the guys with whom Bryant is associating, I'd rather kill the white leaders in government, those conveniently in bed with the ANC and whose prime objective is perceived as being the unashamed levelling of their own people.'

Smith lit a cigarette. 'To some, Cartwright's just as odorous. He is obviously not a political leader but he has underpinned the black power base and thereby created a platform for whoever chooses to use it, be they communists or those with a more moderate leaning. It's a case of extremes, and to the right wing Cartwright's extreme enough. But I don't believe that is what's going on here.'

He dragged deeply on the cigarette. 'I think someone has found that he's standing in the way of something, or more specifically, has something they want. If they were after Cartwright, which I believe they were, I think that he has received something that would pull them apart if exposed. You don't simply pick up guns in Pretoria and go to the Berea just to kill someone without a pretty good reason.'

'I don't get where you're coming from,' said Johnson. 'It sounds as if you're grasping at straws. You haven't said why last night was about getting Cartwright. When does a guy, or guys, who are after something so important, as your suspect, not even know the whereabouts of the man they're after? Unless they are idiots or pretty incompetent they would surely have checked to see if he was at home.'

'Intelligence is not always accurate, especially when, as in many cases, infiltration into the target camp is not easy with the limited resources and access you have at your disposal. No, three things come to mind.' Smith stubbed out the cigarette and almost in the same movement lit another. He knew he smoked too much and that one day it would probably kill him, but he still persisted with the habit.

'First, whoever it was that broke into the house left it in pristine condition. To me that means they were after something else, something not available simply because Cartwright wasn't there, and he was the key. I'm sure Cartwright will confirm nothing was taken.' Smith spun his chair again, reaching for the overloaded ashtray. 'Second, there are the guns. Very few in this country have access to .357 magnums, and then they're mostly white. The other calibre, 9 mm parabellum, is more widely used but it's also a class cartridge, and again nearly all users are white. So what were whites doing roaming around Cartwright's house in the dark of the night? I can't believe they were stealing. The whites are still too well off.'

Johnson leant on the desk, without taking his eyes off Smith. 'And what is the third?'

'Whoever was there was an excellent shot. Both dogs were probably killed from a range of twenty to thirty metres, since you never get any closer than that to an Alsatian that doesn't know you. The groupings were less than two inches. With combat pistols that's exceptional. Guys like that aren't interested in petty theft. They have a greater mission.'

'You're convinced they were after Cartwright and, as you said, something that he might have.' Johnson didn't know where they were going on this. 'Why have you pulled off the police protection? They can help us. Fraser was pissed off, to put it mildly.'

'Fraser will do as he's told,' said Smith. 'I've got the authority when I choose to exercise it. This thing's more complex than he's used to.' He returned to his subject. 'The motive for going after someone you don't know personally, and I'm sure these people last night didn't know Cartwright, is usually covered by the following categories. The first is to cause political disruption, chaos and violence, destroy opposition groups, men and women of political influence, and to right the wrongs you feel have been done by society to you or your people. There are many terrorist cells doing this in the world today, and some of them operate separately from the original group that inspired them, but with the same objectives. The second is purely criminal and for some reason you go it alone or you are persuaded or directed by others to commit the crime for their own reasons.' Smith idly fondled a piratical scar on his cheek. 'The third is that you or others want something that the person you are after has in their possession, such as damaging information or business secrets. I'm sure that's where this one fits in.'

Smith hesitated in thought, then answered Johnson's first question. 'The police are competent at bringing in the man who fires the bullet, even some of his mates if there are any. But they have limited powers, as in most civilized countries, and in cases where the crime or act is more orchestrated, more skillfully planned and organized, they fail to get the man or men at the top. They need evidence, and they always seem to come to an end without getting to the root of the conspiracy. Look how the TRC failed to come up with any evidence they could pass on to the prosecutors that would convict the major criminals of the apartheid period, men who are still as free as birds in the sky. That's exactly why this organization, the DSO, was formed.'

Smith stopped and stared trenchantly at Johnson. 'I intend to hit the guys who went for Cartwright last night so hard they'll crawl into their caves for good. And then I'll root out and bring to trial those who sent them. I'll open this can of worms and I'll go right to its heart. I suspect it's that deep and if we're successful it could open the doors to a lot more, the convictions we've been after for a few years and have never got, ever since we were formed.'

Johnson pursed his lips disappointedly. 'You're thinking of an investigative squad that will take at least a week to set up. When you finally get it going, all this, as serious as you think it is, will be over and the dust will have settled. And if Cartwright is killed you'll become the hunted, vilified and held up for castration at a government inquiry into our operations. You surely haven't forgotten the hit squads that used to work for military intelligence under the old white regime. They were a total mess. It's impossible to get men at short notice who have the ability to take this right to the top and get the prosecutions you and I would love to see. I still think this is fantasy.'

Smith lifted a finger. 'You must learn patience. It's a virtue in love and war. Hear me out. I don't intend to let a bunch of operators, which, by the way, I don't have at the moment, run loose looking for these men. One weak link and the whole lot will blow me apart, especially after I pulled off the police. No, I'll send one.'

'One?' said Johnson, unable to believe what he was hearing.

Smith swayed his head like a swan, his eyes filling with mirth. He laughed knowingly, praising himself, supremely confident. 'One man, that's enough. As long as he's the right type, one man can achieve what I want of him. That's where the military intelligence of old went wrong. They chose a disparate bunch, a few whites and some black cops. They stuck them on a farm in the old Northern Transvaal for some kind of training, and then released the chains. They were a hairy crew, not a brain amongst them. Not surprisingly they screwed it up, then started blabbing to the press without any effect, and some of them even tried to get amnesty at the TRC hearings. I'm not surprised they failed and are now serving long terms in jail. That's not what I have been contemplating.'

Johnson studied his superior cautiously. Smith had been ordered, as one of his briefs, to bring to trial the people who were ultimately responsible for directing the apartheid state criminal acts of gross human violations. The unit in Durban was still relatively small for what was eventually intended for the Directorate, with its two sub-directorates of Strategic and Investigative Support, and Operations. At present the organization comprised a network of undercover operatives like John Bryant in the field, and a well-organized staff of lawyers, prosecutors and other professionals in the central office, a five-storey building in the city. They needed, for all their work, evidence.

'It won't stop them,' said Johnson. 'We're only playing their game by sending one man to dig into their holes. That's nowhere near enough.'

'That's the game I want to play,' said Smith firmly. 'I'm tired of waiting for the facts to come to me. He pulled at his shirt cuff and looked at his watch. 'It's a quarter to one and time for lunch. There's a new steak house in the arcade that's supposed to be good.' He pushed his chair back from the desk.

'Who's the one-man band?' asked Johnson, intrigued by the concept.

Smith sank back, pleased Johnson wanted to know. 'A powerful man if ever I've met one, mentally and physically. He's also very intelligent, educated at Cambridge University in England. He was born in England and is virtually unknown in South Africa. To me he is perfect for getting the results I want. His name is Steiner, James Steiner.'

'What's so special about him? What does he do?'

'You've heard of the martial arts, karate, aikido, and so forth. Well, forget the shit you see practised around the town.' He smiled dismissively. 'They're mere amateurs. Steiner has dedicated his life to *goju-ryu* karate, a major Japanese style. He spent some years in Japan, reached the exclusive rank. If anyone's developed the power of *ki*, he has.'

'*Ki*? Never heard of it,' said Johnson, amazed at what seemed to be pure fiction unravelling in front of him.

'I'm no expert. It's developing strength of mind and being able to channel this energy at will. Trained practitioners pervade an aura of calm, invincibility, as if nothing can stop them, and little can. The old Japanese *budo* masters considered the development of this co-ordinated power a prerequisite to fighting prowess.'

'So?' Johnson raised his eyebrows. 'He'll need a lot more than that. Cunning, resourcefulness, brains, and experience in dealing with this kind of operation. The men he'd be after sound as if they'd sell their mothers if it gave them what they wanted. No one can dodge bullets, whatever the coordinated power acquired by them.'

Smith replied assertively. 'Oh, he's got all that except the experience. But he's as streetwise as you can get, and I've come to realize that even the most experienced operatives are still useless at getting what I want. No one's suggesting Steiner can deflect bullets, and he won't need to. He's too clever for that.'

Smith finalized his case and added as a bonus: 'Besides, he's competent with all kinds of weapons, primitive and modern. He's slick with a pistol, and if necessary I would have no hesitation in backing him any day against those who so clinically killed the dogs. I once saw him at a local target range. His performance was very impressive, what I would expect from a man with his coordination and powers of concentration.'

Johnson cast his eyes on the desk, trying to imagine the man his boss had described. The more Smith spoke, the more he could see the plan succeeding and he felt the first excitement, after months of frustration at the slow pace of their work. 'How will you persuade him to do this job, unless you have already succeeded in getting him to join our group? He's a civilian. Don't tell me he's a psychopath as well.'

Smith sat patiently, casually resting his elbows on the synthetic leather of the desk. 'Let me tell you a little more. I met him a few years ago when I played with karate, like so many others. He ran the club, and I got to know him a bit. He was a likeable sort of fellow, very impressive in appearance and stature, and highly articulate. He certainly had the intelligence of someone you'd expect with his breeding and education. You should have seen him on the *makiwara*.'

'What's that?'

'It's a striking post, and the item responsible for the heavy callouses I'm sure you've seen on the hands of some guys who follow the art. Even in those days Steiner's hands were as hard as iron but his, surprisingly, were like a concert pianist's, relatively without blemish, only minor callouses, strange considering what I saw him put them through.' Smith shifted in his chair. 'I didn't keep it up, too much commitment, absolute dedication required. I didn't see him for a while, three or four years.'

Smith took another cigarette from his pack, vigorously stubbing the plain end on the sole of his shoe. He fixed his gaze on Johnson. 'That was about ten days ago. Steiner was in serious trouble. Apparently he had a friend in the police who asked him to accompany him on a raid in Point Road. Two blacks and a coloured, the latter a habitual criminal tattooed from head to foot, were hiding out in a dilapidated warehouse near the old Smugglers Inn. They found them without much trouble and that was the end. Steiner killed the blacks and his friend did in the coloured. Unfortunately the victims weren't armed, and they were arrested, charged with murder.'

Johnson nodded, somehow expecting to hear the story that Smith had just told him. 'I can guess,' he said. 'Steiner was released.'

Smith lit the cigarette, squinting at the blue flame as it burnt into the tobacco. He was in no hurry. 'I had the charge quashed,' he stated unreservedly. 'He just seemed too good to send to jail. I suggested he take a trip abroad. He did, London, Tokyo. He returned a day before I got the call from Bryant.'

'It couldn't be better for you,' said Johnson. 'So he's your man.'

'Yes,' said Smith. 'He'll also do well out of it if he delivers. He'll get more than he can make in a year teaching karate, and only for a few days' work.' He picked a comb from his pocket and ran it unnecessarily through his well-oiled hair. 'The most dangerous beast in the African bush is the leopard. If you've ever read the diaries of the turn-of-the-century white hunters, men like John Hunter, Karamojo Bell, and those a little before them, Selous, you'll appreciate why the leopard was the only animal they really feared. It has supernormal strength, the strength to lift an antelope its own body weight into the branches of a tree, nocturnal finesse that makes a cat burglar appear inept, and fangs that can strip its carcass clean in seconds. In the human world, Steiner is my leopard, and he's on my chain.'

Smith hauled himself from the chair, gripping the half-consumed cigarette dexterously between finger and thumb. 'I phoned him before you came in, and told him about Cartwright. He's now working for me, and only on this operation. I gave him my word. We just sit and wait.' He poked the cigarette in the ashtray, dusting his hands.

'I'm not sure,' said Johnson getting up. 'How far do you expect him to go? If he achieves what you want you will never release him from the hold you have on him. He'll always be tied to you.'

'How far he goes is up to him,' said Smith ignoring the second comment. 'I'm sure he will see this job through to the very best of his ability.' He shrugged his bony shoulders. 'He can start with those who were at Cartwright's last night, then move further up the ladder. In this operation I'll bet there's a controller, someone who has close ties with the leadership and also directs the men in the field. I want him blasted to hell and then I'll get the big fish I spoke of earlier, the great white sharks. To me the beginning is to find out why those men were at Cartwright's last night and then to track them to their source. I then think the rest will fit neatly into place. It will become a chain reaction.'

'Something else,' said Johnson. 'Where does Steiner begin? All he's got is your supposition that someone tried for Cartwright last night, and a few scraps that Bryant can tell him in Pretoria when and if he gets there. And what's that?'

Smith scowled impatiently. 'You're making heavy work of this. Use your imagination. I don't always need proof before I act. I believe the men who killed Cartwright's dogs will go for him again, like tonight.' He propped himself up against the wall, steepling his fingers. 'This morning his secretary received two phone calls, from men she'd never heard of. According to her this never happens. Cartwright's contacts are well established. It's all high-level stuff. He doesn't get cold calls, unless they come with a personal introduction. No, there's something up.' He went round the desk. 'I haven't been so interested in something since I took this job. I'm sick of the small stuff that predominantly comes to us. We need real achievement to provide some fulfillment, like any professional in this life. Now, let's go to lunch.'

Alone in his *dojo* half a mile from Smith's office, James Steiner looped his drenched *dogi* over a peg on the wall and slumped semi-naked into a chair. A couple of hours previously he had received the call from Smith, but during the session he had blotted it out as he pounded the heavy bags with his feet and worked his hands on the flexible post. When the DSO commander had quashed the murder charge he knew he was in his debt, that some day the dues would have to be paid. The time had come, and as he dried the mat of hair on his chest he thought about the job. He was reassured that it was a one-off, simply a case of penetrating an insidious network that had been at full strength with their crimes during the days of white rule.

After this he felt he wanted to return to England, the home of his birth. That he had killed the coloured and the black, and now faced possibly more killing, didn't bother him any more, and the deaths of the Japanese, Oshima and the *ninja*, were a distant memory, a time when he could have died. The men Smith described were, as far as he could see, simply assassins, on the wrong side, society's miscreants, even though they were apparently after something bigger. The years of hardship had given him the strength to go against anyone without fear. As long as he could get a lead on the men, he didn't envisage a problem. It was simply a case of being systematic and covering his tracks. Smith's protection was not all-embracing, even if he was one of the commanders in the Scorpions.

He showered and sat for an hour in meditation on the unforgiving floor, calming and centring his mind at the 'one-point' in his lower abdomen. When he looked at the clock it was after four o'clock and he retired to the office at the end of the hall, clearing the desk of piles of paper, tedious student records and accounts, and began assembling the bits of information Smith had given him. He had never heard of Cartwright, but he had the address, and Smith's conviction that these men would go for the man's life in the next 12 hours.

After a lunch of prime steak washed down by a quality Cabernet Sauvignon the two DSO men returned to the office, Smith immediately launching himself at a cigarette from one of the packets he left strewn on his desk. Much of the meal had been taken in silence as they filled themselves with the meat and mulled over the scheme Smith had set in motion by his call to Steiner.

Releasing his weight sluggishly into his chair, Smith lit the cigarette, expectantly scanning his colleague for comment. 'What do you think? For me this is where the right-wing activists in this country get a taste of what they've handed to others. It's the chance for which I've been waiting. If Steiner fails I'll send another until they lie awake at night, crapping in their pants, fearing the next visit.'

Johnson smiled at his superior's description. 'They're clever. Not to be taken lightly. These men you think are after Cartwright will be canny, even if they messed up last night. And then there are those above them, the ones you really want, and they will be a lot harder to catch.'

'A man who can concentrate his mind for hours in meditation won't be caught napping when he's supposed to be awake.' Smith waggled the cigarette in his mouth like the tail of a chirping bird. 'Trust him. You still think I'm off beam, don't you?'

Before Johnson could reply the phone emitted a subdued whistle, attracting Smith like a bee to pollen. Cupping his palm around the mouthpiece he took the receiver to his ear. It was a long-distance call. 'Smith.' He listened carefully, instantly in tune. 'Did she give any names?' he asked, interrupting the person on the other end.

He listened for over a minute then replaced the phone and addressed Johnson, conveying quiet satisfaction. 'That was Bryant, and it convinces me that the men he spoke to me about before were the ones at Cartwright's last night. Bryant spoke again to the girl who leaked this stuff to him in the first place. She said that a prominent Durban lawyer, and advocate, was somehow connected, that he was at the centre of things.'

'Why didn't she say this before?' asked Johnson. 'It could have helped.'

'She didn't and still doesn't have a name. For that reason she clearly thought she had nothing more to offer at the time, and her dread was that her brother was involved in something big. With that on her mind she couldn't think of anything else. But the information just given to me by Bryant would still not mean anything, or give us a lead, if the attack had not been made on Cartwright's house last night. And, he is definitely a prominent lawyer.'

Smith took up some papers on his desk and after a glance through them, cast the small pile into the waste bin for shredding. 'Bryant also told me that the man Marais who I sent up to Pretoria never contacted him, which he was supposed to do, before or after doing his job of tailing the girl's brother Richter. Marais was also supposed to maintain contact with me and keep me informed. I haven't heard a thing from him either and now I don't expect to. That tells me that he's had it, that somehow he screwed up and these guys got him.'

'Looks as if you were right in your assessment,' said Johnson. 'I'm beginning to see that we're onto a big one.' He paused, thoughtful. 'There's something you haven't explained.'

Smith urged him to continue. 'Go on,' he said, wondering what was next.

'As I see it, Steiner's brief is to find where these guys came from and who sent them, what they are after, and then get the evidence to convict them and others, those you name as the great white sharks. Naturally Steiner might have to kill the guys who are here in Durban. But I'm sure they are the tadpoles in the pond and it's who they can implicate that is of importance.' Johnson got up and sat on the edge of his boss's desk. 'What about Cartwright?' he asked cogently. 'What if he is killed while we play this game? Besides the ethics, Fraser and those above him will go mad. They'll want you to bleed.'

'Fraser will toe the line, as I've told you,' said Smith. 'I've already spoken to his boss. I explained that I wanted a lead on these thugs and their superiors, that my own men would protect Cartwright. I didn't tell him I'd be using one man, but that is my choice and at the moment I don't want stupid objections from them on the way I operate. If these men kill Cartwright, so be it. He's not the president and I'll explain it as an operational hazard. Anyway, I don't expect him to be killed before we get what I believe he has, and what I'm after.'

Johnson let out air like a pricked balloon. 'So to you Cartwright's expendable, bait, a hunk of meat,' he said.

'Unfortunately that's true,' returned Smith. 'But he's not dead yet, and still of great value. He is essential at this stage. This is a cruel game, Lieutenant. Sometimes it's necessary to play by different rules, where morality is simply a word beginning with "m". I can't help it. If you can't understand that then resign, the DSO or intelligence service is not for you.'

'God, what are we doing,' said Johnson, uncertain, scared. An innocent man was probably going to his death, yet he could do nothing. He was impotent, a pawn directed at will by the masters, those who had spent years doing this. He was suddenly embarrassed at his lapse. 'There is an alternative,' he said. 'Put Cartwright in a safe house and send Steiner to Pretoria. He can work things out with Bryant and get them when they return.' Johnson laughed, his mood changing.

'No, you're not thinking straight. Cartwright stays in his house. We need to know why these men want him and what they are after. They won't get it if they can't get to Cartwright. I've explained this. If they return to Pretoria empty-handed, and without us knowing that they were even here, we'll be left with nothing, and what I believe is a great opportunity will have gone down the toilet. Anyway, Cartwright rejects the notion that anyone is after him, and insists on sleeping in his own bed. That suits me perfectly, because without him around we'll go nowhere.'

'If he knows what you've told me, he's a fool,' said Johnson. 'This is a pure balancing act with Steiner in the middle trying to find out what these men are after, if anything other than to kill Cartwright. The chances of Steiner protecting him are zero if his prime aim is to find a reason for all this, get what he can, and if necessary follow these guys back to their home base.

Smith watched him coldly. 'I agree that it could be bad for Cartwright. But it'll be done my way. Steiner will be there and he will make his move at the right time even if it means in Pretoria. Call it intuition. I rely on it and it never fails to serve me well. I might also add that Steiner has probably got the most perfectly conditioned intuitive mind, the unconscious mind, or as some call it the no-mind. But we won't dwell on that. I simply want to get moving on this job and obtain the results I'm looking for.' Smith got up and walked in a small circle. 'I expect this job to be concluded tonight to my satisfaction,' he said. 'That means we get what I have repeatedly said is the nucleus of their operation. If we don't find out what it's about and get what I believe is there, then Steiner goes on to Pretoria and sorts it out as he sees fit. His first contact would of course be Bryant.'

Johnson relented, his superior's determination to drive the plan through undeviating, resolute. To him Cartwright's fate had been forged, and they still did not know what they would get out of it, or so he thought, whatever Smith's proclaimed intuitive sense.

Berea

Jan Krige watched Cartwright and the second man go

into the house. When the door was sealed he broke from cover, running over the damp lawn that filled his footprints with water like a sponge behind him. When he reached the building he went down the side of the house to the back. The light bore down, for agonizing seconds holding him prisoner, and he wished Cartwright would switch it off. He came to the verandah and peered circumspectly through the metal framework that secluded it from the grounds.

The lounge he and Richter had entered was in darkness, and from his position a few metres away he examined the doors. Richter was right. They had been repaired, with added bolts set into the top and bottom. An axe would be needed to get in now. He considered the options. Box-like bars in the Spanish style covered the windows he could see on the bottom floor and he wondered if Cartwright had secured the entrance. He suspected he had. He was about to leave and find out when the lamps in the lounge went on, reaching out and transforming the verandah into a golden cavern. He crouched lower and saw Cartwright through the net curtains walking up to them. He heard the bolts slammed laterally and then the doors were opened.

Cartwright walked out onto the verandah and embraced the garden he had spent thousands on, voraciously consuming the sweetness. Behind him Kaplan came up, inspecting the locks approvingly, running his hands over the solid steel.

'No one's going to get in there,' said Cartwright, 'without bringing the neighbourhood round his ears. And there's nowhere else. The house is solid brick. It's now the complete fortress.'

Kaplan oscillated up and down on the tips of his shoes. 'You've got enemies,' he stated trenchantly. 'You've spent all these years working for the ANC, transferring money into their accounts and condoning their fight. Someone must know what you have been doing, someone who wants your body ten feet under.'

Cartwright unbuttoned his coat. 'If they had wanted me they would have come before. Why should they now, with all parties working under a nationally elected government, a government that has the support of the majority of whites, and the New Nationalist Party in a coalition with them down in the Cape? That would have been unheard of before.'

'Not all,' corrected Kaplan. 'The demented right-wing resistance groups have to live with political defeat prescribed by the ballot box. Their ramblings are unheeded, their neo-Nazi affiliations reviled by blacks and the majority of whites. They see no hope for their cherished dream, a white-only Boer state. These are men who believe the fires of Hell are singeing their boots, and they mean to do something about it.'

'They're nowhere near us,' replied Cartwright going to the door, disbelief in his voice. 'Their efforts are still concentrated on the large townships where they use whatever assistance they can muster in the police and military to foment violence between groups like Inkatha and the ANC. What they can achieve through insurrection, which I believe is virtually negligible, is infinitely more than bumping off someone like me. I don't think these men you talk about know I exist, and even if they did it's unlikely they appreciate the extent of my involvement. Besides, why come for me now after ten years of black rule?'

Kaplan moved to let his friend pass. 'Maybe you're right, but you were wise to have the house made safer, even if it's only to prevent theft.'

Pressed to the soil below the framework of the veranda, Krige could scarcely believe his good fortune at having Cartwright so near after the hours of uncertainty. He listened to the slow receding steps as the two men went back indoors and he readied himself to go into action.

As Cartwright reached the carpet Krige came out, his feet finding the steps and swinging him in. For a moment Cartwright and Kaplan were motionless, numbed by the terrifying figure before them, the pistol pointing like the evil wand of a witch. Blinking with disbelief Kaplan shoved Cartwright, frantically trying to shut the door. 'Get away,' he screamed. 'It's them.'

Cartwright fell to his knees, his mind a cauldron of ineptitude. He was not used to this. He looked over his shoulder at Kaplan, still exposed, his arms stretched wide as if courting death.

Then came the shots, and Kaplan reeled into the room, his stubby hands going to the holes in his body. 'I'm dying,' he cried, his cheerful countenance disfiguring under the sickness in him. 'Save yourself.' Still pressing himself he sank to his knees, bent over like a praying priest, his body racking as he died.

Cartwright scrambled up and ran for the swing doors that penetrated the bowels of the house. In seconds he was there, pushing them apart and springing into the hall with the eagerness of a gazelle ahead of a lion. Behind him he heard Krige burst into the lounge and he hesitated, glancing at the door, at the multitude of iron that converted it into the entrance to a fort. The killer was too close for him to unloose it and he ran for the stairs.

Nearly tripping over Kaplan's disarranged form, Krige saw the doors come to behind Cartwright and he went after him, hurdling the sofa, onto the sumptuous cushions and high over the top. He pounded through the doors and into the lit hall.

Cartwright had gone, and he had a choice, along the passage adjacent to the stairs or up to the next floor. He picked up no sound, and noting the carpet on the stairs chose the latter. If the man was up there he was trapped and his for the taking. He could see this messy business coming to an end.

Krige began his ascent, his long legs devouring the steps. It got progressively darker as he climbed and he slowed as he went up the last stretch, his nerves as receptive as optic fibre. He pictured the layout he and Richter had worked through before, the sequence of rooms, Cartwright's at the end. Diagonally across the landing were the switches, on the wall next to the first room.

Estimating the position of the door he flung himself at it over the carpet. He hit it in the middle. As it gave he went in, turning on the light with a brush of his hand. It was as before, and standing next to the frame he reached round for the main switches, and in an instant ignited the passageway in a bald glare. He waited a few seconds then looked out.

The corridor was inanimate and he was angry that he hadn't been quick enough to get Cartwright in the lounge. Whites owned guns, either for carrying on their person or kept in the house. If Cartwright had had a weapon on him he would have used it downstairs. By now he'd be armed and as primed as anyone fighting for their life. Krige extinguished the beams and went quietly along to what he had previously decided was the master bedroom.

He could see the door was shut, and everything around him was silent. A venetian blind blanked out the high passage window and he tugged at the cord, parting the slats and allowing in slivers of diffused light from the lamps at the side of the house and the lounge and verandah below. He tried the door but it held fast. He was sure Cartwright was inside, and he prepared to go in the hard way. Then he heard a metallic sound further down the passage. He brought up the gun, trying to shed the feeling that he had been outmanoeuvred, desperately needing something to aim at.

The flash from Cartwright's pistol lit up the passage like a firecracker and Krige reeled as the slug tore into the muscle above his knee, shooting off with a hum and ricocheting off the wall. He saw Cartwright and dived, tilting the barrel and giving the gun its head, extracting pleasure as it recoiled against his firm grip.

The bullets hit Cartwright in the chest a little off-centre, spinning him like a ballerina and taking him neatly onto his back, his legs momentarily flying high and then cascading with him.

Supporting his leg, Krige got up and went to him. He was alive, the blood already resembling a midnight tide on his shirt. The man's short-barrelled revolver lay at arm's length and Krige went to the lights and turned them on. He returned to Cartwright and looked at what he had done. The man wasn't dead, his blue eyes were steady, and he returned the stare without fear.

'Why me?' said Cartwright, gritting against his suffering. 'I don't know you.'

'I don't know you either,' said Krige, feeling the torn ligaments in his leg constrict. He imagined Muller's joy when the obese man heard of Cartwright's death, and he felt angry and helpless. Richter was right. He would be asked again, the same threat. But the file was at the centre of everything, and without it he would have failed completely even if he said that he had only managed to kill Cartwright.

'It's not my war,' he continued. 'I had no choice. I'm driven by others who want a file that was delivered to you by courier two days ago. We know you have it in your possession.'

'There's always choice in who you serve and kill for,' said Cartwright. He twisted his head and looked at his revolver. 'You nearly died. Do you want to live by the gun, hunt a man down, erase his only life, purge that most valuable flame?'

'Where's the file you received?' said Krige, stepping even closer. 'You're not dead yet and your death is not the reason for me being here. Give me the file and I'll let you live.' He held the gun loosely and touched his leg. It needed attention.

'There's bandage in the bathroom,' said Cartwright. 'Your aim was better than mine but then I was never good with guns. I'll need a doctor. You've plenty of time to get out.' He picked at his shirt bravely. 'Who are you working for? And who was your friend? You didn't kill the dogs alone.' He was stalling, as evasive as an astute politician.

'He chickened out,' said Krige. 'And he's not worth talking about. Now tell me where I can find the file. When I get it I'll leave.'

Cartwright placed his hands over the wounds. The flow of blood had miraculously stopped, but he could still feel the pain. If he had urgent medical attention, he felt he could live. He also knew that if he didn't give up the file he would be summarily killed. The desire for life was becoming very important and he wished the file had never been sent to him, as valuable and damaging as was the information contained in it. But his life was infinitely more precious.

'It's in a safe in my room at the end of the passage,' said Cartwright. 'The key to the room is in my pocket.' He moved over a little to give Krige access.

Krige extracted two keys. 'And where is the safe?' he asked.

'It's behind the picture at the head of the bed,' answered Cartwright, feeling a sense of release. 'The number is very simple, the digits one to nine and in that order.' Cartwright shook his head. 'Why can't we live together in peace? Men like you are destroying this beautiful country.'

Krige backed away, picked up Cartwright's revolver and went down the passage to the room at the far end. He inserted one of the keys and then he was in the room. He turned on the central light and went quickly over to the picture on the wall above the bed. He stripped it from the wall. Behind it he found the safe. With care, and almost holding his breath, he rotated the dial according to the numbers given to him. Cartwright had told the truth. After all, in his wounded state he wouldn't have had anything to gain at this stage by lying.

Krige swung the door of the safe open on noiseless hinges and looked inside. There wasn't much in the box, some stuff in small cases, probably family jewellery. But at the centre lay what he immediately believed was what he was looking for, and he felt a surge of elation. It was a package, the contents contained in a thick heavy-duty white envelope used by couriers and without any inscription on it. He pulled it out. Inside was the file.

The file was 3 inches thick, perfectly contained in a black leather-bound outer case with the words 'State Security' embossed in red on the cover. He looked inside and the typed front sheet confirmed that he had at last got it. The title read: 'Security of the State: 1960 to 1994'. A list of seven names was written under the title with the designation: 'Attention only'. Krige didn't recognize any of the names but that was not important. He knew that when he went into the file itself, which he intended to do, he certainly would find the names and details of people he had either met or heard about, the leaders of state security, the police and government under the old regime, those who were as guilty as hell of human violations. He flicked through parts of the file and it looked very detailed and impressive at first glance. It was pure gold. He could understand its significance and why Muller and those above him in the party of no name were so desperate to retrieve it. He returned the file to the white envelope.

Krige partly shut the safe and went back into the passage with the file held in one hand and pressed to his waist. Cartwright was where he had fallen, an arm across his face. He shifted his arm away when Krige came up and looked up without showing any sign of defeat.

'I see you found it,' he said. 'That should make you happy. Now you can go.'

'Did you make any copies?' hissed Krige. 'Does anyone else know about it?'

'There were no copies made,' said Cartwright. 'I told Kaplan about it but you killed him.'

Krige believed him. To copy something like this would take days, and it would have to be done by a trusted person or persons and in total secrecy. He kept some distance from Cartwright, a couple of metres. 'I'm sorry,' he whispered. 'I can't let you live. It's between you and me. As soon as I go you will have everyone in town after me and I still have to get out of the area.'

Cartwright threw his hands up as if that would help him, curling his body feebly. 'No!' he shrilled. His cry was cut short as the bullets drilled into his chest.

For a long minute Krige looked at the human mess before him, mortified at the way he could kill so easily. Muller was getting a complete job. Putting away the pistol in his shoulder holster he tried the nearest door. The bathroom had to be somewhere along the passage and he speeded up, checking again before he found it, a good-sized room with an enamelled bath occupying a quarter of the tiled floor. Above the basin he spotted a cabinet, and went for it.

The dead man had told the truth. Bandages and

antiseptic were on the lowest shelf. He undid his belt and dropped his trousers. The bullet had bored a two-inch wound, half an inch deep. The wound was still wet with blood and he poured hydrogen peroxide onto the flesh, tensing from the sting. Holding a swab over it he wrapped the bandage in telescopic layers and tied it in a double knot. He hitched up his trousers, glad they were dark blue and a full cut. Little blood had reached them and what had was difficult to see.

Outside the bathroom he went to the body then left, suddenly conscious that he had already been there too long. In the lounge he got Kaplan into a corner and then extinguished some of the lights near him, and was about to turn off the others but then decided there was no point. He left the verandah doors open behind him and sped across the lawn to the wall where he had come in. He clambered over and disappeared into the trees.

Chapter 11

Durban

As he started his five-year-old Chevrolet in the city James Steiner glanced at the clock on the dashboard. It was a little after nine o'clock. His students' grading had taken longer than scheduled, an hour longer, well after Cartwright was supposed to arrive. But if the dog-killers were seriously after the man, he couldn't see them doing anything until the dark hours or the early morning, if they tried. He was convinced he would finally turn up in Pretoria with nothing, if Smith still wanted him to go there, and Bryant his only lead. But he had told Smith he would watch the house, at least until dawn.

He parked up on the Berea and walked down to Cartwright's road. A survey map had given him details and he had a clear picture of where the house lay. Choosing his moment, he went through the gates of the adjacent property but one, and came to an arrangement of shrubs that for a moment hid him. He was wary of dogs and he waited, eyes probing the semi-dark. In his coat inside pocket he had an Austrian Glock 9 mm semi-automatic. It was his only weapon. The gun was constructed of a special light-weight, high-yield material and to him it had no equal for accuracy and reliability.

He reached the fence, shinned it to the next garden and set off briskly to Cartwright's wall. He could see a long lawn to some trees and he thought he saw someone darting between them, ephemeral. He wasn't sure and he kept going, coming to the wall and going over into Cartwright's grounds. He wasn't surprised to see two cars. He knew Cartwright planned to entertain a friend and imagined them already relaxing with drinks.

For 15 minutes he watched. There was nothing out of the ordinary and he began to go up the garden. From his angle he saw the open verandah doors with some light inside. Cartwright was either a fool or he thought he was well protected.

Steiner positioned himself so he could see past the cars to the gates. He stripped the wrapper off a chocolate bar and took a bite, mashing the caramel mix on his palate and enjoying the fine texture. He couldn't see much of the lounge, which he assumed led onto the verandah, and inquisitively he went to where he saw the centre of the room and the Chesterfield sofa. Neither of the two men was on it, which seemed odd. The upholstered seats were renowned for their comfort and would provide the best seats in any residence. He watched for a little longer, going nearer, trying to catch voices. Then he went into a run, the total absence of noise and the strange stillness bizarrely pre-eminent. Something was very wrong.

As he went up the verandah steps he held the Glock and he slowed, noting the oval of blood on the carpet just inside the doors. He entered and saw Kaplan's slung body in a corner, the opaque, drained pallor that of a dead man.

The corpse was warm and he peeled the garments from him. He saw he'd been hit by several bullets, within a small circle, and remembered Smith's comments about the close groupings on the dogs.

Leaving the body he went to the hall doors, flattening himself to the wall as he levered one wide with his foot. But from what he could tell, Kaplan's demise was more than 30 minutes before and he was almost sure the killer had left.

Going into the hall, he began a search of the ground floor, ending at the stairs. He started to climb, convinced he was the only one alive in the house and that he would soon find Cartwright's corpse. He was not surprised when he did, and as he went to the body he reproached himself for being late.

He bent over Cartwright and frisked him, glad he had never chosen pathology for a career. The chest and stomach were congealed blood, only random strips of white cotton visible, as if the man had been hacked to death by the machinations of a long-term psychotic given premature release. Someone had wanted him dead badly, and been content to leave without removing the gold Rolex and considerable sum of cash.

A bullet had gone through the chest and he picked it up, rolling it on his palm. It was a 9 mm parabellum, misshapen but recognizable. Further along, he found the slug from Cartwright's gun. So the man had had a chance, however slim. From the number of bullets fired into Cartwright the killer was using more than a standard semi-automatic, not a sub-machine pistol, but something close to it. He looked down the passage and went to the end, the master bedroom. He turned on the light and instantly saw the half-open safe, the picture that presumably covered it thrown onto the bed. The few small boxes that he quickly found contained jewellery and were all that was there. He instinctively knew they had got their prize. He left the room for the passage and looked briefly into the other rooms. When he got to the bathroom he saw the bandage and antiseptic next to the cupboard, the cap of the bottle lying on the tiles. The fight hadn't been totally one-sided. Selecting a large bath towel he returned to the body and tossed it over, covering it to the knees.

There was nothing more he could do up here, and he went downstairs.

There was a phone in the hall and Steiner tapped out the private number Smith had given him. In a couple of rings Smith answered.

'Smith,' said the commander tersely.

'Cartwright's dead and so is his friend,' said Steiner softly. 'They were both hit in the last hour.'

'Shit, where were you?' said Smith, agitated. It was not what he wanted to hear.

'Late. The last thing I expected was for them to be here so early. They were smart operators and they didn't like Cartwright.'

'Why?' said Smith.

'He had half a magazine through his chest,' said Steiner, as cool as a bucket of ice. 'It won't be difficult to tell the cause of death. Much the same applies to his friend. I believe you told me his name was Kaplan.'

'Yes. Pity he got caught up in it,' said Smith, insincerely. 'So we're left with nothing, only what Bryant can give us and that's not much. Neither did I think they would come again so soon.'

'This is not going to look good for you,' said Steiner.

'I've explained away worse before,' said Smith. 'I bet these guys got what they came for. It wasn't simply to wipe out Cartwright.' He was quiet and then said: 'Have you looked to see if anything was taken? Not that it will help you. I think we've missed any chance we had.'

'There was a safe open in the main bedroom with only items of jewellery in it,' said Steiner.

'Then they were successful,' said Smith emphatically. 'I said previously that if this was not concluded tonight you must go to Pretoria and speak to Bryant. The step after that will be to visit the men who he suspects were involved in this and, in my opinion, certainly killed Cartwright. I spoke to Bryant again a while ago and told him about the killing of the dogs. When you meet these guys it is up to you to find out what they were doing here, even though we have no proof it was them. If necessary give them the heavy hand. I'm relying on you.'

Steiner fed a stick of chewing gum into his mouth and tugged at the wrapping. 'I'll get back to you in a couple of days,' he said impassively, his tongue taking in the gum like a chameleon claiming an insect. 'It might even be a challenge.'

'Don't misjudge them,' said Smith, remaining confident he had picked the right man. 'They're not stupid. There's more planning and organization behind this little sortie than I gave them credit for. The deeper you delve into this can of worms the better. And I'm still convinced that it involves something a hell of a lot more than Cartwright's death.'

'Be seeing you.' Steiner terminated the call and stood still in the hall, the audacity of the killings sending a strange thrill through him. He was not used to this kind of work, but it carried an excitement of its own and already he was under its spell.

Stopping every now and again to protect his leg, Krige travelled wearily to the meeting with Richter and Koch. The physical and mental stress had shown him little mercy and he was glad when he crested the rise at the top of the Berea and saw the start of the long dual carriageway that was previously the only route to the Transvaal, now Gauteng. The new freeway system a kilometre to the west took the bulk of traffic and the number of vehicles passing the bridge below him was not difficult to count. If his partners had been there he would have easily seen them, parked in an obvious lay-by before the bridge that was the first choice of anyone with common sense. But the car was not there and with increasing irritation he sat on the bank overlooking the road, feeling around the place on his leg where he had been hit.

At first Krige expected the car to arrive in seconds, but when he had been on the bank for ten minutes he knew they weren't coming and he remembered the last conversation with Richter. He had been as caustic as usual and he had wanted to return to Pretoria. His nerve had gone. Like others of his type they were all talk and couldn't take the heat. The absence of the car made sense.

Krige thought of the options. There were only two – a hired car or the night train to Johannesburg. Rejecting the first as traceable he crossed the bridge and went down a flight of steps to a bus stop. The station was in the middle of town, too far to walk. The timetable, displayed behind broken plastic on a post, confirmed his suspicion that the service was infrequent outside the rush hours when it was primarily used to transport township blacks to the city and the surrounding industrial zone. The next bus was in 12 minutes.

Twenty minutes later when he was about to give up on the bus he saw it lumber over the rise and bear down on the lonely stop. There were only a few on board, blacks, huddled in deformed worn seats that had witnessed the passing years. They scarcely looked at him as he paid the driver and went to a seat, three-quarters down the line, where the elliptical light bulbs had blown. He longed for the vehicle to move on and, when it did, he at last felt he had got away with it.

The bus went through the old Indian quarter, past the mosques and bazaars that carved an Asian micro-city in the centre of the predominantly black and white city. Krige welcomed the anonymity that the numbers on the streets gave him, after the incongruous solitude of the quiet white stronghold of the Berea.

He got out of the bus at the terminus near the station, a twin-towered structure, and hurried to the ticket office. He smiled when he heard that the night train departed in five minutes, his timing perfect, and he booked a first-class sleeper. He took the ticket from the attendant and went to the platform. Like the buses, the railway passenger service was seldom used outside peak hours and the station was a ghost town.

The train was already in and he found his cabin. He placed the package containing the file on the overhead rack. Lying on the bunk he thought of home, his wife Kirsty, how he wanted her in his arms, to make love to her. But with what he had in his possession his work was definitely incomplete, more than he'd ever envisaged, and he didn't know when he would see her again.

James Steiner left the grounds of Cartwright's house through the gate, and later took the freeway inland. The annoyance that the killers were a step ahead passed, and he thought about Bryant, Smith's plant in this 'group with no name' as Smith had described it, and the man who ostensibly could provide the lead he wanted. He had a summary knowledge of Pretoria from his previous visits and he knew Bryant's flat was near the Afrikaans university, in one of the series of parallel roads below on the hill.

What sort of man Bryant was he had no clue: reliable, precise in the information he fed on, or a man who was gullible? That he had accurately forewarned Smith of the imminent job was encouraging, though the name of the central figure was missing and not confirmed, until everything gelled and Cartwright was found dead, clearly the prominent lawyer referred to by Bryant after his later conversation with Richter's sister. What the men were after was still unknown. Steiner knew little about South African politics and had never heard of the men he was supposed to chase down until now, when they were remorselessly starting to pull the strings. But he had been assigned to the job of getting them and finding out what they were up to.

London

Sophie Carswell was thrilled to see Adams when he returned to London. He hadn't contacted her while in Japan and she was beginning to worry for his safety. She had known what he intended to do, and that he was very strong and could take care of himself, but she also knew the strength of Steiner. Of the two, she had to admit that she would have backed Steiner in any confrontation, and that had added to her anxiety.

Now, seated in her flat on the sofa where Steiner raped her, she looked up when Adams came in with some goods from the local shop. He had arrived late the previous evening and they had hardly spoken a word to one another. It had simply been kissing and making love before they fell asleep.

She crossed her legs and said: 'Tell me what happened over there. Did you meet him?'

Adams sat opposite her. 'I didn't see him, but he knew I was coming, probably through this guy Lawson, and he set up a meeting at a place two hours by train from Tokyo, the Nikko reserve. It was obviously a trap, but I had to go. That's why I was in Japan. A friend of mine, Oshima *sensei*, insisted that he accompany me and we went together.'

'How did you know he was up there, and that he

wanted to meet you?' asked Sophie. This sounded like an adventure story, but she sensed it was going to become much more macabre.

'Steiner had left a message with the office girl in the Tokyo headquarters of his style and I went there with Oshima. She gave us the message that Steiner was expecting me and that he suggested a meeting in this reserve. She called it his spiritual home or something like that. I know Nikko well and I can understand Steiner's choice. He chose his own ground. After all, we're in the same business and if I was in his position I would have done the same.'

'What happened when you got there?' she asked, leaning forwards, absorbed and consoled by the fact that Adams had returned unharmed.

'The meeting place was this *ryokan* or inn at the top of the reserve,' said Adams. 'When we got there on the early morning bus we were given a message by the desk clerk to meet Steiner on the other side of the lake that lay in front of the inn. I was getting more sucked into the game that he was obviously playing, and I felt compelled to do as he requested. I also had this pressing desire to meet this guy, regardless of what he had done and why I was there. It was a strange feeling and one I've never had before.' Adams got up and came to her. 'Oshima and I split up. I crossed the lake to the far shore and he went down the road. The intention was that we'd meet in the woods on the far shore. Steiner was following our every move. Very cleverly he got to Oshima first and isolated him. Oshima was killed.'

Sophie knew that was coming. She could imagine the cleverness of the way Steiner had set everything up and the way he moved. He was a killer, but in his own appealing way quite remarkable. 'Go on,' she said. 'I'm sure you never came face to face with James.' She used

Steiner's first name, more and more attracted to him as this extraordinary story unfolded. She couldn't help it.

'After Oshima's death I had to tell my teacher, Shirai *sensei*, what had happened and the reason for my visit,' said Adams. 'He was adamant that Steiner should die. He knew that it was a waste of time trying to get the law involved and he didn't want the organization to be associated any more with what had turned into a mess. I could understand that.'

'So what did he suggest?' asked Sophie, not really wanting to hear the answer, and fearing the worst for Steiner.

'There is a warrior style in Japan known as *ninjutsu*. It is the art of concealment, subversion and assassination. There are other descriptions I can use, but that's enough. In short, they are highly dangerous if they are set after you. There are several schools still existing in Japan, different styles but with the same intent, and prepared to carry out the work for which they've been trained so meticulously.'

Sophie couldn't believe what she was hearing. 'Don't tell me,' she whispered, 'your teacher set them after James?'

'Yes,' he said. 'Shirai said that I should go back to London. That was two days ago and by now it's probably all over.' He touched her on the thighs but she didn't want it. She was too worried about Steiner. Perhaps if he had gone about things differently he would be in front of her now. She even started to long to see him again. He had made love to her in Johannesburg, and that had been pure satisfaction, unlike anything she had experienced since. Her mind was in a spiral of dejection. 'What now?' she asked, almost inaudibly.

'It is late afternoon now in Tokyo. I'm going to phone Shirai.' Adams got up and went to the telephone. He knew the number by heart, and in seconds he was through to the headquarters of his style and then to Shirai himself.

'*Sensei*, it is Paul Adams. What happened in our business with James Steiner? Have you heard anything?' The line was quiet and he knew intuitively that the men sent after Steiner hadn't been successful. This was soon confirmed by his teacher.

'The men were found dead by other members of the sect in a forest a short distance outside the village of Takamiyama, three hours west of Tokyo in the mountains. Steiner is no fool, and to beat men like these, shows that he's in the highest class. I am now sure that he had no difficulty killing Oshima *san*.'

'Do you know where Steiner is now?' said Adams. 'It looks as if it's up to me.'

'According to the office girl at his *dojo*, Michiko *san*, he's returned to South Africa,' said Shirai. 'If you want him, that's where you'll have to go to get him. He's now out of our hair and a totally free man. The more I get to know about Steiner, and his background, makes me realize that he has been trained to have no conscience. For him the past is of no consequence, it's not even a memory. He only lives for the future, and without fear. That is when a man is at his most dangerous. I think that you should forget that he ever existed.'

'I can't,' said Adams. 'Thank you for your help, *sensei*. I'll contact you.' Adams replaced the receiver. For the moment he was not sure what he should do, track Steiner or leave him.

Sophie had heard enough of the conversation to know that James Steiner had escaped his pursuers, and she suspected their demise. She marvelled at the power of the man. 'So they didn't get him,' she said. 'I didn't think they would.' She did not add that she had hoped they would fail in their job. 'Where's James now?'

Adams returned to his seat. 'He's gone back to South Africa, and I'm not sure what I should do.' He covered his face with his hands and said: 'I'm going to phone your father and tell him what has happened. It will help to clear my mind.'

'I want you to leave James alone,' she said. 'Forget this whole business. It's not that important any more.'

He was surprised, but sensed she had had enough of the whole affair. 'What's your father's number?' he said. 'I'll ring him now.'

Sophie gave him the number as he dialled it. 'Do you want to speak to him first?' he asked as he waited for the connection to be made.

'No,' she said. 'I'll have a word with him after you.'

John Carswell answered and was pleased to hear Adams's voice. 'Where are you?' he asked.

'London,' replied Adams. 'I'm here with Sophie. I missed Steiner in Japan and he's returned to South Africa.' He didn't elaborate.

'I was about to try and contact you through Sophie when you phoned,' said Carswell. 'I know that Steiner is back in South Africa. He arrived two days ago.' Carswell paused, like someone gathering himself for a major speech. 'When he was away I contacted people in the Scorpions, or Directorate of Special Operations to you, and guys in the police. Steiner was facing a murder charge when he left this country but it was quashed, for whatever reason. I didn't ask. A man in the Scorpions, name of Smith, phoned me yesterday and said that Steiner is doing a job for them which Smith believes will blow the apartheid period apart and bring the leaders to trial. If he's right, that means he will get what everyone else has failed to achieve, the conviction of the bastards who used to run South Africa.'

'What does this mean to me and Sophie?' said Adams. 'I think you're telling me that Steiner is now untouchable.'

'You are right,' said Carswell. 'And from what Smith told me about Steiner you would have had a hard fight on your hands if you ever met him, whatever your ability in unarmed combat. The message is to leave him alone, forget about him, and let him do the job the Scorpions have got him hooked into. I get the feeling that he will deliver and be instrumental in creating something this democracy of ours so desperately wants, a monumental purging and final reconciliation with the past.'

Adams understood, and for all his strength he felt some relief. 'It's nice talking to you,' he said. 'Thank you for what you've done. Here's your daughter.'

Chapter 12

Pretoria

The journey to Johannesburg was four hours, another thirty minutes to Pretoria, and after a halt for petrol Steiner approached the outer suburbs of the judicial capital in the early hours. Taking the outer ring road, he travelled on before coming to the turn-off to the university. Another kilometre and he saw the majestic, symmetrical buildings on the skyline. He dropped his speed, and crawled along while he read the street names. In a short time he was at the road he wanted, wide, nondescript, and like all the others. He parked and looked across to a block of flats. Vacating the car he went along an unkempt hedge to the entrance where he found the flat numbers and their level. Bryant was in Flat 34 and he went up the naked concrete stairs, external and exposed to the elements.

The flat was at the end of a corridor. There was only a miniscule glow inside and he pressed the bell. It rang efficiently and he waited, the chill air of the high veld causing him to pull the collar of the jacket around his neck. Impatiently he pressed again, and was rewarded by increased illumination through the glazed sheet as someone responded. He heard footsteps and the occupant's voice. 'Yes?'

Steiner went up to the door. 'Unity is strength,' he said, iterating the previous motto of the Republic and the words Smith had given him, without any further understanding of the Afrikaans language. To him the only language in the world was English, even though most of its words had been taken from Latin, Greek and French.

Without replying the man inside fumbled with the lock and opened the door. 'I've been expecting you, but not so soon. You must have driven through the night.'

'I did.' Steiner walked past Bryant into the passage. 'Smith keeps in touch,' he said laconically. 'How much do you know? From the last couple of days, and anything else you can tell me.'

Bryant, clad in striped pyjamas and navy dressing gown, led Steiner into the lounge and they sat down. 'Not much detail, except they were successful. Cartwright's death was in the late news. Callous they called it. The African National Congress is denouncing the loss of one of their most trusted brothers as if he were a saint.'

Steiner smiled. 'All parties would say the same about their own supporters.'

Bryant sprawled opposite him, noticing the faintly calloused hands, the tissue spread aesthetically like reinforced plate. He wondered what had caused it. 'Smith said you wanted information, names and chains of command in what we call the "group of no name",' he said.

Steiner was peculiarly unexcited. 'Smith put a tail on one of the men you named. He disappeared. As a starter, do you have any knowledge on that?'

'No. I didn't meet him but he had the address. He was supposed to contact me. He's simply disappeared. The one I spoke to Smith about, Richter, is not at home and neither is his close mate Koch. It all comes together.'

'I'm interested in Richter's name and address,' pursued Steiner. 'And the one you call his mate. Also, close contacts, the men above him.'

'That's not difficult.' Bryant puffed himself up. 'Richter,

Abe Richter, Venters Straat. He's certainly involved, directly or indirectly. His closest buddy is this guy Koch. They live near one another.' Bryant got up and walked to a table and picked up a street guide of the district. 'There,' he said. 'The street is four kilometres from here. I forget the numbers but they're in the book.'

'I'll get them later,' said Steiner and slotted the guide into his shirt. 'You said Richter is not at his home. How do you know?'

'OK, I guessed,' admitted Bryant tetchily. 'They weren't at the last party meeting. They never miss.'

Steiner's face didn't change. 'Who's above them?' he asked. 'Who's the person who would direct this operation?'

'His name is Muller. He lives alone on the perimeter of town in the old quarter. He's a postmaster.' Bryant laughed briefly. He was glad to find a form of release. 'It's one of those ugly red-brick post offices peppering the country. I'm sure you've seen them.'

Steiner allowed a grin, presenting an immaculate set of teeth. 'I'll need to get whatever you can give me on him. Is there anyone else I need to know about?'

Bryant picked up a pad and scribbled down Muller's address. 'That's it. The way I see it is that these guys are a small sect or cell within the greater party. One cannot underestimate how dangerous they are. And I'm sure they are distancing themselves from the manic right-wing parties to satisfy their own aims. They are using the group as a vehicle, and there are some of the brightest in the country in it, but definitely not these guys. I assume Muller answers to a few men at the top, and then the guy I presume is their immediate leader. He is Viljoen, a cattle baron, and he is always at their select little meetings. He has a big farm twenty kilometres to the north of Pretoria. Beyond him there are the big fish, the ones you never see.'

Steiner appeared disinterested. 'He can wait. I'll find him. Muller's high enough for the present.' He returned to more immediate matters. 'Did Richter lead this skirmish in Durban?'

Bryant looked out of the window onto an architectural nightmare. There was something very odd about Steiner. He thought about the question. 'It's likely that he did. He's a killer and so is Koch. To me they'd be ideal. Does that help?' He had been told to tell Steiner what he knew, but the neatly injected questions were becoming tedious.

'In part it does.' Steiner casually laid his hands on the settee. 'Who was your informant, the person who first tipped you off about this stuff in Durban? It wasn't Richter.'

'If you must know, I've something going with his sister, Sarah.' The pitch of his voice increased in frustration. He wanted to shout, but he held it. 'I've been screwing her. She told me her brother boasted of being selected for a vital operation in Durban. She later told me that it concerned a highly-rated and well-known advocate. I passed that on to Smith.'

He became less flustered. 'She's innocent. She couldn't believe what she felt was going to happen, and has, as we know now.'

Steiner laughed then said: 'I'm not after her. Like you say, she's innocent. There's one last thing. Does she know who you are, your connection with Smith?'

Bryant reacted as if branded by a cowboy's iron. 'Of course she doesn't. I'm not a fool. She knows nothing.'

'Good.' Steiner stood up. 'Let me have the street number of this guy Richter. I must leave.'

Gratefully Bryant took the local directory from under the phone and went to the middle pages. He wrote the details on the pad and threw it on the table. 'All three,' he said. 'Richter, Koch and Muller. 'They're the ones you want.' He marched to the door.

Steiner gathered the paper and read it. 'How long is it from here to this man Richter?'

'It's five, seven minutes by car,' replied Bryant, glad to see Steiner leaving.

'That's close enough. I want to find out if they're there before I go in. Give Richter a ring. I want an answer.'

'Now?' said Bryant reluctantly. He didn't like orders from a stranger, whatever his connections with his boss.

'Now,' said Steiner. 'I have to be sure.'

Bryant went to the phone and dialled the number. There was a compulsion about Steiner, ominous, restless, but strangely calm. He wished he wasn't involved. After a minute he heard Richter's wife. 'Who is it?'

'Forgive me.' Bryant put on a benign tone. 'Is Abe there? I have to speak to him.'

'He's not here. Who are you?' She had only met him once and didn't recognize the voice.

'A friend,' answered Bryant blandly. 'I'll ring again.' He returned the phone to its stand. 'He's not there. Obviously they're not as quick as you.'

Steiner ignored the sarcasm. 'They left before me, an hour, maybe more.' He twirled the black strands of chest hair that poked from his collar. 'They must have gone somewhere else first. Perhaps they went to see Muller. That might give me time if they have. I'd rather not have to get them out of their beds with their wives present.'

'To do what?' asked Bryant quietly. 'Smith said you were collecting information.' Then it came to him. 'God ... you're going to kill them, murder them. What sort of organization is Smith running?'

'If we went through the usual channels to get what we believe they have, we wouldn't even be able to charge them, let alone get a conviction,' said Steiner. 'Besides it would take months. No, Smith's right. Knock the shit out of them and get what we want, even if that means killing them. If they cooperate and survive it will be a lesson in manners and how to behave in society.'

'The girl will think I had something to do with it,' said Bryant, thinking of his skin. 'I know these people. They'll beat the truth out of me. The Scorpions will end up getting the exposure they don't need.'

Steiner walked to within a few feet of Bryant. 'You're exactly right. That's why you're expendable.'

Bryant propelled himself back, dancing into the corridor. He knew he had to get out, yell his head off. The man had a power about him unlike anything he had ever seen. He stuck his elbows flat to his ribs and willed his legs into action. Nothing came from behind and he felt he was moving in a vacuum, empty, devoid of threat, flying as if on a thermal.

The kick struck him below the last rib, and pulped him into the wall. At once he feared it was over, that this man, one of his team, was going to kill him. He wailed miserably, staccato, and slithered down the eggshell paint. The rib was fractured. He could feel it, the end stabbing into him. Tilting his head he looked up at Steiner, a jailer of infinite calm. 'Why?' The word was innocent. 'We're together. I gave you what you wanted.' The pain took him and he slumped further, his fists uncurling in manifest submission.

Steiner said: 'You know too much. This is necessary.' He took Bryant by the collar and lifted him, as if he had hold of a dying moth. Death would be instantaneous, delivered without a weapon. He of few men knew how. It couldn't have been easier. Then Bryant screamed, the waves of sound obliterating the air and tearing at Steiner's ears like the high-pitched notes tuned by a torturer. Using his feet against the skirting, Bryant jettisoned himself towards the kitchen like an athlete out of the blocks. But Steiner recovered in a second, first looming bestially and then chasing after him. He closed the gap, reaching out his arm and taking the gown. He pulled him round, his posture instantly low and powerful, balance perfect. Rotating on the one point in his abdomen he cannoned his fist into his victim's face, his muscles relaxing to dissipate the energy that came from the centre of his being.

Bryant pirouetted like a high-wire artist then hit the floor with the undiluted weight of his 180-pound frame. He landed in a Gothic assemblage, his aquiline nose reduced to an uninspiring profile. He was out cold and the karate man tested his pulse. It was still beating. He had never killed anyone who didn't have conscious life, the will to fight. This was unpleasant. But he saw it was now a part of the job, a job that he wanted to be over, and set him free from Smith's hold.

Raising Bryant's head and shoulders, Steiner cradled the body like a mother holding a child. Bryant's breath came out and he could feel the heart. Holding the neck, he released the rest, letting it go under the gravitational pull. He waited, then he jerked, easily snapping the spinal bones. With the face away from him he jerked again to sever the cord.

Steiner let himself out, securing the lock and removing the key. He left the block, confident after seeing no one that his presence at the flat had gone unnoticed. In the car he examined the map before sparking the engine. He was satisfied he had what he wanted, that things were working to plan. At the end of the road he turned north, for the district where he believed he would find Richter and Koch.

* * *

'You were foolish, both of you. You should have stayed with him.' Muller addressed Richter and Koch, his eyes red from being woken up in the middle of a deep sleep after drinking the evening before. The two younger men, seated at the scrubbed kitchen table and reduced from the trials of the past two days, hadn't expected to hear what they did. Standing next to the 1930s combustion stove and waiting for a pot of coffee to brew, Muller cast an unlikely figure as the one who had orchestrated the operation. On hearing the old buzzer at the door he had hurriedly pulled on baggy trousers up to his vest and he stood with the bearing of an old man, his shoulders drooped, his ample waist covering the brash buckle on his belt.

'He insisted on making a go for Cartwright without knowing he was there,' argued Richter defensively. 'There were only those dogs that nearly tore us to pieces, and we killed them. What kind of leader is that?'

'He's a man who's already done a lot for us, perhaps more than I ever expected of him.' Muller shifted the pot, sniffing at the roasted beans. 'Cartwright's dead, and a friend of his. It was on the news. I still don't know if he got the file and that is why you should have stayed.'

Richter showed surprise. 'He was lucky. I staked the place out the next day. The police were all over it. Krige put himself before the interests of the party. He chose to take one hell of a risk.'

Muller bubbled into a shriek. 'The whole mission was a risk. That's why I sent you along, to work as a team.' He gesticulated like an irate stallholder. 'Where is he now? Did you consider that if he gets caught by the wrong cops, possibly blacks, they'll be barging into your house before the rise of the sun? And then it'll be mine.'

Koch reacted defiantly. 'If Krige's caught he knows better than to talk. His wife and those boys of his are worth more to him than this file.'

Muller banged the pot irascibly. 'That was coercion. I needed him, his resourcefulness, intelligence and experience. Are you going to kill them? Would you kill a white Afrikaans woman and her two young sons because you think her husband failed on this kind of job? At least he tried.' Taking the pot with him he filled enamel mugs with the dappled liquid and pushed a couple across the table.

Reflectively he said: 'Krige would never allow himself to be taken alive. He's of that stock. I think he got out, that he's already on his way here. They would have said so otherwise.'

'And then? He's a danger. You said you'd get rid of him.' Koch looked at Richter for support. 'He'll have to be killed,' he said.

'That's what I thought originally,' said Muller. 'But he's no threat to us. He's a professional, knows how to shut his mouth, a true Afrikaner who is loyal to our people. Destroying him will serve no purpose. He can go. After all I gave my word.'

'And he'll just walk off,' stated Richter sarcastically.

'Why shouldn't he?' Muller took satisfaction in seeing Richter go silent.

'When's the next job?' asked Koch, knowing there was nothing to be gained by pushing the subject.

'It'll come in time,' answered Muller cryptically, filling his mug. He dropped onto a stool, stirring in some sugar. 'I never thought it'd be difficult getting the file. And we might still get it, thanks to Krige. A job like this depends on your preparation and the methods adopted. And, of course, satisfactory achievement is also heavily reliant on the choice of men. Good men can turn the odds against them into success.'

He stilled the coffee with the spoon and poured it into him. 'There might be more that I'll ask you to do, if of course you can convince me that you stay with the pace and see a job through.' Muller took his cup to the sink. 'Now go. I'll talk to you again when I've spoken to Krige.'

He added cuttingly: 'I know he'll turn up, even though you left him stranded there to take the can. Forget you ever met him.'

It was close to two o'clock when Koch drove the American saloon into Richter's drive. He went down the 100-metre corrugated surface and pulled up in the cluttered yard, markedly dissimilar to the wealthy manicured suburbs of the Berea.

'Muller's losing his grip,' he said turning off the V8 engine and the lights. 'Krige's a flaw, an outrider, our bogy man. I'd feel better if he was eliminated.' He grinned lasciviously. 'Then I'd screw his wife.'

'You're letting your mind wander.' Richter reached over for his bag. 'I'm only concerned with Krige. He hates our guts and will be pissed off we left him. I don't know how he'll react to that, and the pressure Muller put on him at the start. He might come for us with a vengeance. He doesn't know he's become Muller's blue-eyed boy.'

'Well for the rest of tonight he's no threat. He won't risk hiring a car.'

'He would have been able to get the overnight train,' mused Richter. 'It reaches Johannesburg at around six and then it is thirty minutes to Pretoria.'

Koch stared into the dark. 'If he comes after me in my own house I'll send him to hell.'

Richter took his bag onto his lap. 'Tonight we rest,' he said. 'If he gets smart he'll join that other retard Marais, the one sent by Bryant, or more likely his boss.'

'And what are we going to do with Bryant? He's worse than Krige.'

Richter got out of the car. 'It'll be a pleasure wringing

his neck. The thought of such a traitor shafting my sister makes me puke.' He put his boot onto the sill. 'In the morning we will decide on Bryant's departure. It must be done without trace. I don't want my sister finding him dead. It has to be as if he's returned to his home, wherever that might be.'

'And then we're clean except for the farmer.' Koch jangled the ring of keys. 'He has an effect on me.'

Richter strummed on the roof. 'Don't let him disturb your beauty sleep.'

'You despise him as much as I do,' said Koch.

'He's only a farmer, and he's also outnumbered,' said Richter idly. He was about to add something when he caught a movement and he cautioned his friend. 'Who's there?' he said. 'Show yourself or we'll come and get you.'

Koch got out of the driver's door. 'What is it?' he said, looking over the roof. Richter didn't reply.

'What did you see?' Koch tried again. 'I can't see anything. This job's got on your nerves.'

'No,' said Richter quietly, reaching into his bag through the clothing. 'There was something there.'

'Leave it. Both of you stand still.' The voice was from behind him.

Richter went rigid, his fingers tantalizingly just touching his revolver. Without retracting his hand he looked over his shoulder and saw Steiner, where he had come from behind a shed, the Glock easy at his thigh, hanging loosely as if wasn't supposed to be there, an afterthought.

On the other side of the car Koch agitated nervously, wondering who the man was. His gun was in his jacket above the back seat and like Richter he had not failed to notice the Glock. How quickly Steiner could bring the weapon up, and his ability, he did not know but he had the long straw. They needed a diversion, enough for Richter to get his gun out of the bag. He was much closer to it.

'What do you want?' peddled Richter. 'Who are you?'

'One or both of you killed Andrew Cartwright at his home in Durban. You also took something from his safe that I want. You know what I mean. Get away from the car.'

'Never heard of him,' murmured Richter, stalling. 'Have you?' He spoke to Koch. 'This guy's an insomniac. Someone's fed him red meat.' He laughed harshly, an attempt at defusing the situation and also an effort to give him and Koch more time.

Steiner circled carefully, as if calculating his steps, the soil crunching in weak resistance. They were as tall as he but a lot heavier, built into masculine V-shapes above their waists. They were dangerous, waiting for their opportunity, and they had guns. He remembered what one of them had made of Cartwright but that was now irrelevant. At the boot of the car he stopped. It gave him the best chance of killing the one nearest him and then the other.

But that was not what he wanted, however appealing the thought. Two dead men were useless without the essential element that Smith believed they were after. He moved forward slowly. There could only have been a document that these men were after all along, something of incredible value. They were certainly not interested in the jewellery. To him it was then clear and, judging by the timing of events, Cartwright had only just been given this precious something. He played his card.

'I want the file you took from Cartwright's safe,' said Steiner, the sound of his voice barely audible, pure ice. He took another line. 'It was sent to Cartwright three days ago. That's what you went to Durban to get. You also killed Cartwright, and that's murder. But I'll let you go to your women if you give me the file.' He was convinced he was right, but didn't expect any cooperation.

'Go home, big boy,' said Richter, ready to move. All that he needed was the gun. He couldn't understand why Steiner waited, perhaps testing him out.

'Which one of you is Richter?' said Steiner, beginning to believe that these two had not killed Cartwright, although they had gone to Durban. There had to be someone else, a man a lot cleverer than these in front of him.

Richter answered confidently. 'Neither one of us went to that hole. You have the wrong house. Can't you hear when I speak?' As he spoke he took the gun in the bag and pulled, at the same moment dropping into the car. He felt the gun come out and saw Koch go for the door. Steiner seemed slow to react, more or less still, standing in the same place, and Richter came out of the car. He was thinking ahead, the effect the flat-nosed slugs would have on the human body before him.

Then Steiner came in, his head low, his eyes on Richter and his arms moving in measured harmony with his legs.

Richter tried to line up the gun and then his insides exploded as the foot struck his chest with a savagery that rammed him into the door. His lungs deflated and he struggled in the impotence that engulfed him in misty cycles of grey and white. Too weak to stand, he held the centre column, the weapon loosening in his grip, and sank to the chrome finish next to the seat.

Any respite was illusory, for Steiner hit him again, taking his knee into his face, a man totally in control of what he had learned to do. Blood rained on the metallic paint and Richter tried to clear his eyes.

Hoarsely he shouted to his friend. 'Get your gun. Shoot the bastard.' He slumped, his hand raking through the sand and minute stones for the gun. But before he found it the blow behind his neck took him down and he fell from the car, thumping his blond head on the high-tensile edge of steel.

Rising robotically Steiner lifted the Glock, poking it through the cabin of the car to where Koch had cunningly vanished on the other side. He was quiet, too quiet. Suddenly there was the scuffling of boots and he saw Koch through the window as he ran from the car. In an instant Steiner was at the bonnet of the vehicle, steadying the Glock in his fists. The fleeing man was already at 30 paces and he had difficulty getting a bead on him in the dark. Twice he fired, and then to his annoyance Koch disappeared.

Going after Koch, Steiner reached the spot where he had last seen him. But Koch had gone and he pulled up, his acute senses like antennae. There were no signs of blood, and he probably hadn't hit him. Then he saw him again, a brief hulk of moving shadow and he went after him, realizing the man would know the yard, and that he knew of a way out. His fears were confirmed when he saw Koch touch the top of a wall and vanish. He closed in and, stepping on a pile of rubble, hauled himself up the wall. It was constructed of brick, in poor condition, and pieces of mortar crumbled as he looked to what lay beyond. Hanging by his elbows he saw a wilderness of trees and indigenous high veld bush, long-stemmed khaki weeds. Koch could be anywhere. He released himself, dislodging the rubble in a minor avalanche, and went to the car. He was angry that he had played with Richter instead of making certain of his death with his hands or with the Glock. Now one of them had got clear and the advantage of surprise was gone. The house lights were still out and he was glad the pistol was silenced. He could finish what he had started.

At the car he went to where he had beaten Richter. The body was still, supine along the length of the chassis, one arm hidden. He couldn't see the revolver and he took hold of the trousers to get the man out. As he gripped him, Richter came to life, lashing out with prehensile strength. The blow caught Steiner, throwing him off balance, and for a moment he stared disbelievingly as Richter took the magnum from under the car. The noise from the gun was shattering in the yard but Steiner had already moved, going down before it blasted out the lead. He rolled over and grabbed Richter's nearest outstretched leg. He pulled the beaten man to him, crashing his knife edge onto the exposed groin as he did it. Then he sprang on top of him, driving his knuckles under his jaw. Richter went into an oblivious state and Steiner got up, holding the Glock. The noise was unfortunate and he glanced at the house. A light at the far end came on.

Positioning the Glock centimetres from Richter's temple, he let out two slugs and as the head went limp he fired into the heart. As he smelt the burnt powder a woman came into the yard from the kitchen, her golden hair billowing in the teasing gusts of air, almost translucent in the light. She cried out for her beloved husband and ran for the car.

Prizing the revolver from Richter's fingers and poking it into his jeans, Steiner left, and with the car between him and the woman ran into the dark. He slowed then went for the road. He had nearly reached it when he heard the woman scream and he hurried on, going over the fence and onto the pavement. His car was nearby and he carried on as she screamed again. It was a cry of one under torture and a picture of her embracing the body flashed into his mind. He expelled it and reaching the saloon got in. The wheels harsh on the tar, he did a three-point turn and drove up the road.

Twenty metres into the plot Koch heard Steiner at the

wall. He was unfamiliar with the grounds and if Steiner came in he knew he would have to attack or try to escape to the road. That he had not been able to get his pistol irked him and he wished he had kept the weapon with him.

When he heard the noise from Richter's gun Koch recognized the sound immediately. There was no other like it. The gun Steiner had been carrying was too small, and he had noticed the silencer. He returned to the wall and went up. Across the yard he saw his friend's wife, Marie, leave the house and run for the car, calling Abe's name. Jumping down he kept to the trees, inching his way to the vehicle, ashamed that he did not try and stop her. He feared the worst, and watched as she reached the car. She became obscured and then he heard her scream, a dreadful wail that told him what to expect. Abandoning his cover he went on, the terrible cries finally making him disregard his own safety.

As he came to the car, Koch heard the woman's wretched cries and he opened the door, gratefully getting the .357 magnum from his coat. Going past the boot he saw her kneeling, cradling Richter's head to her bosom, and he stepped up behind her, the hacked body and lifelessness of his friend involuntarily contracting his stomach.

Marie Richter spun when she heard Koch, her tear-streaked face a canvas of grief. 'Johannes,' she murmured, bowing her head over her husband, recognition of his trusted friend instant. 'He's dead, my lover, and the father of my children.' She sobbed in gulps, smothering Richter as if her warmth and love would give him life. Koch caressed her, his touch tentative, helpless. He realized he had taken a risk coming to the car, and he looked to where he had first seen Steiner. He half expected the killer to appear again but as the seconds passed he knew he had gone, like a phantom into the night.

He sat beside her, confident with the revolver, and drew her to him. 'The swine will not rest until he has more notches on his gun,' he whispered cogently. 'There are others at risk in the party. I must leave.'

'Who could do it?' She wept again, ignorant. 'What has Abe ever done to anyone? He only showed love.' Her voice rose in subdued hysteria, her shaking fingers stroking the ridge of muscle on her husband's neck. Recoiling at the stench of blood and her cheap scent, Koch took her from the corpse. She was a picture of pathos and trembled against his chest, his arm wrapped around her waist. 'You must go inside and do something for me. I'll look after Abe. He'll be taken care of.'

'Call the police,' she said regaining some calm. 'They'll know what to do.'

'Not now. Someone else will do that. I want you to phone Muller, and then Viljoen at the farm. Tell them Abe's been killed and that I'll be in contact. They must send someone to collect the body. Leave the outside lights on.'

'Where are you going?' She wiped away her tears, frightened at the thought of being left alone.

'You're safe,' he said, wanting her to keep quiet. 'The killer's not after you. He's a fanatic who's broken from his cage. Come, we must hurry.' He led her from her husband to the house. She cooperated meekly and he guided her to the steps. 'Make the calls,' he said as she went up into the kitchen. 'Trust me. I'll return when I've finished off this guy.'

She left him, closing the door and bolting it. In a hurry he went to the car. He removed a blanket from the boot and after draping it over his friend took out his bag. He placed the revolver inside and set off for the gate, leaving the keys of the car in the ignition.

Seven minutes later Koch neared his home. Entering

the neighbour's garden, he went to the fence, a stone's throw from the garage where he kept his car. He looked through the hedge that towered above the wooden planks, the brutal death of Richter still with him. Not seeing anyone, he went to the end where the hedge tapered, and climbed over, falling low onto his knees. He went through a small orchard of apple trees, came to the garage and opened the doors. They creaked and scuffed the earth. Ever conscious of Steiner, he got into the old Pontiac and took it past the house and into the road. At first he wondered where Steiner had gone, who else he wanted to kill, and then he thought of one man, John Bryant, the person who he believed would provide the key. He must have had something to do with Steiner's visit.

Cursing his failure at not killing Koch, Steiner drove fast from where he had committed his crime. Initially he planned to go to Koch's house, but after a kilometre north he took the car due east for the old quarter of town. Muller was more important, and if Richter and Koch had got the file they would have given it to Muller, who they had almost certainly been to see before they arrived at Richter's house.

Steiner easily found Muller's house, double-storeyed, and standing in a small plot. He left the car further up the road and returned, going into the garden and to the back. A light was on inside. Unlike the homes of the wealthy, security-conscious whites of the Johannesburg suburbs 30 kilometres south-west, Pretoria homes were relatively unguarded and in the warm weather he was not surprised to see windows open, some on his level. Perhaps it was a sign of defiance. Choosing one, he poked his hand in and released the metal catch that held it.

Within the building a telephone rang and he lowered himself, half-closing the window and propping it in position with his thumb. The phone was answered but he could not hear anyone speaking, and climbed in. He was in a room containing eighteenth-century Dutch furniture, a solid dining table, eight chairs pushed up to it, and a free-standing sideboard. He went to the door, slightly ajar, and listened. The deep, local accent of a man reached him and he stuck his head out as far as he could to pick up what he was saying. The man had to be Muller.

'Where's he gone?' Muller's tone was terse, irritated. 'Why didn't he come here?' Then repentance: 'I'm deeply sorry, Marie. The perpetrator of this hideous crime will not escape. It's directed at our people and it involves something that it is of vital importance in protecting those who led us in the past, before the blacks were allowed to claim this land as theirs.'

For a short while Muller was silent. Then he said: 'I'll speak to Viljoen and arrange for your husband to be removed. It will be done in half an hour.' Muller carried on: 'And Marie, no word to anyone, not even the children at this stage. The murderer will be punished, I assure you.' The receiver was replaced and Steiner heard the rustling of paper. After a short delay the phone was lifted and Steiner entered the room. Seated at a little table with the telephone on a pile of books was a fat man, and Steiner knew he had set eyes on Muller, ready to start dialling.

'Put it back.' Steiner came behind him. Muller turned as if bitten by a dog. He dangled the phone, and then placed it on the cradle. 'I knew you would come,' he said, his attention quickly on the Glock. 'But I didn't think it would be so soon. You know your way around.' He added the last perfunctorily, his manner outwardly collected despite the latent threat before him.

'So you're the one who directed the killing of Andrew Cartwright in Durban,' said Steiner. 'You must be hard-pressed to select thugs like Richter and Koch. I wonder how many more people you're working on. But for my purposes he's enough and the reason I'm here.'

Steiner stepped closer, ever wary, never taking his eyes off Muller. Even a fat man could move fast when cornered. 'I want the file that I believe was taken from Cartwright's house, the file that you and your breed so eagerly want. Richter and Koch came to see you before they went home. They must have delivered the prize. Give it to me and I'll go.'

Muller slid his chair back on the rug. The reply came easily. 'You're white. I'm fighting your war, getting rid of those who've risen to pollute this land, those who have now been given the freedom to annihilate us. Start to think, man.' He was unafraid. The tenets of his ingrained beliefs were being questioned, and that was what he could not accept from anyone, even a man who might kill him.

'Cartwright was also white,' said Steiner. 'He was innocent, doing his best for conciliation between black and white.'

'You call someone who funded the ANC innocent?' spat Muller. 'This man was as culpable as those who planted the bombs, that tore our woman and children limb from limb. You've been misled by the rhetoric spewed out by the liberals. Where are they now? I'll tell you. They're hiding in their palatial homes behind iron bars that would make Pretoria central prison look like a chicken farm.'

Steiner admired the man's resolve.

'You're wasting your breath trying to convert me. I'm not one of your nasty boys, the two you sent to Durban to kill Cartwright. Besides the file, I'm sure that you and your type have always wanted men like Cartwright dead. His death was the delicious icing on the cake. To you, he betrayed the Afrikaner people. You're a disgrace to what the majority of whites now want in this country, reconciliation with the crimes of the past and acceptance that the blacks are the new rulers.'

'Three men,' blurted Muller. 'Can't you count? You seem to know everything. And the file was ours, compiled through years by one we trusted, and who then betrayed that trust and sent it to Cartwright. It belongs to us and we'll get it back.'

Steiner had learned something, but it was not enough. The file was still not his. 'Three?' said Steiner quietly. 'Where's the third man?' He came closer. 'Tell me. I only saw two. I haven't much patience.'

He was still, Muller's words beginning to sink in. Somehow he should have guessed that Richter and Koch were too stupid to have been sent alone on a job like this. They were mere bully boys, no brains and purely there as a backup.

Muller grinned mockingly. 'You'll never find out. Now get out and return to your paymaster. The blacks will never govern us.'

As Muller finished his sentiments, Steiner whipped him on the teeth with the barrel of the Glock. The fat man bucked in the chair, banging his head on the wall, his mouth a swelling rictus. The chair tilted precariously then gave in, and Muller went to the floor, belatedly reaching for the table to lessen the fall. Wiping his mouth, he unconsciously smeared blood on his cheek looking like the victim in an American horror film. He glared defiantly at Steiner. 'That won't help you.'

'It's of no matter,' said Steiner. 'Bryant has already given me the names. How do you think I found Richter and Koch? He had already worked it all out.'

'Bryant? He's one of you,' spluttered Muller, his bleeding lips and gums temporarily of secondary importance. 'I should have known. He wasn't from these parts, never a loyal member of the party.'

'He's dead now,' murmured Steiner. 'I got what I went for.'

'You'll never get Krige,' said Muller. 'His family has farmed in the White River area for generations. He's of the old stock. When he hears you're after him he'll hunt you like the animal you are.'

'You chose a farmer for your hit squad?' teased Steiner. 'That's why you'll fail in the end. You need trained men, professionals from an elite unit, organization, not men of the land.'

Muller scoffed at him. 'Krige was a first-class police officer before he returned to the farm.' He laughed disdainfully. 'And Koch, the one you missed. He turns into a maniac when someone takes pot shots at him.'

'Where's Krige?' said Steiner dispassionately. He cocked the Glock with a near-frictionless rasp of the slide and returned it to hang at his side.

'So Bryant couldn't tell you,' said Muller, a note of pride in his voice, and that he had managed to stage the operation in secrecy. 'He was lucky to know as much as he did, the weak little fool.'

'He didn't tell me about Krige. I must thank you for that,' said Steiner, feeling that he was at last getting somewhere.

Realizing he had been tricked, Muller heaved the chair at Steiner and, miraculously for a beaten man, got to his feet. With a staggering turn of speed for one in his physical condition he went for the passage like a pig ahead of the butcher's knife.

Steiner evaded the chair and raised the pistol to waist height. The bullets hit Muller in the liver, piercing the fat that hung on him like a torus and channelling his guttural inflection into a scream. He tumbled, turning his face at the last moment as his head struck the grained boards. Lying still, he stared at the opposite wall.

'You shot me in the back,' he said. 'You're a coward. You'll never succeed and get what you want. We're too strong for you.'

Steiner aimed as if on a target range and shot him in the head. 'You didn't deserve a better death,' he said, sorry he had wasted the bullets and already going to the table, where he picked up the diary Muller had before him when he entered. The book was parted by tags where a register of names and numbers ran for several pages. Briefly scouring the list, he found no entry under Krige and thumbed to the section that covered daily events in the October period. Many of the pages were blank, and he was about to take the book and go when in a box dated 4 October, three weeks previously, he spotted what he was looking for.

It was simply: Jan Krige, White River 1667. He turned over a few more pages and then put the diary in his pocket. From what Muller had said, Krige had led the operation. He had to have the file. Only he could have taken it. And it was near certain that he hadn't visited Muller before now. Something had happened in Durban between the three men that was a mystery. But Krige was definitely the leading player in this strange course of events, and he held the pot of gold.

Paying no more attention to Muller, Steiner went out the way he had come in. Killing him had been easy and in the process he had learned of Krige's involvement. The car was parked on a bend and as he got in he saw a car pull in up the road. Someone approached the house and went into the grounds. He thought it was Koch, but he could not be sure and he decided against going back.

By now others would know about Richter and they might arrive at Muller's when he was there, adding an unnecessary complication. Richter and Muller were enough for a night's work. Koch could wait until after Krige, and then he would take great pleasure in killing him.

When Koch reached the block of flats where Bryant lived he parked in the residents' area and went up the fire escape to the third floor. He had been to the flat before on one occasion with Richter. The revolver was tucked in its holster under his coat and he prepared it unconsciously as he pressed the bell. It was loud for a small flat, and he knew if Bryant was in he would hear it.

He gave the man a while but there was no reply and holding his hands to the frosted glass he looked through. It was dim, a light on further in, and he pushed the bell again, beginning to accept that Bryant was out. There was no other reason for him not to answer the door. The corridor night lamps were still on, an ethereal radiance, and just before departing he bent to see through the flap on the letter-box. He gave his pupils a moment to dilate. At first he only saw the cramped entrance hall and passage but as the objects became more defined he frowned in astonishment as he saw Bryant lying where the passage ended.

The unnatural juxtaposition of the head and the engineered rigidity carried the design of death and Koch glanced along the corridor. Only one man could have done it, the man who had killed his friend. But why had he killed someone who must have been working on the same side?

Koch went from the flat in a hurry. This was more serious than he had imagined. Muller had to be next.

Chapter 13

Pretoria

Before the train pulled into Johannesburg station Krige stirred from his sleep and eased his legs over the bunk. The bleeding had ceased, leaving a stain the size of a saucer on the bandage, but the muscle was tender and he gingerly drew up the trousers that he had thrown on the floor. He still felt drained, and as he washed over the scallop-shaped basin he reflected on the evening before, the completion of the job, the betrayal by the men who had been there to help him. He was still angry at being dumped but also glad, now that he was in his home area, that he had the file and would never see Richter and Koch again.

When the carriages reached the platform he took the Beretta from under his pillow and, with the file in its envelope suitably encased in a supermarket carrier bag he had found, left the compartment, testing his leg with more weight as he went to the exit. There were only a few others on the train, an amalgam of families and old people returning to the Reef from a holiday on the coast, and he went through the ticket barrier, noting from the departures screen the next train to Pretoria. For such a short distance they were frequent, and within ten minutes he left the Gold City on the last part of his train journey.

Pretoria station was from the past, built on prime real estate in the centre of the old town, of magnificent and compelling architectural design, created from the Dutch ancestry of the Boer farms in the districts. Off the train, Krige went to the only toilets, and in a cubicle peeled off the bandage. The wound mocked him, the unhealed flesh a mutinous weal, and he bound it with the roll he had removed from Cartwright's bathroom store. Wrapping the soiled cloth in toilet paper, he stuffed it into his coat and crossed the main concourse to the taxi rank outside.

The morning was overcast and he thought of the farm where the tenanted labour would already have spent a couple of hours on the land, gathering the crop for the seasonal drying. The first cab in line was a two-tone 1957 Ford Galaxy, the protruding wings an anachronism in present styling, and he spread out gratefully as it routed its way to the jeep. Being a little after 6.30, the roads were clear and in several minutes they were in the area he wanted. He instructed the driver to drop him in a road down from where the vehicle was parked, and he let the car go before moving on. The jeep was exactly as he'd left it, no vandalism, and he sank into the driver's seat with relief. He longed for a cup of coffee but quelled the thought and took the file from the carrier bag and white-paper holder he had found it in. He looked up and down the road, conscious that he was in possession of something of incredible importance, nationally and internationally, and he started to read it from the first page.

For two hours he read the contents of the file in blocks, skipping as he chose, and could see that it was the most comprehensive and meticulously compounded dossier that he had ever set eyes on. The detail behind the names, some of whom he recognized, particularly those in the infamous and all-powerful State Security Council, initiated in 1979 and disbanded in 1989 by de Klerk, would make any prosecutor, here or at an international court, weep with joy.

He thought of the difficulty that the prosecutors of the Serbian leader, Milosevic, were having in getting the man convicted, and other cases where it was almost impossible to bring the supreme leaders to trial, the ones with blood dripping from their hands. In the case of Milosevic he recalled the prosecutor saying that as with Hitler, nothing had been written down. But in this file, on human rights violations and criminal murder, it was written down, but no one who wanted these men had been able to find what he now had on his lap. There were 47 names in the file, each one separately identified, and details of false documents that had been prepared for them.

At 8.30 Krige closed the file, replaced it in its envelope, and started the jeep. It had become perfectly clear to him what he had to do, and he drove into the centre of Pretoria, the place of finance, legal firms and high business. There was one man he trusted, as he had his father, a very clever lawyer who had close contacts in South Africa and abroad.

Krige parked his jeep over the road from the lawyer's offices and waited patiently, knowing that men of this type were seldom at their desks before nine or ten, which was not surprising as they had probably spent the large part of the previous evening going through cases. At a little past nine he saw his lawyer emerge from a side road and amble towards the building. In seconds Krige was out of the jeep and across the road. The lawyer was surprised to see him, coming as if from nowhere. The expression on Krige's face rapidly told him that their meeting was not mere coincidence but deliberate and of great urgency.

After the usual greeting Krige said: 'I've got to see you

in the privacy of your office. This is the most important matter you will ever come across in your career.'

The lawyer, David Staples, immediately captured by Krige's words, waved his hand to the offices and led the way, Krige following with the file under his arm and nervously looking to see if anyone was watching.

'What's this about?' said Staples when they were seated in his office, cups of steaming coffee in front of them, Krige across the desk. 'You've already made clear the serious nature of your visit.'

'I have here a dossier, a file, that contains the names and activities of the leading men in power during the apartheid period,' said Krige. 'These are the men who should now be facing criminal charges of gross human rights violations, and who have so far escaped justice for lack of evidence. Their crimes were sanctioned by the state.'

'Carry on,' said Staples, leaning forward in his chair like a schoolboy watching the denouement of a thriller on screen.

'The evidence of their atrocities, or crimes, is here in detail,' said Krige. 'I'm sure there is more, but the damning stuff is in this file. It was compiled by, shall we say, the inner circle, and they would have put the guts of anything that could convict those men, their brothers, in this work. I'm not a lawyer but it does not take one who reads this to realize how incriminating it is.'

'Pass it to me,' said Staples. 'If what you say is true then we have something that, if revealed, would shake this nation to its very core and give immense satisfaction to the people who were denied human rights in the past. It's the satisfaction they deserve for years of oppression.'

Krige took the file from its wrappings and passed it to Staples. The lawyer read through some of the contents for half an hour, while Krige sat quietly, now and then dragging at one of his cigarettes. He was smoking more than usual.

In a calm expulsion of intensity, Staples broke silence and said: 'This is what you say it is, and how you described it. Clearly, I've not read it all or even digested fully what is against each name, some of whom I know personally, but if we lived in a state that had capital punishment, these men would face the hangman.'

Staples closed the file. 'What do you want me to do? I think I know what you are going to say, but let me hear it. You haven't told me how you got hold of this file.'

'The file was prepared by people working for the leaders of the previous regime,' said Krige, who had been expecting the question sooner or later. 'These leaders are men who are now in prominent and important positions in this country, intelligent men who despise the ramblings of the present opposition parties, from the Democratic Alliance, downwards through the racist rabble parties.' Krige swigged coffee from his mug and then went on. 'One of the guys, central to the compiling of what you see in front of you, apparently got cold feet and his conscience started to upset him. He sent this file to one of the leading criminal lawyers in this country, Andrew Cartwright.'

'I've heard a lot about him,' said Staples. 'He's pure genius in court. I wouldn't want him to be against me if I was on trial, as good as I am.'

'I was asked by someone in this group, to them known as the party with no name, to retrieve the file,' said Krige. 'I went to Durban with two of their guys, unbelievably members of what I think is a sophisticated if misguided group, to Cartwright's place. I was compelled to do what was asked of me, and I succeeded without help from the other two.'

Krige, for all his background and strong self-belief, felt the penetrating gaze of the lawyer, as if he was on trial in the country's high court. 'Unfortunately, I had to kill Cartwright and a friend of his who was in the house at the time. It was me or them. Before Cartwright died he told me, with some persuasion, where to find the file. I was supposed to meet the other two at a prearranged point, but they didn't show. I then caught the train to Pretoria, and here I am.'

'An amazing story,' said Staples. 'I won't ask you what kind of hold these men had on you, but you got the file they wanted. It was a pity you had to kill Cartwright, but for the moment we'll forget about him. I assume no one can trace you to his murder.'

'Not to my knowledge,' said Krige, thinking of Muller, Richter and Koch. They surely wouldn't bleat, because they would incriminate themselves as accessories.

'Why have you come to me with the file, and not gone straight to the men who commissioned you?' asked Staples, absorbed by the intricate saga that was unfolding before him. 'Surely they must know that you got out, and are expecting you at any time now.'

'They're not necessarily going to get it,' said Krige flatly. 'And no one knows I have the file except you. I will go and make contact with them this morning. I'll tell them I killed Cartwright but couldn't find the file. There is no reason for them not to believe me, particularly when they read of Cartwright's death in the newspapers, and taking into account the fact that I have reported back to them.'

'What's your answer to the first question?' said Staples, persevering. 'What do want you want me to do?'

'I want you to make authenticated copies of the file and to store them all, including the original, in the most secure places, here and abroad,' said Krige. 'This must be done immediately. I will contact you within a few days or before. At the moment my intention is for you to send the certified copies to the Scorpions, or the DSO, and to two leading newspapers, one in London and the other in New York. These are the *Guardian* in London and the *New York Times*. The original must be produced when and if required. There must be a covering letter with your name on it, but without reference to me. The file is enough to bring any of the recipients to their feet and when they look at it they won't care who originally obtained the file. They'll only know it was sent to them by you. I'll leave the letter up to you.'

'I will do as you request,' said Staples. 'I'll get on to it as soon as you leave. Might I ask why you seem to have chosen this route, rather than giving the file back to the people who created it in the first place and commissioned you to retrieve it?'

'The answer is quite simple,' said Krige. 'I want the people who committed heinous crimes in the suppression of the blacks to be caught and spend the rest of their days in prison. They are our country's arch murderers, as were the Nazis of the Second World War. Some of those paid the price, and others escaped and are still on the run. This file will get all the leading criminals of the apartheid period in one go. And, I emphasize, their activities were not war crimes but rather state-sanctioned crimes. That is the most damning. I recognize that the distinction between crimes that are pure criminal acts and politically motivated acts is blurred, but ninety per cent of those who applied for amnesty, all of them the pawns in the game, were refused. Only a few who had acted for what were deemed honest political reasons were granted amnesty.'

Krige ran his hand over the stubble on his cheek and then continued. 'But, however strange this might sound to you, I might change my mind. That is why I have said I will contact you and give my final decision. At the moment I won't give you the possible reasons for doing it this way and you must accept the instructions I have given you. All I can say is that if the file is not released to the DSO and the foreign press, it might be returned to the people who sent me on this job in the first place.'

'I understand perfectly,' said Staples. 'I'm sure there would be a very good reason for you not to want the file released to the press and the DSO and I will do exactly as you say. As always, you can trust me.'

Staples thought for a moment and then said: 'What happens if I don't hear from you in a few days? From what you have told me, there has to be a risk that something might happen to you.'

'You will hear from me,' said Krige confidently. 'And I think it will probably be as early as tomorrow. If you don't, you will receive my instructions from someone else, the only person who knows that you have the file and can convey my final decision. I know there is a risk, but it is one I am prepared to take.'

Staples nodded. 'As far as I'm concerned your name will never be linked to any of this, whatever you finally choose to do.'

'Thank you,' said Krige.

'He left the office and mentally prepared himself for his next job, a meeting with Muller. But the meeting held no fear for him, and it was almost inconsequential. It would merely complete the assignment, and he felt an enormous burden being lifted from him.

Koch stood at the rear door of Muller's house, tense. Everything seemed all right but Steiner had had a good enough start to get in and out. Coming in, he had noticed the windows, naively welcoming when the Afrikaner people were under siege. But Muller was like that, bold against any possible threats that might come his way.

Koch knocked, enough to be heard anywhere in the house and waited by a brick column. He gave Muller a couple of minutes then climbed in one of the windows. Not hearing anything, he crept into the hall. The sight of his still boss brought him up sharp, then he went nearer, the fears that Muller was dead taking hold.

Muller was on his stomach, his eyes slits, the lower part of his jaw demolished where the final bullet had made an exit. The blood from his back had been absorbed by his vest, forming a scarlet belt that was supported by the fat underneath. As he lingered Koch saw a stirring in the ivory-grey old man and he went to him, touching him tenderly. He had meant something to him.

Like shutters, Muller's eyes opened wide, his pupils aimless. The lids closed and Muller rumbled, his Adam's apple bobbing grotesquely. Then he spoke, salivating through the blood on his lips. 'Krige. Help Krige. He's going to kill him.' With a quantum expulsion of breath the body contracted and Koch tried to catch more, feeling inside Muller's vest for the beating of his heart. It was weak, a near-undetectable injunction, and he went to the table. Keeping the gun outwards, he dialled Viljoen's number at the farm. He looked at Muller, the signs telling him he was about to die, that there was nothing he or anyone else could do.

Almost immediately, Viljoen answered, his tone curt. 'Who is it?'

'Johannes Koch. I'm at Muller's place...'

Viljoen interrupted callously. 'When did you return? Where's Muller?'

'Dying at my feet,' said Koch. 'There's someone after

us. Richter is dead and so is Bryant. Whoever is doing this work has also got Muller. Of that I'm certain.'

'Bryant?' said Viljoen, disbelief in his voice.

'He was an informer,' said Koch, pleased with the surprise he had caused. 'I believe he set this guy after us, but he wasn't smart enough. He was obviously disposable, got his nails clipped.'

Viljoen went quiet, rearranging the information he heard over the line. 'Stay there,' he commanded at last. 'I'll send someone for Muller. How bad is he?'

Koch gave Muller another look. 'Unconscious. Shot to hell, blood everywhere. He won't make it.'

'I'll be there,' said Viljoen, and severed the call.

Koch went to the body. He felt the pulse. It had gone and he bowed his head, numbed. His best friend, and the man he had come to regard almost as a father, both murdered in the space of an hour. The shock pumped tears, overspilling and running in trickles down his taut skin. Like a nemesis a picture of Steiner appeared, so far the winner, the pistol hanging as if moulded to his hand.

He shut out the vision, suddenly leaving the body as if it was diseased, his grief replaced by a monstrous compulsion for revenge. He remembered Muller's last words, the strained plea to help Krige, as if the farmer's life was in danger.

How had Steiner learned of Krige? He and Richter had only been informed of his name a day before the trip, after Richter's sister had spoken to Bryant. And Bryant was undoubtedly the link in the chain. Cocking and uncocking the gun, Koch tried to put himself in the position of the farmer. It seemed he would at least see Muller, give a statement on the job before returning to the farm. Koch still despised him. Muller had been a fool to bring in a stranger, one who ridiculed the beliefs of the party and its very existence, and was totally behind the blacks.

Sauntering over to the chair, he pulled it upright, seating himself and tilting the frame. Growing like a fecund seed was a plan of retribution, a plan to kill the two men he had come to hate most, Steiner and Krige.

White River, near the Kruger Reserve

Several kilometres from the farming town of White River, James Steiner stopped in a lay-by. The dense cloud overhead covered the low veld like a cloak, and when he switched off the headlights he was in a catacomb of black. In a broken circle around him the lights from distant farms were like fallen stars, and his thoughts narrowed to the farm further east where he hoped to find Krige. If Richter and Koch were back, then so was their leader. The diary carried no address, but even if it had he was aware that his chances of finding the farm in the dark were tenuous, without the directions of someone who knew the area. He was annoyed that he was unable to push ahead and make use of the night hours.

Reaching into the rear foot-well, he took a flask of coffee and a packet of sandwiches from his bag and ate and drank greedily, filling his mouth with bread and cheese and slurping crudely from the plastic cup. When he had satisfied his hunger he lowered the seat, almost instantly falling asleep.

Pretoria

Nearly half an hour after speaking to Viljoen, Koch heard a vehicle draw up in the yard. As he rocked off the chair there came the sound of another, and he went into the kitchen, tentatively lifting the jaded lace that partnered a turret-like window. A delivery van and car were parked by the garage and hurrying over were Viljoen and two other men he had never seen. Before he reached the kitchen door they were there and on their way in, Viljoen stalking to the table and placing the Borsalino hat he always wore onto it. He carried himself well, and his dark suit, which he favoured when off the farm, fitted him perfectly. His privileged upbringing had endowed him with the facility to mix confidently in all strata of life, and he was equally comfortable with labourers on the farm and businessmen in top city circles.

'Show us to Muller,' he said, as if talking to himself.

Koch was already going to the passage and Viljoen called the others to follow. One of them carried a portable stretcher and he started unfolding it.

When he saw the body Viljoen conveyed no emotion. The shot man was a minor impediment to achieving their objective. Concluding Muller was dead, he let the others perform their task. 'Take him,' he said unnecessarily. 'I'll ring you.'

As the corpse was carried out on the canvas Viljoen went to the table. He was quiet until the body had gone. 'Now tell me what happened,' he said, giving a slight smile. 'I know Cartwright and two of the blacks are dead.' He buttoned his jacket and walked into the lounge, sinking onto the ample sofa as if it was his own.

From a matching seat opposite, Koch summarized the events since meeting Krige at the farm. He was clinical in his treatment, telling the facts without embellishment, leaving out the resentment he and his friend had felt for their appointed leader.

Viljoen listened, never taking his eyes off him. 'So you ditched Krige in Durban?' he said. 'For what reason?'

Viljoen had never liked Richter and Koch, and regretted he had ever let Muller send them with Krige on the job.

'The police knew,' said Koch. 'They were crawling all over the place. The risk of being caught and implicating the party was too great. Krige was determined to get the file but the risk was too great. We had no alternative other than to pull out.' He was sure the older man would see the virtue in his reasoning. He was ready to resume his account.

'You were wrong,' said Viljoen, before Koch could continue. 'Unity is vital to success in this work.' Viljoen's nails marked the leather, his knuckles a neat series of miniature icebergs. He went on. 'You need men who are responsible and able to fight together for a common cause.' He sank more into the feathered cushion, his hands held like a bishop about to give a sermon. 'Where's Krige now?'

Koch looked down. 'I don't know,' he said, containing his irritation. 'He wants out. This work sickens him.'

'He still carried it through to the best of his ability,' said Viljoen, 'even though he might not have got the file. For that he has credit. He'll not be instructed again.'

'He hates the party,' said Koch repetitively, not knowing what else to say.

'My father and his built farms in this territory when it was a lawless land. They did that from nothing. Krige is a true Afrikaner even if he is not a member of the party.'

'You asked him to do our work?' said Koch, incredulously.

'The job had a distinct purpose which is still urgent and unresolved,' said Viljoen. 'It was necessary to demonstrate that a clever man can serve us adequately. There are not many about.' He looked pointedly at Koch when he said the last words.

Koch wasn't interested. 'And me? What about me?' he said, scared that he was dispensable. He knew how these men operated.

'You're a loyal member,' answered Viljoen, without further commitment. 'But you must learn to obey orders.' He lit a cigarette, blowing most of the smoke through his nose. 'But we digress. What happened when you reached Pretoria?'

Koch continued in a monotone, relating the visit to Muller and the encounter with Steiner. 'I asked Marie to phone Muller,' he said, 'and then went to see Bryant. The door was bolted. I saw him through the box, lying out on the floor. He was dead, a busted neck I think. I came here but I was too late. Muller had bought it.'

Viljoen cleared his throat, stubbing out the cigarette, not wanting it any more. 'Why go to Bryant?' he said evenly. 'How do you know he was an informer?'

Koch knew the question was coming. 'For weeks we sensed Bryant was playing a double. When the killer appeared I knew it was no accident. The leak couldn't have come from anywhere else. It had to be Bryant.

Viljoen got up like an advocate in court, smoothing his oiled hair. 'You're leaving something out. I want the truth.'

Koch wished he had never mentioned Bryant. 'Abe let slip to his sister that he had been assigned to a job in Durban and that it was of vital importance to the group. She was horrified and later told Bryant.'

'Why him?' shot Viljoen.

'They were sleeping together,' said Koch, in a matter-of-fact tone.

Viljoen swore and then said: 'Sex. How often that has precipitated the demise of men. Go on, don't let me stop you. This is becoming interesting.'

'At about the time when we were given the job, Richter suspected Bryant of living a lie,' said Koch. 'He wasn't as committed to the movement as he pretended to be. Richter had his line tapped and in twenty-four hours heard Bryant repeating the information he had told his sister to some guy in Durban. That was a couple of days before we joined Krige.' Koch hoped he had said enough.

'Why didn't you tell Muller?' asked Viljoen.

'We were going to do that on our return,' said Koch, lying. 'They had nothing to go on, no names. She had no idea why we were going to Durban.'

'Except your names,' said Viljoen, dryly. 'And they have your link within the party to Muller. That will also lead to me. God knows what he revealed. They couldn't catch you in Durban, for whatever reason, but they are on to you and have set loose a gunman amongst us. He's going through us one by one, the price of a simple slip.' He went to the window and looked onto the road.

'This is how we'll play it,' he said after a while. 'If necessary we'll appear as the victims of a plot inspired by traitors in the security services.' He returned to the centre of the room, lighting another of the filtered cigarettes. 'I have friends in high places. This will all go through the usual departments. The deaths of Richter and Muller will be logged as cold-blooded murder. If any finger is pointed at us it'll be in the press, a carefully prepared report. For the moment I'll wait until I hear from Krige, which I'm sure I will. If he hasn't got the file we will make other arrangements to get it, and you won't be involved.'

Koch listened, admiring Viljoen's cool manner. 'I want the man. He killed my best buddy.'

'You're out of it,' stated Viljoen emphatically. 'Find a friend to shack up with, preferably out of town. You're vulnerable. I'm saving your life, or can't you appreciate that. Let me know where you are.'

Koch reacted like a child denied sweets. 'I want him,' he repeated angrily. 'Why leave me out?'

'I don't want you blazing away in town with that gun of yours,' said Viljoen. 'In the current climate my protection is limited. I'll also take the appropriate steps to have this person eliminated, hopefully before he's done what he came for.'

'What about Krige?' said Koch, calming himself.

'I'm coming to him,' replied Viljoen, searching the younger man's face. 'I need another answer.'

'What is it?' said Koch, hating the continual questioning.

'Did Richter mention Krige to his sister?' said Viljoen.

'No. He didn't have Krige's name when he spoke to her,' said Koch. 'We were told later.'

'Then the killer knows nothing about Krige,' said Viljoen, not sure he was getting the truth. 'Do you agree?'

Koch thought of Muller's last utterance. 'Yes,' he lied. 'Unless he has another source, of which I am unaware.'

Viljoen seemed satisfied. 'Unlikely,' he said. 'It would be too much of a coincidence.'

'Where does that leave Krige?' said Koch.

Viljoen smiled blandly. 'Safe,' he said. 'He's out of it as far as I'm concerned. When I see him I'll tell him to stay on his farm, for a while at least.'

Koch laughed roughly. 'And how will he know? We don't know where he is.'

'He'll phone Muller when he arrives,' said Viljoen with certainty. 'That's the sort of man he is, the sort who never leaves things undone.' Viljoen went to let himself out. 'I'm going to the farm. Stay here for what's left of the night then leave. I'll return shortly after dawn.' He disappeared, and a while later Koch heard the car reversing in the yard and leaving.

He made some coffee and drank it in the lounge, thinking over the conversation with Viljoen. He was forbidden to play a part in killing Steiner, and that filled him with anger, but as he drank the brew he contented himself with the plan formulating in his mind that held him like a vice.

* * *

When Viljoen returned to Muller's house at 7.00 the next morning, Koch had gone, and he sat at the table in the kitchen, smoking profusely. He was certain the man after them would try to kill Koch, and earlier he had taken measures to bring the man in. He didn't know when he would show himself or make his next move, but through the years he had learnt patience and he was prepared to keep his men in position for weeks if necessary. It was not that he cared for Koch. The man had risen as high as he was going to in the party, and at times had showed a disappointing lack of guile. The killer was far more important, a bitter pill that in the past six hours they in their group had been forced to take.

As he drew on his fifth cigarette since reaching the house, a pall of smoke floating above him, Viljoen remembered the look on Koch's face when he had asked him about Krige. There was something he was keeping to himself. His hatred for Krige was as evident as rancid meat, and he would be the last to mourn his death. And, Viljoen knew that Koch wouldn't sit still. He would go after Krige.

Taking the ashtray with him, Viljoen went into the hall and paged through the phone book. On an envelope he jotted down the names and numbers of four people, all members of the party and, aside from Richter, Koch's closest friends, those he would turn to for help. He was about to ring one of them when the phone went and he wavered before lifting it.

It was a public phonebox and he felt for his cigarettes as the routine mechanics of the system cleared the line.

'Yes,' he said when the noise ceased.

'Muller?' said the voice at the other end.

'No. He's not here,' returned Viljoen. 'Can I help?'

'Where is he? It's important.'

Certain of who it was, Viljoen replied: 'Krige. My name is Viljoen. Muller worked for me in the party. We must talk.'

The silence was tangible. Viljoen went on, not needing an answer when he was sure who he was talking to. 'There's someone gunning for us. He's well informed, and he'll get to you.'

'My name is as you guessed,' said Krige. 'How much do you know about this business?'

'I know as much as Muller,' said Viljoen. 'Where are you?'

Again, there was silence, and then: 'I'll see you now. I have to trust you.'

'You can.' Viljoen heard the connection go and walked into the lounge, stopping when he could see the street. It was 7.30. Somewhere out there the killer roamed. He wondered what kind of man he was. He was certainly a clean operator, intelligent and deadly. The group could use someone like that. From a cut-away holster behind his hip he pulled out a snub-nosed .38 Special revolver and released the cylinder, checking the six rounds. The gun sheathed, he let himself out and went to the gate. He looked up and down the road, not sure from which direction Krige would come. Ten minutes went by before a green jeep pulled into the road from the north and parked a way up on the verge. Viljoen had never seen Krige and he watched the tall, powerful frame of the advancing figure. As the farmer neared he said. 'Krige?'

Krige gave a nod, wiping his hand over his clothes, the rings under his eyes and growth on his cheeks projecting him in a debauched light. Viljoen led him into the house and through the hall to the kitchen. He showed Krige to a chair and put some water on to boil.

'I can see you're tired,' he said. 'I don't regret what

we asked you to do. It was of the greatest importance, which I'm sure you realize.'

'Where's Muller?' said Krige. 'He's my contact.'

'Muller's dead,' said Viljoen, scattering ash. 'There was a leak before you left.'

Krige thrust himself back. 'What do you mean a leak?' he said. 'This operation was only known to us. What the hell's going on?' He grated the chair as he came to his feet, banging his fist on the table. 'Come to the point.'

Viljoen made a soothing gesture. 'Relax, my friend. It's not as bad as you think. You're safe.' He didn't add his doubts.

Krige sat back into the chair, weighing up Viljoen. 'Safe? I want answers. I'm not one of your gangsters.'

Viljoen paled under his tan, unused to such aggressive bluntness. 'Stay there and I'll tell you,' he said savagely. 'Until this thing is through we're together, and then you're a free man.'

'I'll listen, but I want the truth,' said Krige brutally.

Viljoen seated himself warily. He resumed in his native tongue. 'According to Koch, Richter blabbed to his sister that he was involved in an important job which meant going to Durban for a couple of days. At that stage Richter didn't know any more, and certainly not Cartwright's name. She told her lover Bryant who was apparently a party member but seems now to have been a plant, National Intelligence Agency or one of the other security agencies, perhaps even the Scorpions. They've sent a guy after us, and he's a cold-blooded killer.' Viljoen paused for a deep breath and then carried on. 'When Richter and Koch returned last night they saw Muller then went to Richter's house. The killer was already there. Richter is dead.'

Krige lit a cigarette. 'They left me in Durban,' he said unsympathetically.

'I know. They behaved badly.' Viljoen went to the stove and spooned ground beans into the pot, filling it to the top with the boiling water. Without letting it brew he poured it into the mugs, setting one in front of Krige together with a bowl of sugar and a spoon.

'Koch gave the killer the slip and drove to Bryant's flat,' said Viljoen. 'He and Richter knew Bryant had sent the information on before you left Pretoria but, as I've said, it was limited and they didn't think it would affect the operation.'

Krige laughed bitterly. 'They were always a bad choice. If I had known I wouldn't have tried the second time to get the file from Cartwright. Clever men can draw conclusions from even the bare threads of information they are given. And I'm sure we're dealing with clever men.'

Viljoen raised his eyebrows. 'What do you mean, a second time?'

'Koch was obviously poor on the details he gave you,' said Krige. 'We went for Cartwright on the first night but only ended up killing his dogs. I am surprised that Bryant's boss, who must have been told about the dead dogs, didn't add it up and suspect Cartwright was somehow involved in this operation. It would have been logical to stick a fence around him, or put him in a safe house.'

'We can only speculate,' said Viljoen. 'All I know is that someone is methodically killing those who were involved.'

'Where's Bryant?' said Krige. 'He must know that this guy is loose amongst us.'

Viljoen grinned like a clown. 'Koch saw him stretched out in his flat. It looked as if his neck was broken. Anyway, he was dead.' The grin departed respectfully. 'Koch came here and found Muller dying. He had been shot. Whoever did it is in a hurry because he didn't bother to finish Muller off before he left.'

Krige left the dregs in his mug and shoved it away. 'What else does he know?' he said. 'Why am I supposed to be "safe", as you so elegantly put it? We don't know what Muller told his killer.'

Viljoen looked at him steadily. 'Koch said he and Richter only knew of your existence after Richter leaked the information to his sister. Bryant concluded Richter was part of the team. It must have been obvious. And Koch, he was Richter's closest friend and it wouldn't have taken a master brain to deduce that he would also be implicated.'

'What are you doing about it?' asked Krige, switching to the present. He had been told enough.

'The killings will be made public through the press as an unprovoked attack on innocent people. I will also get lawyers involved. But I'm not releasing anything in the press at the moment. I want to wait and lure the guy in.' Viljoen reached behind him and replenished the mugs. 'Sooner or later the killer will have another shot at Koch. It is essential that he does not reveal anything about the file. I've told him to stay with a friend but I've also posted a couple of men up at his house. The man, if we find him, will be dealt with privately.'

'Where's Koch now?' asked Krige.

'As I said, he's gone to ground, a friend's place,' said Viljoen. 'I don't know where, but he'll contact me.'

'All very clever,' said Krige coldly. 'That leaves me. How can I be certain our assassin hasn't got my name on his list?'

'Koch…' started Viljoen.

'Screw Koch,' rasped Krige. 'He'd trade his children if it suited him. He left me to grill. That's not exactly affection.' He added caustically: 'Or do you see it differently?'

'We can never be certain,' conceded Viljoen. 'As far as I'm concerned, you're out of it. Remain on the farm.'

Krige laughed mirthlessly. 'And wait until you find him, or he finds me. What do I do with my wife?'

'You have little choice,' said Viljoen. 'When he makes another move we'll get him.' He got up from his chair. 'Now with all that cleared up we get to the most important item on this agenda. Did you get the file?'

'No, unfortunately Cartwright was killed before he could tell me where I could find it,' said Krige. 'He was with a male friend of his when I first confronted them. I killed the other guy and went after Cartwright who had gone upstairs. It was dark and he came at me from behind, opened fire, and I retaliated out of pure instinct. He hit me in the leg but my aim was more accurate. It's as simple as that. I searched the place but couldn't find what we went there for, the file. I then had to get out and meet Richter and Koch. But they didn't show, as you know, and I returned to Pretoria on the night train.' Krige looked at Viljoen evenly. 'I'm sorry I didn't get the file. I don't like failing on a job I have undertaken to do.'

'I'm sorry as well,' said Viljoen. He added philosophically: 'But there is no room in this life for regrets, you just learn and move on. I don't believe Cartwright had the time to digest the contents of the file, which for a lawyer would have been his first action, and therefore no time in which to make certified copies, the logical next step. That means the file exists somewhere, and it might never be found, except by his family, and they won't know what it's about. They'll probably think it's more of his legal work.'

'Can you take that risk?' said Krige.

'You are right,' said Viljoen. 'We can't take the risk but I'm not going to send in men like you again. I plan to assign lawyers to the case and instruct them to get involved with Cartwright's family. In other words, they will act as executors of Cartwright's estate and have access to his effects. We have very strong contacts in the legal profession in Durban and I'll now use them.'

'Why didn't you use them in the first place, rather than get me involved?' said Krige.

'Cartwright was still alive then, but now he is dead,' said Viljoen. 'The game has changed, and the previous methods that could have worked with a bit of luck are now defunct. We have to try a different approach, like the one I have described.'

'Very clever,' said Krige. He went to the door. 'I'll ring you daily at your farm. I want to know everything you're doing to remove this guy in our midst. Then I don't want to hear from you or your group again. And make sure Koch shuts his mouth.'

For a while Viljoen dwelt on his mug. Then he gave Krige a cryptic look. 'You have my word,' he said, and watched Krige. An intelligent, experienced man like Krige, and forewarned of a deadly threat, was the most dangerous species alive. He didn't want to be in the killer's shoes if they ever met, but if they did he relished the thought of being there as an observer.

Chapter 14

Near the Kruger Reserve

On the north-eastern perimeter of Pretoria, Koch took the grey Toyota onto the freeway. During the previous three hours he had slept badly, but he was on a high and did not feel the need for more rest. The day was overcast with threatening rain clouds filling the sky and he increased his speed on the empty road, wanting to cover as much mileage as he could before the inevitable storm. He was no stranger to the vast tract of low veld that comprised the farming district west of the Kruger Reserve. Over the years he had hunted the southern part during the season and he was familiar with the general area that included Krige's farm.

The rain started shortly after he left the freeway for White River and the wipers struggled to cope with the water that beat on his windscreen in a deluge. He reduced his speed to a crawl and wrapped himself around the wheel, his eyes glued to the road, visibility down to 50 metres. The rain continued for the next 10 kilometres, through White River, and then abated a little, settling into a downpour that seemed as if it wanted to stay for days. Then, 7 kilometres north of the town, he saw the turn-off to Krige's farm and two others, but he kept going, thankful for the strip of macadam that made driving easier in the poor conditions.

Five kilometres further on and just before Hectorspruit,

a one-store town with hotel and bar, Koch turned off the tar onto an irrigated dirt road. A sign nailed to a fence simply said 'Leeuveld'. It was the name of the farm belonging to Claasen, Krige's western neighbour.

When Steiner reached the town of White River he rolled to a stop at the store. He crossed the raised planking and went in. Diagonally from the door, he saw a man standing on a ladder behind the long counter, digging into one of hundreds of cardboard boxes on the shelves. There were about a dozen blacks in the store, and he went to the white, past bags of flour and *mielie* meal, and various cans of food. The man twisted on his ladder as Steiner approached, the veins on his hands standing out like blue rivers as he held the rails. He was an old man, known locally as Oom, and the flesh on his cheek hung in folds that reached below his jaw. But his weathered, aged appearance was at odds with the alert piercing yellow eyes that lurked below his heavy brow.

Steiner spoke first, resting his hand on the glass counter, above an assortment of poor-quality folding knives. 'Good morning,' said Steiner. 'I'm a visitor in these parts.' He smiled, disarmingly.

Oom turned and climbed down the ladder. 'Yes Mister?' he said in a husky wheeze. 'I have everything in my store.' He had spent much of his life running the business and he was proud of its contribution to the local farming community. His father had farmed further south for as long as he could remember, but the harshness and uncertainty of the life had never appealed to Oom and he had seized the opportunity to purchase the store, 40 years previously and in those days a small fraction of the present size.

'I've a friend in these parts,' said Steiner without deliberating. 'We were in the police together, nearly ten years ago.' He spread his fingers on the glass. 'I want to surprise him.'

Oom came closer. He looked at the hands on the counter. He always did. Over the years he had come to categorize farmers by their hands, the roughness and raw strength of a man born on the veld to the fresh abrasions of a novice. Clearly the man he faced was neither, for his hands were smooth except, he observed, for the slight callouses that lay on the first two knuckles and stretched like corn tissue to the base of the little fingers. The hands were unlike any he had seen before, obviously trained for something hard, but as delicate as an artist's.

'Who's the friend?' he asked, lifting his eyes.

'Krige, Jan Krige,' answered Steiner immediately. 'We were very close. I believe he married a woman from here.'

'Jan Krige, I knew his father,' said Oom, looking past Steiner, reviving his memory. 'He was one of the first in this district. Jan is like him, bold and proud. He has a beautiful wife and lovely sons.' He focused again on Steiner. 'The farm is north of here, maybe twenty minutes. Call him, he'll meet you.' Extending a gnarled forefinger, he pointed to the public phonebox over the road.

Steiner grinned. 'I want to surprise him,' he repeated, glancing at the shelves. 'Do you have something for his wife, chocolates or something that would please her? I don't know her name.'

'Kirsty,' said Oom. 'She's not from here, but she's strong in mind like her husband.'

'Where can I find the farm?' said Steiner. 'I want to get on. He'll be glad to see me.'

Oom detected a hint of superciliousness, impatience. He attributed it to Steiner's eagerness to go, but he still did not like it. 'Take this road. You'll see a sign, Krige. They never called the farm anything. That's a pity. It's the best around.'

Steiner hid his annoyance. It was so simple. He could have found it without help, earlier. He started to walk from the counter.

'What about the chocolates? They're the best,' said Oom.

Steiner ignored the old man and quickened his pace. Enough time had been wasted.

'Pig,' muttered Oom, taking his pipe from under the counter. He poked his stained finger into the bowl of burnt tobacco. 'No manners. He's not a friend.' He lit the hardened leaf, alternately pressing into the bowl with his thumb, thoughtful, and went back to his shelves.

An hour-and-a-quarter after Koch took his car onto the freeway in Pretoria, Krige joined the same road at a junction closer to the city. He damned Richter's indiscretion and for a moment he had thought of making enquiries amongst those in the security services he once knew. But he was now a killer, and under the transition men had been replaced, allegiances changed, and the chance of exposure was too great. And whoever had killed Richter and Muller would be working in the greatest secrecy, with only a few at most privy to the operation. He also recognized that Viljoen could not give him any protection. He was on his own, and glad that he had given the file, with the instructions, to his lawyer. For him, that was infinitely satisfying, and justification for doing the job, even though he never thought that he would do what he had done. He had to admire the way they had hit back rapidly, no fuss with a heavy-handed police investigation, simply a man working alone, going from one to the other and silently going about the murderous job to which he had been assigned.

The rain came when he was 50 minutes along the road

and he stopped the vehicle on the side, waiting for it to die down. He rested his wounded leg on the seat, trying to give it relief. Viljoen had not seen it, although he had alluded to it, and he wanted it like that. It was a blemish that tied him to the work in Natal, and the fewer people who knew about it the better. None of them could be trusted. Ideally it needed stitches, but they were out of the question. Any doctor would have his suspicions aroused. And then there was his wife. She would soon see it but he trusted her more than anyone to keep quiet.

He shook out his last cigarette and slid the window along a little to vent the smoke. Before he had taken the last drag the clouds dispersed, reducing the ferocity of the rain and he pulled out, keeping in the slow lane. A few cars flashed by, throwing up an iridescent spray and he swore at them, wondering what kind of madness went through their heads.

Travelling at below the speed limit, he finally saw the entrance to White River. He craved a cigarette and he was thankful when a little later Oom's store appeared through the rain. The old man was serving when he went in, and he hung around at the near end of the counter where the selection of cigarettes and pipe tobacco lay untidily on a shelf.

'Ah, Jan Krige, where have you been?' Oom hobbled along the counter to the till, a warm smile on his cracked lips. 'Your wife was here yesterday. I haven't seen her for months.' He threw coins into the tray and reached for a carton of Texans. He knew Krige's brand.

'Business,' said Krige taking the pack, as always so perfectly wrapped in cellophane. 'I had to leave the farm.'

Oom took the 5-rand note and went back to the till. 'Someone wanted to know how to find your place,' he said jerking, down the handle of the obsolete machine.

'That was less than thirty minutes ago. He said he was a close friend of yours from years ago.'

As if pierced by a lance, Krige stared at Oom. 'What did you tell him?' he said.

'I told him to phone you from the box, but he insisted on surprise.' Oom lifted his frail shoulders defensively. 'I gave him what he wanted. He was a strange man, and his hands...'

'What about his hands?' said Krige.

'They were delicate but with thick skin here, which was most unusual.' Oom touched his largest knuckles and ran his fingers along the top. 'He was...'

But Krige was already on the move, sprinting for the door, forgetting the pain in his leg. He went over the pavement, landing in the squelching mud that clung viscously to him. In seconds he was through and across the road, clawing for the handle on the phonebox.

He dialled the number of the farm. The wait for the call to connect was interminable, and he ripped the cellophane from the carton of cigarettes. The phone started to ring and he held the packet of 20 to his teeth, tearing off the silver paper strip. With one hand he levered out a cigarette and lit it, pulling deeply on the acrid smoke. The phone went on ringing and fear for his wife's safety constricted his stomach like a gin-trap. Banging down the receiver, he bolted from the box for the vehicle. Oom stood in the doorway, clasping his body abjectly, but Krige ran past him and leapt into the seat of the jeep. The tyres spewed mud, eating through to hard earth, and then they touched the tar, projecting the vehicle with a high-pitched wail towards the farm.

To the north of Claasen's substantial acreage, Koch went along the main track that he came across. From memory he assessed his position, and when he felt he had gone far enough he took to the veld in an easterly direction. Clearance on the car was higher than most, but barely sufficient to deal with the obstinate terrain, and he winced each time unseen rock and mounds of brick-hard earth slammed into the underbelly of the metal chassis. It could have been worse, he told himself, for the ground was mostly level, unlike parts he had encountered before where scabious boulders and dense thickets of thorn were an impenetrable screen. Occasionally he saw antelope and he grinned, for they did not flee, somehow understanding in their peculiar way that he was not hunting them.

After what seemed an age, with 2 kilometres on the clock since he left the track, Koch came to a fence, the partly corroded wire between crude wooden posts almost invisible in the dappled setting. He pointed the car back the way he had come and got out, filling his lungs with the perfumed air. Beyond 150 metres, the car was invisible through the grass and scattered knobthorn and *matsondi* trees, as were man and beast. He plucked his jacket from the seat and opened the boot. Nestling in a scabbard was a superb rifle, a Mauser in mint condition and chambered for the 7 mm Remington magnum cartridge. It was perfect for what he had in mind, and he drew the weapon from the boot. He peeled off the bag and tapped the telescopic sight pensively. He remembered sighting it for 300 metres, and like all scopes it was ideal for long range, but he did not think it would be of use to him so he dismantled it, placing it in a corner of the boot. His work would be conducted at far closer range. Sliding the ten-shot magazine from its housing, he added a round, and with the gun soldier-like on his shoulder set off towards the fence.

* * *

Less than 3 kilometres south-west of Koch's parked car, Steiner brought his own vehicle to a halt. Minutes earlier he had passed through the gate leading onto Krige's land, and now in the distance over a plain of ripe tobacco he saw the tall barns in an oasis of trees. They were in a cluster to the left of a *kopje* that he guessed obscured the house and sheds on the other side. The crop occupied a significant part of the land in his view, swathed between rows of bluegum trees that neatly sectioned the fields. On his right the ground climbed to a low arboreal ridge that extended down the flank of the shallow valley like the spine of a dinosaur, eventually curving towards the Kruger Reserve.

The only people in sight were a group of pickers in the field beyond the first line of trees. He studied the scene for a while then turned the car onto the veld. Within 100 metres he found what he wanted, a *donga* that dropped a couple of metres to its lowest point on the flat bed. Wary of getting trapped in soft soil he walked into the depression, testing the cohesive strength of the earth at intervals. Satisfied, he returned to the car and let it roll down the gradient, braking it when the bank rose above the roof.

After retrieving the Glock, he moved off at a run along the length of the *donga*, gradually coming to higher ground. He kept to the trees as much as he could, and soon he was climbing the lower slope of the hill. Little by little he could see the other farm buildings and he was able to make out the roof of the house and some of the sheds between it and the barns. He went a third of the way up the hill, then levelled out, striding evenly, his feet skilfully finding the spots that made his passage easier. After a time he rested, looking out over the plain to the *kopje* and the house. The pickers were still the only people he saw.

When the noise came he dropped like a stone, moving his body to get closer to the earth. It was the noise of a vehicle, the engine revving hard through the low gears. He could see the entire length of track, across the plain to the *kopje*, but there was nothing. He raised his head, finding it difficult to judge the direction of sound, then to his left a jeep shot into the open, ejaculating a mud-tinged spray in its slipstream. The driver was tall, his head nearly touching the roof, and he gripped the wheel violently as he pushed the engine into the red.

As the jeep came to the buildings it went behind the *kopje*. For a while the diminished sound continued and then it was cut, leaving only a hush in the valley.

Once through the fence, Koch was on Krige's land, and he lumbered over the veld in a westerly direction expecting in a couple of kilometres to come to the main buildings. He first glimpsed the long shed where Krige stored his machinery, and then a little further on he saw the rear of the house itself. He carried on and saw the tall barns, almost hidden by small outhouses and a row of bluegum trees next to the orchard. The *kopje* poked above the shed, the rocky silhouette a divergence against the geometric lines of the roof.

For a few minutes he watched from a shelter of bush. There was no indication of life except a laminar emission of smoke from the kitchen chimneys and he went closer, moving quickly between points that obscured him from the house.

When he was near the long shed a black woman carrying a pot and mug left the back of the house, two dogs bounding expectantly around her, and walked across the yard. They vanished for a moment and then he saw them moving through the orchard to what he assumed were the servants' quarters, a longitudinal four-door structure in a clearing. They went in and after a minute when they did not reappear he sprinted over the open to the shed and entered through a door at the end. Three tractors stood in the middle, and various implements were on shelves and suspended in racks. The shed was more than a storehouse, for a workbench and heavy-duty machine tools occupied a quarter of it. He moved the length of the shed to the window nearest to the house. Laying the rifle on a pile of sacks, he got close to the dirty glass. He could see the back and some of the front yard, the worn patch where he knew Krige parked his car. It was not there.

He looked again to the back where a few outhouses had been erected, red-brick and corrugated, in need of renovation. At the end a lean-to stood like an afterthought, aged timbers supporting a flat roof. Poking out of the ramshackle shelter and just visible was the tail of a small car. A prurient grin lined his face. Kirsty, Krige's wife, how had he forgotten.

Folding up the cuff of his jacket, he checked his watch, unashamed desire for her body already dominating his thoughts and obscuring his judgement and the reason for which he was there. But he reasoned that the absence of Krige's car surely meant he had failed to get out.

With the departure of her husband, Kirsty Krige had dutifully gone about her chores, grimly trying to dispel the fears she had for his safety. She longed for his return, the resumption of a normal life, and she hoped he would phone and say he was coming home. But by the second evening she had not heard from him and the worry built up inside her, sending her into a spiral of depression. In an open nightshirt and pants she finally went to sleep on the settee, the verandah doors open to allow in cool air and provide relief from the heat.

She overslept and woke with a start when Claasen's half-ton pickup entered the yard. Covering her breasts, she sped to her room, appearing later on the verandah, barefoot and in a blouse and short skirt. Claasen was a lean powerful man in his sixties and his handsome craggy face broke into a grin when he saw her dishevelled state.

'Kirsty, my dear,' he said. 'Did I disturb you?'

She shook her head apologetically, a little embarrassed. 'No, you are always welcome Meneer.' She addressed him formally, in keeping with the respect she and her husband had for the older man.

He halted at the steps, his gaze going swiftly down the length of her figure. She was one of the most attractive women he had seen, and he wished he had met her as a younger man. His wife had died tragically of cancer years before, a protracted painful death, and he had never remarried.

She turned to go and get coffee, but he stopped her. 'I'm not staying. I hope everything is alright.' Beyond him she saw a team of men lugging their tools to the fields. It was a comforting sight.

'Jan will be grateful that you came,' she said, coming up to the rail. 'You're very kind.'

'It is nothing,' he protested, touching his felt hat and going to the truck.

She watched as the vehicle went past her to the private road that joined the two farms. The truck had soon gone and she went into the house. She felt better after seeing Claasen. The man had a quiet towering strength that she found consoling.

The rain came as she was brushing her hair in her room, and she listened to the drumming on the iron roof, like the noise from thousands of rivets being driven methodically into their predrilled holes. It was a satisfying sound, with the soil powder-dry from a particularly hot spell.

But the thundering lasted only minutes, and she looked with disappointment at the insipid shower that took its place. She finished in the room, her sleek hair tied in a ponytail and her face lightly made up, and she went to the kitchen. It was mid-morning and Maria was leaving through the screen with her breakfast and a mug of sweet tea. The dogs were squatting patiently for her in the rain, and when they saw her they began romping excitedly, eager for the morsels she always gave them while she ate, even though their stomachs were full from the large bowls of food they had just eaten.

Kirsty stayed in the kitchen, preparing venison for the freezer, working on a low table set along the wall where the ceiling came down to head height. It was a spot she loved, for it had an excellent view of the orchard that she and her husband had spent hours planning and nurturing. Through the multi-paned window she saw Maria and the dogs walking between the trees, the three eventually hidden by a runner-bean trellis that isolated the woman's quarters from the house.

A little further away, the machine shed lay perpendicular to the house. It had been built by Jan's father with a vision of future growth, a requirement for self-sufficiency in the maintenance of heavy equipment the farm would require. She never went into it, her understanding of mechanical things vague, but she recognized the vital part it played in the successful running of a large mechanized farm.

Skilfully she cut the meat into cubes, removing surplus fat and laying the tender pieces in a small pile. She had nearly completed the task when she glimpsed movement through the nearest window of the shed. At first she thought she was mistaken. Only her husband and two others ever went inside, and all three were away. Then the movement came again, forcing a cry from her as it transformed into a face, one she would never forget, that of Johannes Koch.

She dropped the knife onto the table with a clatter and stepped back. For a moment she was stock still, transfixed by what she saw, her fist held like a baby's to her mouth. The presence of the man, and fear for her husband, heaved her stomach and she gulped at the influx of tension. His nose was on the glass and his attention was held by something in the yard. She glanced through the screens. There was nothing there except the small sheds. She looked to where she had seen him but he was gone, as suddenly as he had appeared.

Near panic enveloped her, and she leaned over the diced meat, checking the area around the shed. She thought of the dogs, wishing they had stayed, and then flung herself into the passage. She fell to her knee but pushed herself up and ran on, making little sound on the carpeted boards, and in a dozen paces reached the study. She could see part of the lounge, the verandah doors, and she stopped, despairingly trying to decide what to do. But he was out there somewhere, perhaps already at the house and coming to the front, and she burst into the room. On the wall was the gun cabinet, and she went to it, knocking her thigh on the desk, reaching for the large handle that jutted boldly from the gleaming wood. She tugged but it held fast, and the hope that it had been left unlocked was gone in one crucifying blow.

She fled from the study and bolted down the passage to the lounge, wanting to get out onto the veld. She paused at the entrance, looking about for Koch. He was not there and she carried on, running to the door that filtered into the second part of the house, her canvas shoes skimming the floor like a carpenter's plane. She was nearly there when she knew she was not alone. Turning, finding it excruciating to breathe, she saw him, an erect gross figure, one foot on the porch, the rifle supported loosely at his waist. He came in, unsmiling, and she screamed, a cry that pierced the tranquility like a visitation from hell.

In measured steps Koch advanced, his dirty boots discarding chunks of chocolate mud. 'Shut up,' he said icily. 'Scream any more and I'll kill you.'

She gaped at him, her shallow breathing pumping her chest out and in, unable to believe what was happening. There was no question that he was a violent man who would beat her, or kill her, if she disobeyed.

'What do you want?' she said softly, recoiling involuntarily as he got closer, and forcing herself to be calm. 'Where's my husband?'

He gave an unpleasant laugh. 'He's of no importance,' he answered, putting the rifle on a chair. 'It's just you and me.' He groped for the buckle on his belt and plucked the hook from the hole in the leather.

'No!' Her scream hit him. She sensed a chance and ran for the porch. She could see he was stunned and she straightened her path to shorten the distance. It took her closer to him and in a few steps she was abreast, her unquenched desire for escape diluting his pervasive presence. He was still immobile and she increased her stride, her hopes soaring like drops of water coming to the crest of a wave.

Then with the incisiveness of a surgeon's knife he reached out with a long arm, his fingers encircling her wrist like a vice. He pulled, his knotted muscles rippling under his skin. With a whimper she strained to get loose but he was on her, bowling her over with his primitive strength.

She collapsed under his leaden weight, the hem of her skirt billowing immodestly to the top of her pants. She wriggled beneath him, her fists beating his chest, but he took no notice, instead pulling at her clothes, her all-woman smell fuelling him. Using little of his strength he ripped the buttons from her blouse, gulping like a toad at the vision of her breasts pounding in her bra.

In an effort to wrest from him, she rolled her buttocks and struck up with her knee. But he was too quick and twisting at the waist he deflected the leg adroitly with his fist. 'Lie still,' he said, 'or I'll kill you.' He took off his jacket and unholstered his revolver.

She had not seen it before and it made her realize he would have his way even if it meant killing her. Placing the weapon next to him, he fed his hand underneath her, and unclasped the bra, becoming gentler as he neared his goal. He applied his mouth to the warm bare glands, his tongue mercurially sensitive and tender, delighting in the satin texture of the skin with a thrill that charged him to his marrow. Closing her eyes, she turned, revolted by the wet of his spit, the sour breath that came over her. She prayed for release, vainly trying to detach herself from the hell that mortal life had become.

For a while his giant palms caressed her chest, ineptly plying her nipples to make them stiff. He licked noisily, laying his saliva in a glutinous trail and then took his hand to the valley between her legs. His breathing intensified and he came up on his knees, undoing the buttons on his fly and taking his trousers down as far as they would go. She was deathly still, her slim arms held pathetically over her face, and he reached for his jockstrap.

Engrossed by the heat in his groin Koch did not hear the drone of the four-cylinder engine until the vehicle neared the *kopje*. He looked up and growled in frustration. He looked at her half-naked body before him. She had also heard and instantly recognized the unmistakable sound, but her longing hope for her husband was replaced by dread. That he was alive she had dared not conceive, but even now with him surely close they were still separated by the enemy, in the form of Koch.

Rising quickly to his feet, Koch pulled up his trousers, jerked up the fly, and fastened the belt. 'Get up,' he said angrily. 'It'll have to wait. I'm sure you know who that is.' He took the gun, pointing to the corner next to the doors. 'Move over there and shut up,' he said. 'Any sound from you and you'll die.' He pushed her, like an unrestrained bully in a school playground.

She complied, the muzzle of the weapon stabbing her like a spike on the low reaches of her spine. With Kirsty where he wanted her, Koch retrieved the rifle and lowered himself behind the settee so he could see the middle section of the yard. Loading a cartridge into the chamber, he balanced the rifle on a cushion, then took the pistol. As he stilled himself, the jeep careered into the yard.

Using the co-driver's door, Krige bolted from the vehicle and went up the steps to the porch, careful as he came to the entrance, the Beretta ready. He deliberated, and then walked nearer. On the carpet he noticed the mud from Koch's boots. Someone had been there, not long ago, the mud was still wet. He looked at the worn section going into the passage. It was clean.

As he moved up to the wall the noise came from Koch's gun. Before it ceased Krige had dived into the room. He saw his wife, arms flung out in a wanton plea, and then the leer of Koch.

Koch's head was poking up like an infant playing hide and seek, his forearms supported on the sofa, and he brought the weapon onto his foe. The gun belched, blowing out another suffocating stench of smokeless powder. The 140-grain slug caught Krige in the deltoid muscle, knocking him back as if he had been kicked by a mule. The Beretta was pulled from him as if by an invisible hand. Kirsty Krige jumped up and ran to him, not caring if Koch shot her in the back. She dropped to her husband, flattening herself over him, stroking his head and drawing it to her neck. He embraced her, pressing her breasts against his shirt.

Full of confidence, Koch came from behind the sofa, his cheeks cleaved by a malignant grin. 'You didn't expect me, Krige,' he said. 'You thought someone else was here, maybe the one who killed Muller.'

Krige lifted his wife off him. 'I always knew I couldn't trust you,' he said, 'and that friend of yours.'

Koch's grin spread. 'How much does your wife know, Krige, about your nocturnal habits?'

Krige glanced at her, ashamed, but she held him as if she had not heard. He saw the Beretta lying there beyond his reach. He had to get it.

'I'm going to kill you, Krige,' said Koch, removing the shells and filling the cylinder. 'Then it's me and her. We were only starting when you barged in.'

'Viljoen will castrate you,' said Krige, moving innocuously on the carpet. His chances were poor, but he couldn't give up without trying. 'Everything you wanted out of the party is fouled up because of your hate.'

Koch laughed. 'He'll never know. He thinks I'm in the city.' He circled, scrutinizing his intended victims, salivating on what was to come. He did not hear the dull scrape on the red stone outside but when it came again he turned his head a little, all the while watching Krige.

Krige had also heard it, and he remembered what Oom had said. Koch's hands were smooth from city life. It had not been him at the store. He touched at the bleeding and bundled his shirt against it to help arrest the flow.

Bit by bit he started to roll his body over, preparing for what to him was imminent.

When the scrape was not repeated, Koch relaxed and the grin returned. 'For a moment I thought someone had come to save you, Krige,' he said. Koch advanced, hungrily appraising the unblemished skin of Kirsty's back. She had calmed herself, wanting to care for her husband, but quiet, waiting, sensing his readiness and that he was going to go for the Beretta.

When the shadow fell into the room, Koch's hand tensed round the butt, conceding that he should have checked the porch. He was about to turn with the gun, then thought better of it, cautiously revolving only his head instead to the intruder. When he saw the man who had killed Richter, his ambitions evaporated like milk spilling onto a heated grate.

'Release the gun,' said Steiner. 'I should have got you before.' The Glock was raised a little from the vertical.

'And if I don't?' said Koch. If he dropped the gun his chances of getting out alive were slim, but so was the alternative of trying to outgun this nemesis.

There were several feet between them, and Steiner took another pace. 'You've only one option,' he said, 'but you don't like that either.' As he spoke he redistributed his weight and came up with a kick that pounded Koch's wrist like a baseball bat wielded by a professional.

Koch let the magnum go, contorting like a man inebriated after a night on the town. He was helpless, the hope that Steiner would somehow be diverted finally dying in him as the butt of the Glock hit him on the neck, sending him back as if caught in the blast from a fireman's hose.

The attack took Krige by surprise and when he thought of the gun, Koch was already down, holding his throat as if his fingers would provide an antidote. Steiner stood motionless, as if nothing had occurred, the Glock returned to where it was when he came in. His composure told Krige he dared not make a move, that Steiner was monitoring every stroke. His wife was still clinging to him, transfixed by the clinical assault that had materialized so theatrically before her. Suddenly she relaxed, as if giving in to her despondency.

Coughing on the internal bleeding, Koch lay on the carpet, dribbling tainted saliva onto his collar. Steiner observed his work, dissatisfaction in his eyes like opaque screens.

'He should be dead,' he said. He sighted the Glock and fired once into the body, then let the weapon hang. He went to the Beretta and picked it up. After a while he said: 'This is very neat. You must be good with it, Cartwright and the other guy. Was it worth it?' He lifted the Glock. 'Now is the time to settle the debt,' he said.

With a demented cry, Kirsty hugged her husband, smothering him with her chest. 'Leave him alone,' she cried. 'He means everything to me.' She wept, holding him beneath her like an animal over its young. Krige moved her clear, returning Steiner's stare.

Memories of the killings flashed through him. It had gone a full circle, except that the man in front of him held the gun. 'You're no better,' he said quietly. 'You're just like the rest of us. We're all killers, whatever the cause.' The words were suspended like stale smoke.

'I'm sure you know why I'm here,' said Steiner. 'I want the file you took from Cartwright's house before you killed him.' He looked at Kirsty. Seldom had he seen such an attractive woman, her long dark hair, flawless features and perfect voluptuous shape. He returned to Krige. 'I went to Cartwright's house when his body was still warm, like the body of his friend downstairs in the lounge. You took something from Cartwright's safe and Muller told me what you had gone there to retrieve. It doesn't take brains to put the two together and conclude that you got it, the file. And Richter and Koch were not involved, probably because you couldn't stand their company, which is no surprise to me.' He walked closer, ignoring Kirsty's look of abject appeal. 'Give me the file and I'll go,' he said. 'You and your wife will never hear from me again.'

'I don't have it,' said Krige, incongruously beginning to like Steiner, his obvious intelligence and the way he worked. They were of the same breed, distinct from types like Richter and Koch. 'The file which you rightly conclude I retrieved is with my lawyer.'

Steiner believed him, and wondered where he could go from now. He couldn't kill the man, there was no point, and he would have little chance of achieving the success he wanted in this job by now going after the lawyer. 'What is your lawyer going to do with it?' asked Steiner.

Krige came to his feet, not badly hurt by the bullet from Koch's gun. 'When I saw my lawyer and gave him the file, I instructed him to wait for three days and, if he did not hear anything to the contrary from me in that time, to send it to the Directorate of Special Operations, the Scorpions, and then the international press, starting with the *Guardian* in London and the *New York Times*.

'Very clever,' said Steiner. 'And are you going to change your mind? The options, if you stop the release of the file as you have stated, are that it dies with you or you return it to your masters.'

Kirsty Krige had remained silent, quickly understanding what this was all about, and then she said: 'It has to go to the DSO. The other bastards do not deserve to get it back, after the cruelty they perpetrated during those years of oppression.' She did not know what was in the file but she sensed that it was damning and that Muller's group had compiled it, and it had been sent to the wrong hands. And that was why her husband had been approached, quite simply to retrieve it. Everything was coming together.

Krige moved towards Steiner and stopped several feet away. 'The file will be delivered to the Scorpions and then the press as I originally intended,' he said, unequivocally. 'The men in the group who asked me to retrieve it, will not know how it got there. Even with Cartwright's death, his wife could have found it and, with her contacts, realized its importance and passed it on. Or it is conceivable that Cartwright acted as soon as he received the document, and gave it to people in high places with instructions to have it certified and given to the press and the DSO.'

Steiner stared at Krige for a moment and then said: 'I'm satisfied that you will go ahead as you first planned. If not, I or someone else will come looking for you.'

'Who are you working for?' said Krige. 'It's not the police, so it must be one of the intelligence agencies. And what's your name?'

Steiner smiled. 'My name is Steiner, James Steiner. I'm doing this work for the Scorpions. Richter's sister told Bryant, who was a DSO plant in this group up here, that her brother had a crucial job to do in Durban. He passed that on to his boss in Durban. She then said that a prominent lawyer was at the centre of things. When you and the others killed Cartwright's dogs, Bryant's boss concluded that he was the lawyer and that you people were after something a lot more important than his death. Of course he was right. Now I must go.' He bowed his head slightly to Kirsty Krige.

Steiner went round Krige to Koch. He gathered the magnum perfunctorily, and went to the step leading onto the porch. He addressed Krige. 'You're right. We're all dogs, killer dogs. For whatever reason that's what we are, ensnared by the circumstances that caught us. By the way, I'll keep the Beretta, it's the best I've ever seen.' He put the Glock away and turned to leave. As his boot touched the stone, the quiet in the yard was split by the supersonic crackle from a high-powered gun.

Steiner jolted like a condemned man tied to the post, taking the impact where the shoulder joined the chest. He went limply for the Glock, detachment on his face as if he had expected it finally to happen like this. Then in a resurgence of strength he fell into the room, tumbling over and over until he regained his feet. For a moment he flexed his shoulder, testing the damage. Although he was losing blood he was satisfied it was superficial and he looked through the window into the yard.

Running to the house from the *kopje* were three men, abreast and a few metres from each other. Two held Kalashnikov AK47s to their shirts while the third, the middle one, held only his hat, a felt Borsalino that he waved up and down in synchronization with his stride.

Krige's wife went to him and the pair watched Steiner as he came from the window. 'Your friends have arrived, Krige,' he said. 'Perhaps they aren't your friends, but my business is closed.' He went to the passage then said: 'Goodbye Mrs Krige, you're a great woman.'

As Krige heard Steiner reach the kitchen he moved hurriedly, tenderly unlocking Kirsty's arms from his neck and retrieving her blouse that had been flung aside by Koch in his eagerness to get to her body. He draped it over her. 'Take it,' he said urgently. 'Wait in the bedroom. You've nothing more to fear.'

'I'm not leaving you,' she replied obstinately, putting on the blouse. 'I want to be here when they come in. If they're your enemy I'll confront them with you.'

Her loyalty, after what she must suspect he had been involved in, sent a feeling of remorse through him. He ran his fingers through her dishevelled hair, taking her head to his cheek. She was a woman he loved deeply. Why had he ever started it, complicd with Muller and become his hired killer? Shaming a loved one was worse than death, and he had shamed her.

When he heard the men who shot Steiner march onto the verandah, Krige didn't know for sure who they would be or who they belonged to, but his guess was right when Viljoen appeared, his suit buttons fastened, his demeanour as calm as if he was about to sit down to dinner. His lieutenants crowded him on either side, the deadly AK47s held in readiness for the unknown, but when they saw Krige and his wife, and Koch laid out, they dropped the muzzles. Their khaki clothing and combat boots were in keeping with the bush soldier, commando philosophy of their organization, contrasting with Viljoen who even under the circumstances had chosen less aggressive attire. They recognized Koch and went closer, astonished, forgetting the man who had received their bullets.

'Leave him,' commanded Viljoen, aware that Steiner had escaped. 'He's dead. The man you shot has gone. He was the killer who has been working his way through us. Go outside and wait for me. Be careful, he's hurt and may be holing up.'

The two left and Viljoen spoke to Krige. 'I arrived at the right moment,' he said with satisfaction, slapping the Borsalino against his thigh.

Krige came between Viljoen and his wife, as if wanting to keep her away from him. 'You credit yourself,' he said cuttingly. 'He was going. How do you know your men fired on the right man?'

'Wasn't he?' said Viljoen. 'Or maybe it was just coincidence that with what is going on amongst us we see a white male, who from his appearance is a stranger to these parts, standing in this room with two pistols in his hands.'

Krige nodded. The question had been pointless. He hated the whole business. 'What made you come to the farm?' he said.

'I believe Muller revealed your name to the killer,' said Viljoen. 'As I told you, it was unlikely he knew before.'

'How do you know it was Muller?' said Krige.

'When I spoke to Koch he was too evasive,' said Viljoen. After you left I checked his close friends. They hadn't seen or heard from him. After that I was sure Koch was on his way here hoping to find the killer and get rid of him. That would have meant you too, if the opportunity arose. He has no particular love for you.'

'If I'd arrived a little later he would have raped my wife,' said Krige ungratefully. 'But the man you really came for is still out there. Do you have any idea how he got here?' Krige was playing a double game. Steiner had to escape with what he knew about the file and Krige's intention to give it to the DSO. If Steiner was caught, Krige personally would be in it up to his neck, and no one would be able to save him from this group's revenge.

'No. Your jeep is the only heap of metal we saw, which indicates he's got a long walk to get to his transport. On top of that he took a pile of lead in the chest.'

'Not enough,' said Krige. 'He came up like a spiked buck. However, you're right. There's only one obvious route onto this land and that's the one I assume you took. If you didn't see a car then he would have parked it in the bush nearer the gate, on the other side of the fields. To reach it without being seen will mean a long walk.'

'Obvious?' stated Viljoen. 'How else can someone get onto the farm?'

'There's a two-wheeled track that goes west to my neighbour's farm,' said Krige. 'It comes to the only other gate in the fence. You'd need an insider's knowledge of this area to find it, which our friend doesn't have.'

Kirsty Krige listened quietly while the men spoke then came up to Krige, gently touching him. 'You should be getting after the killer,' she said to Viljoen, certain from the conversation that he was the boss of the repulsive Muller, one of those responsible for involving her husband. She carried on: 'And how did this creature get here? I take it you saw no car.' She looked at Koch's still form, without sympathy.

'Most observant Mrs Krige,' said Viljoen smoothly. 'I doubt he's familiar with this area so he must have come in where we did. Where his car is I have no clue, but we'll find it.'

'Do you know him?' she said evenly, already knowing the answer.

'Yes,' replied Viljoen brusquely. 'But I'd rather forget him. He betrayed us and I'm sorry for your distress.'

'Like hell you are,' she cried bitterly. 'You're no better, a human butcher who got my husband to do your foul work and mix in your swill. I wonder how you threatened him into doing it.'

Viljoen purpled in anger, his lips quivering as if he was about to go berserk. With an enormous effort he contained himself. 'I'm no butcher, Mrs Krige,' he said. 'One day you'll thank people like me. Now, as you suggest, I'll go and get the killer.'

'You're forgetting Koch,' she said, before he could move. 'The sight of him disgusts me. I want you to remove him.'

Krige interjected. 'I'll help you carry him into the yard. Your men can collect him later. I'm coming with you.'

'No, you can't.' Kirsty Krige went in front of him and wrapped herself around his neck like a winding scarf.

'I have to,' said Krige firmly. 'I want to see that person out there, physically taken out of our lives for good, just like this one. Only then will peace return to this place.'

She hung her head, then turned to Viljoen. 'I want a brief word with my husband, alone.'

'Carry on,' said Viljoen. 'But it has to be quick. That man is not going to hang around and we need your husband's knowledge of the area to find him.'

Krige and his wife went into the passage and he waited for her to speak.

'After what you told the man Steiner, I'm sure you are playing a double game,' she said. 'If I was that guy I would go in the least obvious direction, and then circle back to where he must have hidden his car. You must lead these men in the direction of the front gate, to at least give Steiner a chance to get ahead.'

'You sound as if you're attracted to him,' said Krige. 'If you are, I can understand why. He's extremely good-looking and utterly ruthless, characteristics that are appealing to women.'

'You know I love you,' she said, knowing he spoke the truth. 'I just don't want them to get a hold on you.'

'Leave it to me,' he said. 'They will never find Steiner.'

'Why didn't you tell me what you were involved in?' she asked. 'I would have understood. How many others know?'

He kissed her on the cheek. 'No one except Viljoen, the other two out there, my lawyer and Steiner. With these three the trail ends, and I also know that Viljoen is listed in the file.' He freed her arms from around his neck. 'Stay in the bedroom,' he said. And then, as if it had just come to him he said: 'Where are the dogs? I want them with you.'

'They went with Maria to her room,' she said. 'But no one is a danger now, certainly not James Steiner.'

'I've told her not to take the dogs to her room,' he said. 'Their place is here at the house. If she'd have listened, Koch wouldn't have got so far.'

'I'll get them,' she said, taking her arms from him. 'It's my fault.' Emotion took her and she cried: 'How was I to know this would happen?'

The patter of feet outside prompted Viljoen to go for his gun but he went rigid as the Alsatians came into the room and went past him to the passage, instantly seeing Krige. Joyfully, they leapt up to him, almost bowling him over with their combined weight, their tongues probing for a taste of his skin.

Embracing them and then tugging them off by their thick coats he got up, boyishly pleased at the unbridled welcome. 'They've got the strength of lions,' he said proudly. 'I wouldn't like to have to go against them if they didn't like me. Where's Maria?'

'Here, Master.' The black servant appeared in the doorway, holding her apron, waiting for the signal to enter. She startled slightly at seeing Koch but hurriedly directed herself to Krige, telling herself it was none of her affair. She remembered Koch from a couple of days before and had thought then that he would bring trouble. She was thankful he wasn't black. 'I heard the guns, Master,' she continued falteringly, apologizing for arriving unannounced. 'It was a big noise.'

'It's not over,' said Krige. 'Did you see anyone out the back, in the yard?'

'No, Master, the dogs would have chased him,' she said.

'Obviously,' growled Krige, chastened by the simple logic. 'I want you to stay here with the Madam. Keep Blackie inside, Caesar comes with me.' He went to Koch and took him under the armpits. 'Let's get him out,' he said to Viljoen.

They lifted Koch and carried him into the yard, half-dragging him over the damp earth to a place near the *kopje*. Leaving him sprawled on his stomach, they returned to the lounge.

Krige briefly held his wife. 'This won't take long,' he said. 'Then we're rid of the whole nasty business. I'm sorry I ever let it come into this house.'

She tried to hold him longer but he took her hands from him and walked to the passage. Viljoen trailed behind him, glad that at last they were getting to the business of the killer. He was suddenly conscious of the wasted time and their quarry might not after all have been badly hurt, although that was unlikely.

The two men who had arrived with Viljoen were looking through the wire mesh screens in the kitchen when their boss and Krige joined them. 'Glad of the dog,' said one, studying the Alsatian cautiously. 'I've seen what they can do to a man. We'll need him with the start our friend out there has on us.'

'The dog stays with us,' said Krige clipping a leash onto Caesar's collar. 'I don't want him running ahead to be riddled by bullets.'

Viljoen went to the door, planting the Borsalino on his head. 'Let's move on. I want him taken alive, before we kill him. It would be interesting to know where he comes from.'

Krige grinned to himself. The likes of Steiner would carry no identification, and nothing would make him reveal his source, which he already knew. Kirsty's idea was identical to his own plan, the double game as she called it. These men were certainly not going to find Steiner.

Chapter 15

Running across the yard, Steiner was conscious of the first stiffening in his shoulder, and incipient stabs randomly administered like the thrusts of a matador's spear. The inevitable drain on his reserves of strength would limit his speed and he was unlikely to outrun those who would certainly take up the chase. He couldn't rely on Krige, although he knew the farmer would do what he could to sidetrack them.

For a while he went north-west from where he had left the car in the *donga* on the southern range, trying to anticipate the thinking of his pursuers. If he were them, he would have deduced that it was likely he had come onto the farm through the gate and hidden his car in the uncultivated area between there and the expanse of tobacco. That's where they would expect him to go, and he had to be patient even if it meant them finding the car and reaching it before him.

When the rugged terrain dipped into a broad-based gully Steiner went north, eventually leaving the low land and going in a large circle to his left. The house was out of view and he loped on with the even rhythm of a marathon runner, altering his course every now and then to maintain the circular path that he expected to carry him down the western flank of the drying barns he had noticed previously. The pain was still there but it was growing no worse, and the initial jabbing was less regular, the blood a trickle as if staunched by the now clotting profusion of what had escaped before. In several minutes he was moving south, leaping over the holes in the earth that reminded him of descriptions of a lunar surface.

The rain had started again, an indecisive weltering of water that alternated between brief intervals of intensity, that seemed to want to wash everything clean, and the renowned English drizzle. His clothes were soon soaked, but the wetness was refreshing. At one point he stopped, the Beretta and heavy revolver clamped in one hand. Almost immediately, and with a tinge of distaste, he poked the magnum into the soil, pushing it deeper with his boot. It was not the type of weapon he would have chosen. He checked the Beretta and it was full. He had read somewhere of the three-shot automatic mode that Beretta had devised, a mode inbetween the usual single shot for each trigger pull, like his Glock, and the total automatic facility offered by SMGs. He could see the sense: sustained automatic fire of more than three rounds in a small gun tended to drive the weapon off target, whereas with the Beretta it cut out allowing the user time to adjust.

He weighed the gun in his palm, watching the drops of water skating on the blue frictionless surface, seemingly desperate to escape, and then he carried on, confident he was alone, and beginning to feel hunger and thirst. Travelling at a reduced speed he was suddenly surprised when Krige's long machine shed rose from nowhere ahead of him. He had thought he was further to the west, and he changed direction appropriately, but then after a while he hesitated, wanting a drink of water, and went to the building.

There was a tap at the end of the shed, screwed to a wobbly pipe and obscured from the house. He drank the pure liquid gratefully, careful not to consume too much and bloat his stomach. Wiping his mouth on his sleeve, he had begun to retrace his path into the scrub when he heard a cry that, even with his conditioned nerves, jolted him like a high-voltage electric current. He would have gone on but it was an abject cry for help, and it came from Krige's wife Kirsty.

Lying where he had been dumped by Krige and Viljoen, Johannes Koch waited until the two men had returned to the house before going onto his knees and assessing his strength. To him it was a miracle the bullet fired by Steiner had missed vital organs and passed instead just beneath his collar bone. By comparison the blow to his neck had hurt far more and for long minutes after it was delivered he had thought it would result in his end, from the acute difficulty he had breathing and the gush of blood into his mouth, a mucous flood that seemed bent on drowning him. But he had been able to swallow most of the fluid and slowly recover, gradually switching his concentration from his own affliction to the happenings in the room. He had heard the conversation between Krige and Steiner, and that Krige had after all recovered the file and passed it on to his lawyer. The man was a traitor and he was betraying his own people, for which he would pay. Through barely open eyes, Koch had seen Steiner shot in the doorway and the subsequent arrival of Viljoen and the men with their AK47s, to whom, ironically, he had taught the fundamentals of combat shooting. He had chosen to feign death. Viljoen was unreliable and he did not know any more where he stood with the man, and he knew the woman wouldn't keep quiet about the fact that he'd molested her.

From the ensuing conversation Koch had learnt that Krige and the others would go after Steiner, but he also sensed that Krige would mislead them and give Steiner a chance to escape. As the energy was injecting into his body he worked out how to get away. It was a relief to know his car was parked on Classen's farm and far from where the men's searching would take them. His first regret was that he had no weapon – he was lost without one – and he remembered the rifle he had left behind the sofa in the house. He got up and went behind the rocks at the base of the *kopje*, climbing a little higher until he could see the house over the roof of the jeep. He couldn't see anyone and the doors of the house were still open.

He thought the men would have gone by now, and he grinned. Kirsty Krige obviously thought that she was finally safe. As he watched he heard the bark of a dog a distance from the house. That was all the confirmation he needed that the men had gone on their search for Steiner.

Putting the jeep between himself and the house for as long as he could, he ran across the yard to the verandah. He went over the rail and along to the window. No one was in the room and he could see the tip of the rifle protruding a couple of centimetres above the sofa. Unless someone had known it was there, it would have been almost impossible to detect. He crawled under the ledge to the doors and, giving the room another look, entered, retrieving the rifle and giving it the kiss of a father finding a lost son. He started for the porch, then halted as he heard someone coming down the passage.

He had just scrambled to the sofa when Kirsty Krige came in, and he saw her go to the doors and look out. She was in a T-shirt and jeans and her hair was untied and wet from the shower she had just had. Her figure in the tight clothing was magnificent, and as he watched he still longed to have her beneath him. She was alone, and it was the perfect opportunity, but he knew he had to get out, with her as a hostage if needed.

He came out, lifting the rifle like a handgun. She stared at the man they had all supposed to be dead, defensively wrapping herself with her arms.

Before she could make a sound he said: 'Not a murmur, Mrs Krige. Our business was rudely interrupted by those vermin. We'll continue it later. For now you're coming with me.'

For seconds she went limp as a doll on strings, the thought of again being his captive, helpless as he ultimately satisfied his carnal desire, more hideous than anything else she could imagine. He was still a third of the length of the lounge from her and, doing her best to disguise her action, she lurched for the passage. Her spirited rush had him flat-footed, but the distance was too much and he speared out the 26-inch barrel like the dropping boom on a railway crossing. She tried to go underneath it but she lost momentum and he pounced, grabbing her hair and halting her rush. She tripped and went to the floor, and then she cried, following it with the name of her dog, Blackie.

From the kitchen came the answering bark of the dog. Koch ran to the passage door and heaved it into its frame with a compounding force that shook the timbers. The door had glass in the top half and he peered through it as the Alsatian bounded towards him. It was a paralyzing sight but he was secure. The dog leapt at the barrier, lifting its body up in frustration at the unyielding obstruction, and revealing the blaze of soft fur of its stomach. Giving in to the temptation, Koch broke the muzzle of the rifle into a pane and put it flush against the dog's chest. He fired.

The sound of the gun was silenced, but the dog's snarl was converted to a blood-curdling howl as it left the floor, bending its body like a high-board diver. Its yellow eyes were filled with hate for its arch enemy. It collided with the wall, fatally wounded, its claws ineffectively scraping at the surface and lagging behind as the head and body came down for final rest. The shot had done the job, and Koch was morbidly fascinated by the twin emissions of blood that began to saturate the lustrous coat, one from the stomach wall and the other from where the bullet had expelled itself after fracturing the spine.

And then Koch saw the black servant appear in the passage, and he lined up the weapon on her. As he took up on the trigger Kirsty Krige threw herself at him, clawing at his clothes.

'No!' she cried. 'She's harmless.'

Koch shook his shoulders roughly but she was not easily removed and then thrust his elbow into her solar plexus. She collapsed, her lungs calling for the air that did not come, and he concentrated again on the servant. She had gone, and he was torn between going after her and making his escape but then he remembered the other men. The noise would have carried, and he prodded Kirsty, angry that he might have used too much strength. He needed her on her feet so she could travel unaided.

He rolled her onto her back and pressed on her chest to restore the breathing. When it came he gave her several seconds before hauling her up. 'Out the front, you bitch,' he said. 'That was unwise. If your husband gets near us you're dead.'

For some distance after leaving the house, Krige appeared to give the dog its lead, with the others following, but he controlled it with the leash and made it take them in the direction he wanted. A north-easterly route was the one he guessed Steiner would take at first, and then if he was clever, which he obviously was, he would go anticlockwise, the most vegetated path, rather than clockwise. He would then make tracks for wherever he had parked his car, which would be well concealed. After a while Krige could feel the dog pulling him round to the left, anticlockwise, but he drew in the leash, walked for several paces in a clockwise circle, and then, with Caesar away from the scent, pointed him directly to the south. Caesar barked as he was pulled from the scent, but he had to obey his master as he led the men to the southern ridge that lay before the main gate.

Viljoen was pleased. 'I knew we would pick up his trail,' he said. 'We would have been heading for the gate and I'm certain that we will soon have him. We are better armed than he is, and we'll pick him off as easily as a duck on a pond.'

'Don't you want to know his name and find out where he is from, who sent him?' said Krige, beginning to enjoy himself.

'I know as much as I need to,' said Viljoen. 'He is clearly from Bryant's crowd in Durban, and they will never see him again.'

In the lounge, Kirsty Krige looked on as Koch busied himself with the rifle. 'I need a coat,' she said. 'It's raining.'

'No time,' answered Koch, thinking of the men. He added: 'Besides, I like you wet.'

Putting the rifle strap over him, he made for her then halted, his jaw sagging mechanically. Ahead of them, motionless in the doorway with a foot in the room, was Steiner, suddenly apparent, as if he had just been beamed in from another world. At his side was the ever-present Glock, and when Koch made no movement for the rifle he walked in until he stood on the apex of a triangle from them.

'You cheated the devil,' said Steiner to Koch. 'I was careless. Step away from her and get rid of the gun. She's not yours, as much as you desire her.'

The icy tone made Koch shiver. He had been reminded how powerful Steiner was and the speed at which he could move. Without the rifle he was finished. He also had to have the assistance of Krige's wife to secure an unhindered escape. 'Take it,' he said, slowly removing the weapon from his shoulder. He noticed how Steiner held the Glock as if he had no intention of using it and it unnerved him. The man was sure of himself but he had to go on. As the rifle came loose he went for the woman.

With the centrifugal force of a bolas Koch's huge forearm embraced Kirsty's neck and swept her between himself and Steiner. She fought ineffectively against his strength as he brought the flash hider up to her chin. It was nearly there when the bolt of the rifle caught in his belt and the barrel fell at an angle. He latched onto her and tugged at the gun. All his attention was on it and when the calloused hand fastened on the wooden forestock and ripped the rifle from him it was the last thing for him and it was clear that he had spent his last coin.

Throwing the rifle away in a disdainful arc, Steiner took the Glock to Koch's face, then lengthened his stance and hit him with his fist over the heart, giving out the war cry of an ape. For seconds Koch was immobilized, a sculpture, and then he was down. He was unconscious and Steiner knelt to him, holding the Glock to his head. 'This time I'll make sure,' he said casually, but with lethal intent. He fired twice into the brain then left the body.

As much as she had come to detest Koch, Kirsty Krige looked away and convulsed at each shot. When it was over she watched Steiner going to the porch.

'Wait,' she said. 'Who are you? Why did you come back?'

'You were in trouble,' he said simply.

She was astonished. 'You can kill like that and yet you risked your life for me. The others will have heard the shots and they will come back. My husband will do what he can to protect you, but he cannot expose himself and reveal his intentions concerning the file. He'll be powerless, and those bastards will do what they like with you when they catch you.'

'They'll never find me,' he replied. 'If they did they would wish they hadn't.' After a moment he said: 'Where were they going? How do they think I came onto the farm?'

'They believe you parked your car in the bush near the main gate,' she answered after reflecting for a moment.

'How else can someone get onto this land?' he asked.

'There's a track that leads north-west to our neighbour's farm,' she said. 'It goes through a gate in the fence. Its existence is known only to a few.'

'The old man in the store?' he said quizzically, smiling faintly.

'He knows these parts as well as we do.' She returned his smile. 'Is that what you want me to say to them?'

'Yes,' he said. 'Tell them that I learnt of your neighbour's gate from the old man, and that's how I got in. Also tell your husband that he will be leading the men in the wrong direction. I'm sure he will take pleasure in doing it.'

'Trust me,' she said. 'And thank you.' She walked up and threw her arms around him. She kissed him full on the lips and then said: 'I wish I had met you at a different time in another place.'

'Those are my feelings as well,' he said. 'Perhaps we'll meet again. But now I must go.' He freed himself.

'Take care,' she whispered. 'We owe you our lives.'

But he was already running across the verandah, and

she saw him vault the rail and continue to the barns, a tall lone figure, so sensually powerful and graceful in the way he moved. She couldn't help wondering what he would be like in bed. She cast the thought from her mind.

Maria appeared from the passage and she wept when she saw that Kirsty was unharmed. Together they dragged Koch out into the front yard, the second time for him, but this time he was dead, killed by two bullets to the brain.

Seven minutes after Steiner left, Krige and the three men reached the house. They had heard the shots. Kirsty was seated on the verandah, in the rocking chair that Krige loved. He ran to her, the relief that she was alright, tangible. 'What happened?' he said, cogently. 'We heard the shots. Who was here?'

'There was someone,' she replied, calmly, the faintest smile on her lips. 'In fact there were two, and James Steiner was one of them.' She enjoyed stretching out the intrigue.

'Who was the other?' said Viljoen, mystified.

'That thug of yours, lying where Maria and I have just dragged him,' said Kirsty. She pointed to the base of the *kopje*. 'He's on the other side. I don't want to see him again. He wasn't dead the first time but he is now. Miraculously, if you believe in miracles, he came alive after you had gone on your chase. He came for me. He was going to take me away with him. Even now, with him dead, the thought revolts me. When he was about to take me, James Steiner appeared. He had heard my scream. He killed Koch. That was ten minutes ago.' She looked at Koch. 'Put him in that Land Rover of yours and get him off this land,' she said.

'We'll do that,' said Viljoen, 'and then I want you to tell me anything that might lead us to this man Steiner.'

She didn't reply and waited until Viljoen and his henchmen had left to remove Koch's body. As soon as they were out of earshot, she turned to her husband. 'You have to lead them on a false trail,' she urged. 'James Steiner asked me to tell you that he came in through our neighbour's farm, and that is where his car is parked and how he intends to get out. You can tell Viljoen that Steiner found out about that way in through Oom at the store. Please do it.'

'If Steiner had stayed any longer, you would have fallen in love with him,' said Krige. 'I can see it in your eyes. But he has gone, and it's in our interests to allow him time to escape. You will get over him and then we'll be together again.' He watched Viljoen and the other two lift Koch into the back of the Land Rover.

She didn't say anything, knowing that what he said was true. James Steiner had that appeal for her, an appeal she hadn't felt for any other man, not even Jan.

'I'll lead these guys with pleasure on a wild goosechase,' said Krige. 'And then I'll phone my lawyer. I have decided what to tell him.'

Several hundred metres from the house in a well-concealed position, James Steiner watched the men return. He saw them with Kirsty Krige on the verandah, and then shifting Koch into the back of the Land Rover. It was not difficult to guess what Kirsty was saying to her husband. When the men were ready, the four of them went on the track that Steiner was certain led to the neighbour's farm. As soon as they were out of sight, he left his position and carried on to where he had parked his car in the *donga*. It was easy to reverse it out up the slight slope, and in minutes he was on the main road to Pretoria and Durban. Smith of the DSO would be ecstatic when he heard about the file, and he would wait with relish to get it in his hands and then hunt the men down. To him it would be almost unbelievable that they would finally get those who he thought had evaded justice, a lifetime achievement.

Krige was true to his word. Minutes after the four men returned after a fruitless search, Viljoen and his men left the farm in the Land Rover. They knew that they would never get Steiner. He was too good for them.

Early the next morning Krige phoned his lawyer, David Staples, from the house. 'Have you made the copies?' he asked, knowing that it would have been done. A man like Staples didn't hang around with something as important as that in his possession.

'The certified copies have been made and they are ready to go by courier to the people designated by you, complete with the covering letter,' said Staples. 'Do you want them sent? Don't disappoint me now.'

'Send them,' said Krige. 'Now the shit is really going to hit the fan.'

Glossary

Scorpions	In September 1999 President Mbeki established a crime fighting capacity to investigate and prosecute national priority crime in South Africa. The creation of the Scorpions was the first step and its brief was, as a multi-disciplinary agency, to investigate and prosecute organized crime. The Directorate came into being on 12 January 2001 and is governed by the National Prosecuting Authority Act 32 of 1998, which was amended to provide the Directorate with the necessary investigative powers. The DSO has the two main Directorates of Strategic and Investigative Support, and Operations.

Afrikaans

boerewors	traditional spiced Afrikaner sausage
donga	a ditch in the bush or veld
kopje	an outcrop of rock or very small hill of earth
sosatie	skewered lamb
volk	the Afrikaner people or folk

Japanese

aikidoka	student of aikido
ashi barai	technical term for a front foot sweep
budo	martial way (do is the word for way)
dogi	standard Japanese martial arts training suit

dojo	martial arts training hall
hakama	traditional divided Japanese skirt, as seen on the samurai of old
karatedo	the way of karate
ki	energy of the mind
kotegaeshi	technical term for a specific aikido wrist throw
maai	the distance between two protagonists; inside *maai* means you do not have to move your bodyweight to deliver a telling strike with hand or foot; outside *maai* means that you have to shift your body closer before delivering the strike
makiwara	flexible punching bag used in karate schools for strengthening the hands; it is usually bound with straw over the striking area
ninja	art of stealth and assassination
ninjutsu	techniques of the ninja
ryokan	Japanese inn
san	term of respect (similar to Mr or Mrs)
sensei	Japanese teacher
shoji	traditional sliding doors usually used in older buildings
tatami	traditional straw matting used in many homes and often in martial arts schools such as *aikido*
tonkatsu	skewered chicken pieces usually found in lunch boxes
uchideshi	inside disciple of a martial arts school and one who will probably become a teacher
yukata	informal loose-fitting cotton bathrobe
zen	At the heart of disciplines such as *karatedo* and *aikido* is *zen* and at its core is the concept of *ki* which, as taught in premier *budo* schools, is the form of energy – unrelated to muscular

power and physical size – generated by the mind and directly related to the level of mind and body coordination attained. Intuition, the unconscious mind, or the state of no-mind is the *zen* mind, the mind that is the focus of the *zen* method. Training in the *budo* disciplines is extremely demanding physically and mentally and leads to a high degree of coordinated power.